BOCHICA

BOCHICA

— A NOVEL —

CAROLINA
FLÓREZ-CERCHIARO

PRIMERO
SUEÑO PRESS
_____
ATRIA
New York   Amsterdam/Antwerp   London
Toronto   Sydney/Melbourne   New Delhi

PRIMERO
SUEÑO PRESS

ATRIA

An Imprint of Simon & Schuster, LLC
1230 Avenue of the Americas
New York, NY 10020

For more than 100 years, Simon & Schuster has championed authors and the stories they create. By respecting the copyright of an author's intellectual property, you enable Simon & Schuster and the author to continue publishing exceptional books for years to come. We thank you for supporting the author's copyright by purchasing an authorized edition of this book.

This book is a work of fiction. Any references to historical events, real people, or real places are used fictitiously. Other names, characters, places, and events are products of the author's imagination, and any resemblance to actual events or places or persons, living or dead, is entirely coincidental.

First Primero Sueño Press/Atria Books hardcover edition May 2025

PRIMERO SUEÑO PRESS / ATRIA BOOKS and colophon are trademarks of Simon & Schuster, LLC

Simon & Schuster strongly believes in freedom of expression and stands against censorship in all its forms. For more information, visit BooksBelong.com.

For information about special discounts for bulk purchases, please contact Simon & Schuster Special Sales at 1-866-506-1949 or business@simonandschuster.com.

The Simon & Schuster Speakers Bureau can bring authors to your live event. For more information or to book an event, contact the Simon & Schuster Speakers Bureau at 1-866-248-3049 or visit our website at www.simonspeakers.com.

Interior design by Jill Putorti

Manufactured in the United States of America

1 3 5 7 9 10 8 6 4 2

Library of Congress Cataloging-in-Publication Data has been applied for

ISBN 978-1-6680-6257-9
ISBN 978-1-6680-6259-3 (ebook)

For Ana, who taught me to love stories—ours was my favorite one.
I miss you.

UNO

ONE IS ALWAYS SUBJECT TO THE INFLUENCE OF SPIRITS
Antonia rested her weight against the wooden desk and stared at the words carved on the gray concrete wall above the blackboard. She didn't appreciate the reminder because she didn't believe the words to be true, but the nuns insisted that the girls should learn about the weaknesses of the flesh and the soul.

The hazy gloom of burned incense settled in the room, but it didn't mask the earthy graveyard smell. The nogal's dead branches click-clacked off the half-open arched stained-glass windows; cold lurked inside, crawling up her nostrils, creeping down her throat. Antonia swallowed. When would this oppressive gloom finally pass over Bogotá?

Rain droplets pelted her face. Antonia pulled up the zipper of her black woolen coat and rushed through the young girls—bent over their notepads on their weathered wooden desks—to shut the windows, then patted her hands dry against the thick fabric of her black dress.

Antonia glanced briefly at her students, and at hand's reach were the Catechism and the Bible. Antonia shook her head; the girls spent hours being told what to say and think.

While boys learned math, algebra, and geometry, girls learned all about domestic economy. Nothing more than simple mathematical operations were required.

Although Antonia had been working at the Escuela para Señoritas de Bogotá for over a year, she still wasn't used to what the nuns called "the nourishing of the minds of the youth."

Girls were taught manners; how to be good daughters, docile and benevolent ones, and obedient and caring future wives and mothers. The majority of them would be married by the age of fourteen. And if they were lucky, marriage wouldn't come until they turned eighteen or twenty. But those were exceptions. And even then, they'd remain in captivity. Captive to their condition as females. Doomed to a life at the service of men, determined by religious beliefs.

For when a woman dared escape home, it was frowned upon. A woman's duty could only be housework.

There was nothing that could even make them consider the idea of leaving.

For a while, Antonia had longed for an escape regardless of what people would say. She'd daydreamed about Paris, London, Rome, and Istanbul. About studying the origins of Gothic literature where it had all begun.

Unlike these girls, who attended Catholic school, when Antonia was a child, she had, for the most part, been tutored by Carmela in math, algebra, and geometry. Still, Antonia's position in life was no better than that of any other woman.

So, here she was.

Just a few more hours until the day was finally over. She snapped out of her stupor and continued with the lesson:

"But the influence of the demons, as we know from the scriptures and the history of the Church, goes further still. . . ."

Antonia wished she could tell the girls that demonic possession was as much of a fantasy as every other folktale they'd been told. Such as La Llorona—the spirit of a grieving woman in search of her dead kid—or La Pa-tasola, a one-legged woman-like creature with vampire-like lust for human flesh and blood.

Antonia's stomach churned at the notion that in 1936 Colombia, mon-sters were female.

"The Devil may attack one's body from without or assume control of it from . . . *within*." Antonia parsed through her words as her gaze fixated on the girls stiffening in their seats, panic flaring in their eyes. This was terrorism.

She placed the *Catholic Encyclopedia* on top of her desk; her brown eyes stared at the navy-blue leatherbound behemoth of a book for a bit. Her chest tightened. She was complicit in this brainwashing.

A hand rose at the back of the dimly lit classroom and brought Anto-nia's focus back to her audience. She nodded, and a black-haired girl stum-bled away from her desk.

"Miss Rubiano, how do we know . . ." The girl paused, her elbows pressed into the sides of her beige uniform, making her look even smaller. "How do we know when someone's possessed by the . . ." The girl's voice trailed off as though she couldn't even dare say the word.

Devil.

Antonia scratched her forehead and pondered what to say next. To her, possessions were nothing more than illnesses of the body falsely seen as the works of the supernatural. The only ghost that had ever truly haunted her was regret. She could've escaped, but now it was too late. And she had to live with the consequences of her own choices. Those were often the heavi-est burdens to carry around.

"There hasn't been real proof of this happening," Antonia said at last, not quite answering Esperanza's question but hoping that would be enough. The least she wanted was to further terrorize these girls. "Most of the time, these . . . *possessions* aren't real."

Antonia's focus darted around the room. Hanging on the dull-colored walls were Christian frescoes caulked into place, their frames rusty from the ravages of time, depicting different religious figures from a portrait of young Pio XI to one of Francis of Assisi—the first person to allegedly suffer stigmata—to a painting of the Resurrection. The latter of which her eyes could never skip over. Her flesh crawled under her skin each time, so she had to force herself to look away.

A spiral of fear traveled down the back of Antonia's neck. But there was more than just fear in it, there was uncertainty underneath it as well.

Dead people stay dead. If they didn't, wouldn't Antonia's mamá be back?

"How do we know?" Esperanza pressed.

Antonia breathed in deeply, pulled a piece of chalk out of her coat, and turned to face the blackboard.

"Unusual violent movements," she said as she scribbled the words with her right hand, the chalkboard screech prickling at her eardrums. "Shrieking, groaning, and uttering disconnected or strange speech. Having the answer to questions they couldn't possibly know the answer to . . ."

The sound of her heartbeat thrashed in her ears as the images cycled through her mind like aging puzzle pieces, worn-out, faded. Antonia knew they were locked in her brain somewhere, but at times she'd rather not access them.

Papá bound to a chair with chains and rosaries, candles the only source of light. He tries to scramble away. He twists and screams so loudly he forgets he is screaming. Then he stops. He rubs his hands together, mumbling to himself, and hunches over as the Latin chants from Padre Juan and the nuns become louder and faster. There is a darkness about Papá that spreads inside the already darkened room. The chanting stops, and as Papá cocks his head up slowly, his eyes open, revealing nothing but white. Blood from his mouth and eyes flows down onto his white shirt. He grins and stays completely motionless for a while. Then his expression falters; he looks dazed and confused. Padre Juan approaches him and places a towel drenched in

holy water onto his forehead, and so the chanting resumes. With one last
convulsion, Papá forces out the "demon" before collapsing against the floor.

Antonia's thoughts left her unsettled. She reached for the glass of water
on her desk and downed the lukewarm liquid in one gulp in an attempt to
steady her heart, threatening to lunge out of her rib cage. After a few seconds that felt like minutes, she managed to compose herself. The memory
had escaped the innermost corner of her mind. Those dark places . . . she
had to stop reaching into them if she wanted to move forward. Or perhaps
the only way she would ever move forward was by confronting them, just
as Carmela often reminded her. But how would she ever overcome so much
death while keeping what was left of her family together? She couldn't afford to consider any of it now. No. She and her papá had survived, barely,
and Antonia couldn't put their fragile recovery in jeopardy.

Antonia sucked in another breath before resuming the lecture. She
wouldn't let catechesis get to her too. No more digging up her past. Not if
she wanted the dreams to stop.

"Occasionally the person becomes incapable of prayer, utters blasphe-
mies, or exhibits terror or hatred of sacred persons or objects," she continued. "However, scientific studies treat these things as psychophysical
manifestations to be dealt with medically. Lunacy and paralysis, for in-
stance, are often mistaken for possession. Results are then attributed to a
diabolical agency when they're really due to natural causes. . . ."

The door creaked open.

Antonia wavered where she stood and stumbled as she turned around.

La madre superiora stepped through the door and over the threshold.
A chill washed over Antonia, raising fine ashy-brown hairs all over her skin
at the sight of the old nun approaching her. Her veins turned to ice, and
she stood still.

Madre Asunción's voice rolled like thunder across the room. "I am sure
Miss Rubiano meant not to deny the existence of such phenomenon." She
grimaced at Antonia, then her eyes flitted to the girls, who quickly got on

their knees, their skin exposed to the cold stone floor, their gazes locked down on their laps as they silently began praying to themselves.

Dread coiled in the pit of Antonia's stomach. Nasty white hairs on Madre Asunción's chin escaped the brown coif of the habit and swung along with the damp wind coming in through the now-open door. Antonia squirmed and her toes curled up inside her black leather shoes, but she forced herself to not look away. It wasn't Madre Asunción's presence that bothered Antonia the most, it was the memories she brought with her.

The air got thicker with every lazy step Madre Asunción took around the room. Her feet sagged and the dusty hem of her robe flipped a switch and unlocked something about Antonia's past. Something Antonia hadn't dared to look into.

Antonia had been a student in this same escuela once, and although she didn't come from a Catholic family, her parents had no choice but to leave her education to the nuns. For a little girl her age, at that time there weren't many options. But it wasn't long until the nuns considered her unfit in their institution and thought it was better, despite her papá's donations to the Church, to expel her. Antonia was, after all, her mamá's child, and that posed a threat to everything the nuns believed in.

"Whatever view rationalists choose to adopt, for a sincere believer there can be no doubt that possession is possible."

Madre Asunción, cadaverous and frail, nearly stripped of her humanity, was almost too old to be allowed to run an entire school. Her skeletal hands carried a ruler and a holy rosary.

Pain and forgiveness, Antonia thought.

Through sunken black eyes surrounded by wrinkly discolored skin, Madre Asunción stared into oblivion with a dead gaze. Slowly, her thin lips parted, and a vile smile crept across her decayed face.

"The most common cause is that someone has turned to the Devil or the occult. Usually, when they try to escape the demonic world, they get attacked by it, and sometimes . . . *most of the time,* they are killed."

The girls gasped in unison, and fifteen sets of small eyes bulged out. Cold sweat trickled down Antonia's spine. She glanced at Madre Asunción, who stood motionless, unbothered.

"Madre Asunción, I just want the girls to gain some perspective. It's 1936, they can use a bit of context. Given how many charlatans one can encounter these days, I want them to ask questions, not to simply believe whatever people tell them. That's all."

Antonia wasn't lying about that. Working at Escuela para Señoritas de Bogotá wasn't easy for her. She was not a believer. After the tragedies she and her family had suffered, her papá had avoided the subject altogether.

Antonia found no solace in spirituality. She wouldn't worship any God who would rob her of everything she cared about. She'd found no comfort in it when her mamá passed. She'd tried to pray, but not a single one she'd whispered during sleepless nights had been answered. What had really happened? Why couldn't she heal? As the years passed, she stopped expecting an answer. She didn't want one anymore.

The nuns were aware of Antonia's beliefs, or lack thereof, but they hadn't found someone else as qualified for the job as she was.

Antonia knew more about literature, Latin, theology, math, sewing, and mending than every other candidate the nuns had come across. She spoke five languages. All of them self-taught. A woman as ambitious as she was unwelcome in any school, let alone any university in the country. Female ambition was a threat to the very foundation of society.

"To deny the words of Jesus himself?" Madre Asunción turned her burning gaze to Antonia. "That's sacrilege. That's not teaching them to be faithful but skeptic, one of the worst behaviors any Christian could adopt. Unless they want to burn in hell, that is."

"I'm sorry, Madre Asunción, but in order for a case to be labeled as possession, there *needs* to be proper medical examination, and in many cases, there's rather a lack of any sort of procedure. . . ."

Madre Asunción's wrinkly and moistureless lips pressed together in a slight grimace as she approached Antonia, causing her to step backward and nearly tip her chair over. Antonia pressed herself to the wall as far from the old nun as possible, but she was trapped. When Madre Asunción's grip reached her hair, Antonia's insides turned to thick slime.

Antonia swallowed a screech, and her heart hammered in her chest as her head tilted slightly toward the old lady's face in a soft but firm pull. According to the nuns, violence was allowed but not encouraged, especially not physical violence. But they also considered themselves God's servants, and if someone did wrong, they didn't bear the sword in vain.

For he is the servant of God, an avenger who carries out God's wrath on the wrongdoer.

Antonia's temples squeezed together at the thought.

She'd seen such violence take place—Sister Luisa slumped to the floor, twisting in pain. Her own blood pooling underneath her.

One. Two. Three. Four—

Sister Luisa was whipped to within an inch of her life.

She wanted to die, she'd told Antonia. All along she thought one more whip should end her pain.

But Madre Asunción wouldn't kill Sister Luisa. No. That would've been too easy of a punishment. She had to survive; she had to live and remind herself and everyone else not to ever transgress the rules. Ever again.

Madre Asunción leaned even closer, her sour breath caressing Antonia's cheek. "You go around hiding behind that skeptical facade of yours thinking that it will keep you safe. But the things that haunt us will do so forever. Don't you forget what happened to your mother."

Madre Asunción's voice was harsh and sibilant. A lump gathered around Antonia's throat—the saliva in her mouth went dry and her stomach filled with acid. How dare Madre Asunción talk about Estela in front of the girls?

No, Antonia hadn't forgotten; a lot of her memories were locked in the darkest corridors of her brain, but Estela's death wasn't one of them, even if there were only flashes of that day.

Antonia had been somewhere, pacing, working up the nerve to share her big news. She would tell her parents she was moving out, that she couldn't stay at that house another moment. She'd found a job as a tutor at a Catholic school in Bogotá and she needed to live in the city to fulfill her schedule. The pay was a few pesos but enough to help cover rent and food. She could still visit them over the weekends. It wouldn't feel as though she'd left at all.

Antonia was as joyful as she'd ever been. She had a plan at last and felt as though she had control over her life. Over her future. That she could finally hope for something more, instead of simply enduring and playing the role everyone expected of her, of every woman. She could work for a few months, earn enough so that she could leave the country. Make her dreams of studying Gothic literature in Britain come true.

But the minute she walked into that cursed house, her dreams died. Since then, a hole had formed in Antonia's chest—sometimes she felt as though it only grew bigger and wider, emptying her from her insides.

Death is often gentle to the person it takes away, but cruel to those condemned to stay.

Antonia felt stunned by Madre Asunción's words and didn't have enough wit to haul herself out of the nun's grip. All she could do was twist her head a bit and force herself to keep direct eye contact.

"Don't think that choosing not to believe will make evil disappear; it will not. Nor will it protect you from anything. In truth, when you finally encounter it, you will be weak and unprepared. *Defenseless.* And not believing will not serve you anymore." Madre Asunción's pointy and bony fingers scratched the back of Antonia's neck before she released Antonia from her grip. "Now, why do you hide? Who, *or what*, are you hiding from if such things do not exist? What is it that you fear?"

Antonia winced at the pain in her neck and managed to straighten in place, her head still hurting and her neck partially stiffened by the twist.

Madre Asunción's voice was grainy as it slid between her cracked lips. "Miss Rubiano, take a break for the rest of the day, will you?"

"But I still have an hour left of catechesis—"

The girls' faces were still trained on the ground as if they were too scared to stare at Madre Asunción. Why wouldn't they be? She embodied everything they should be afraid of.

A life subjected to Catholic rules. A life of caring for others without ever caring for themselves. A life taking care of a man's children. A life subjected to the desires of a husband who would see them as not much other than a birthing machine and an acquisition to have sitting at home.

"*Leave,*" Madre Asunción cut her off, "we will see you tomorrow."

In the now hollow deafness that spread inside the crowded classroom, Antonia stumbled to get to her desk. She reached across it for her bag and left without saying another word. The girls resumed their chanting as they rose back up. Terror poured through their eyes, and Antonia couldn't stare at them for long. Their eyes told her, *Don't leave. Don't leave us alone.* But she couldn't stay. And she didn't want to.

But what would it cost her, and her family, to escape for good?

Today the land felt mine for the first time.

The sun gleamed through the midmorning air, lighting up the dirt path around us as I watched my breath gloom in the cold. Sixteen thousand sqft, and they were all ours, at last, after back-and-forth offers and promises to take care of the abandoned land. And I would take all the turmoil, corruption and all. I would have it even when Ricardo tried to convince me otherwise. No price was too high to pay if it meant living in a sanctuary that one wanted. No, needed. These were holy grounds, and it needed a fortress, it needed a leader to rule in order to survive. I saw myself like a mirage, looking over the land and its vastness, a throne-like balcony from where I could stand. I felt my chest inflate with pride, with joy. I'd never felt so powerful, like the world was at hand's, reach and I was closer to Bochica at last. Money had always failed to make me feel whole—even though I'd grown up with nothing, and the little I had, my family, the only thing I truly could call mine, was ripped from me years ago. I felt like a transplant in the city—I never thought that I belonged. But this place, secluded from everyone else, already felt like home.

As I stood on the ledge, El Salto hummed with life, its waters tumbling down the mountain and onto the rock. Its melody tingled my soul and the scent lingering in the air filled my lungs. Thick ghostlike scarves wrapped the area in a maze of mist, writhing and coiling with delight. We weren't spared—its spineless tentacles clung to and enrobed us. Could it swallow us whole?

My heart froze, then pounded against my rib cage. How much decay was there that the eye could not see? How much rot was underneath the veil of thick fog? Beauty was deceitful, a mask, a disguise, and it always kept what was broken below the surface. Under it, barren soil extended rapidly like a silent plague. Ill-infused ambition can dry life out of anything. But I intended to restore it, to give it its life back.

Briefly, everything around me stilled, and I was rooted in place. I closed my eyes. I wanted to take in this moment, capture it as it was and lock it inside my brain, like a precious treasure of my own. Something no one could take away.

Warmth radiated throughout my body, and I opened my eyes again. A hug of browns, the wild encenillos provided a shelter of extended limbs, resting beneath foliage hues. El Salto belonged to Bochica. It was a holy sanctuary. A place of ancient souls, of spirits who dwell with the sweet sounds of moving water, cóndores, and owls. Somehow, this was more home than home. Perhaps one day my family will understand that too.

Ricardo's voice was muffled by the waterfall; where he stood, there was a trail of hardened black-and-white candle wax, along with filthy rags, feathers, and grime. "Workers will get all of it cleaned up," he said reassuringly, and whatever he said next, I didn't listen.

This thing in front of us—our future right across—was bigger than Ricardo could ever imagine. Than I could put to words.

I wished Antonia had come with us. This was a better setting than any of the Gothic novels she obsessed over. Would she appreciate it as much as I did?

How could she not? This was hers too. It lived within her, dormant, patient, simmering inside. The day would come when it would lay on her hands.

DOS

The road was empty, cast into shadow by the imposing nogales standing on either side. It was covered with dirt, smears of mud, and clots of black filth. Antonia stood in its center, only a few yards away from the escuela's main black iron gates. Her crimson scarf, soft and gentle, almost like a colorful flag waving in the wintry winds, sat snug on her neck to protect her from the cold. As she marched away from the escuela, the last bits of light faded in between the clouds, and the cobbled streets of La Candelaria opened to her. The two-story homes painted in white, with worn-out red roof tiles and black wrought-iron window bars, saluted her as she walked by.

Antonia did not turn around. The idea of going back sent a tremor of nausea down her throat. Slicked her palms with sweat. No. She couldn't allow herself to lose her temper in front of Madre Asunción again. Not if Antonia wanted to keep the job. And she *needed* to keep the job. Madre Asunción's patience had already run thin, even before the day's events. The nun had forgiven her for skipping the biannual peregrination to Monserrate, for not wanting to walk up a steep hill to pray to the shrine of El Señor Caído and taking the girls to the National Institute of Science instead. She'd forgiven Antonia for refusing to take the habit. Not to mention, for being twenty-six and still unmarried.

And, no, Antonia would not consider the habit. She felt cloistered enough in her everyday life. She'd barely survived her own Gothic nightmare. She wouldn't make it any harder on herself.

Sixty pesos a month was worth the hike, the weekly lessons of catechesis, and everything else the nuns put her through if it meant being able to cover for her papá's medical expenses. It also meant that she could one day finally leave for good—start a new life somewhere far away, away from the trauma she'd been trying to leave behind.

But even with all these reasons to stay, she couldn't help but think that perhaps it wouldn't be so bad if she was fired. Maybe there *was* a way out. After all, her blighted childhood home had been converted into Colombia's first luxury hotel. El Refugio del Salto, sprawled over the Bogotá savanna, and overlooking a 515-foot waterfall, where French haute couture met Native Andean traditions, offered a gateway to splendor and exclusivity a mere three hours away from the city. According to *La Nota*, the city's local newspaper, the five-story hotel consisted of a lobby and a ballroom with bold geometric architecture, lavish golden details, paneled murals, mosaics on the floor, and crystal chandeliers, as well as sixteen well-appointed rooms with gold snake-medallion doorplates. The hotel also boasted, along with electricity and telephones, three restaurants offering numerous dining options from local cuisine to international dishes, and two lounges on the main floor with spectacular views of the waterfall where guests could sip on beer and wine from the property's own Bavarian-style cellar made of walnut wood, while listening to live boleros playing in the foyer. Its spa offered a comprehensive list of natural treatments for any ailment, inspired by local rituals.

An odd mixture of horror and hope overcame Antonia just thinking about the place that she used to call home. It offered no shelter to anyone, and it was certainly no haven. That awful house, the place where it all happened, was about to open its gates to the public. But at least she would be able to save a few pesos. Precious funds she hadn't been able to save since her mamá had left the world four years ago, and her papá had fallen into a depression that had left them in ruin and threatened to swallow him whole. A thick haze clouded his mind, making it impossible for him to work, dream, or hope.

Demonic possession, Antonia thought. Those kids had no idea what true darkness looked like. But all that talk of the Devil meant they still weren't going to sleep through the night.

Then, Antonia heard it.

It wasn't quite a noise but a displacement of air, a feeling of something big coming up from the depths of the grimy stone streets, one that was somehow rapidly moving toward her.

Antonia quickened her pace, not turning around, her pulse pounding in her ears. She was only one block away from her house, but she'd heard too many stories about what had happened to unaccompanied señoritas to not be afraid even in the middle of the afternoon.

But Antonia knew real evil.

How can I be afraid when I've survived real darkness?

Antonia raised her hands from where they hung loose at her sides and pulled the hood of her coat up to cover herself, as though that would be of any help, but something about it made her feel more at ease.

Still, she made the mistake of looking up—and gasped: a dark silhouette stood across the street, just outside the threshold of her house, bright red eyes staring back at her.

She was momentarily stunned, planted to the moist asphalt beneath her feet, but then she recoiled. The air felt warm and suddenly stale as she scanned the empty street. Those eyes . . . she knew she'd seen them before. . . .

Around her, the houses stood so still, giving no sign of life inside them, and the tall nogales reached their bold green limbs across the somber sky as though their very presence was enough to beat back the darkness and command light to fall on their rain-soaked leaves.

But it wasn't the emptiness nor the stillness of her surroundings that frightened her. It was the silence. The utter deafening silence, the kind that muffled and muted everything. Normally, she'd hear the endless roar of the cars and carriages up and down the streets, the click-clack of the soles of each passerby, the nonstop chatter of old ladies after the midmorning mass at the cathedral. But now . . . nothing. It was as if she had crossed into an entirely different place, yet it remained familiar. And it was because of this familiarity that she didn't run. Instead, she forced herself to keep staring at the motionless figure standing in her doorway.

The face she couldn't make out, for it was covered in a black veil, as though something, or someone, had smudged its features, leaving nothing but indistinct knobs of shadow.

But those red eyes . . .

Antonia's eyes shoot open. She gasps for air, cold sweat trickling down her spine like icy, treacherous hooks, threatening to slice into her flesh. She clings to the white sheets, hands trembling, pressing her back against the bed frame. She blinks rapidly, trying to shake off the fear pressing on her chest. Memories flicker in her brain—red eyes looking back at her from up close, Antonia standing still, cornered, moist weeds coiling around her bare feet.

She opens her mouth to scream, but she's unable to utter a single sound, as though the space has been emptied of all air. No. No. No. She won't let herself fall back into the somber dream. It had to be a dream. She whispers to herself, "Antonia, you're here," a reassurance that she is awake. She scans the darkness of her room as a tiny trace of moonlight seeps inside through the window; the familiar tap-tap of the water splashing against the crystal feels comforting.

The menacing nightmare loosens its grip on her, but the echoes of terror linger like an ominous whisper, mocking her fragile sanity.

"I-i-it couldn't be . . . ," Antonia let out faintly.

"Señorita Nona?" a muffled, rusty voice whispered against her ear.

Antonia recognized it and whirled around. Emiro, her papá's young chauffeur, stood behind her.

"Señorita?" he called again. Antonia remained motionless, her gaze now locked down on her lap. "You're standing in the middle of the street—"

She nodded, not even able to utter a word, and stumbled to her side. She turned around and looked up, the silhouette no longer in sight.

"Are you okay?" Emiro insisted.

"There was someone . . . at the door. Papá . . . is he?" Hadn't Emiro seen it? "I . . . I was walking and—"

"Your father is inside the house. There is no one outside with this horrendous weather."

"Yes. I was just . . . I was distracted." She curled her lips upward into a half smile. "Long day at the escuela."

Emiro's brows furrowed. His long, straight dark brown hair moved alongside the wind, almost completely covering his face. He brushed it back before his rounded eyes met hers again. "Señorita Nona, can I ask you something?"

Antonia nodded, but her eyes were still locked on the house's porch.

"How do you manage to do so much? La escuela, taking care of your father, this house, the business, the other house . . . You're doing too much, and I don't think you see that."

Antonia turned to face him. She considered his words for a moment, but it was pointless. Women had no choice but to stay. "I don't have a choice—"

"There's *always* a choice."

Antonia swallowed. She'd *had* a choice. She could've escaped many years ago, but now it was too late.

"Not a word to Carmela or Papá. I don't want to worry them with my clumsiness."

<hr/>

Antonia twisted the key that opened the rust-covered padlock. She slid the stone-cold bolt and swung the chestnut door open, revealing a flickering dim light at the end of the arched hallway. Her house was arranged around a central courtyard, on it a marble fountain surrounded by a lush garden composed of tropical flowers, pink cone gingers, bromelias, gardenias, and anthuriums, alongside several species of orchids that welcomed guests as they strode inside. At the north end of the central wing, a wooden staircase led to a second floor consisting of bedrooms, a study, a library, and various empty drawing rooms. The house was bigger than her family needed, but Antonia didn't mind the vastness of the space, especially after spending almost half of her life in a five-story mansion on the outskirts of the city.

The nutty smell of freshly brewed coffee permeated the air. She shut the door behind her and dropped her thick black coat and her crimson scarf on the green velvet sofa framing the parlor, not removing her eyes from the yellow flashing light. The warmth coming from the golden chandelier felt good against her now-exposed skin.

Antonia wasn't certain what, or whom, she'd seen moments ago, and she wanted to believe that it had been the work of her imagination. Whatever it was, it had left her thoughts disarrayed.

It all started a little over a year prior to her mamá's death. Antonia would wake up screaming, shrieking for help in the middle of the night, her room enclosed in darkness. Mamá, Papá, and Carmela would rush inside. Ricardo was always quick to let her know it was nothing more than night terrors. But her mamá hadn't looked as convinced, at least not after the first few times. Antonia felt Estela knew there was more to it, but she was keeping her mouth shut. Antonia sensed it in the way her mamá watched her, how she'd open her mouth to console Antonia but would hold herself back.

But no matter what consolation Antonia got from her mamá, the dreams didn't recede. The images were a recurring loop that played when she closed her eyes at night—the red gaze always there to greet her, to welcome her to her nightmare.

Antonia thought putting distance between her and the house would make it all go away. And it worked . . . until it didn't. Then she began to believe she'd gotten rid of the nightmares while awake. That reality protected her from the thing that haunted her while asleep. And for a while, it could. For a while, it was as easy as being awake. But what if she couldn't escape the nightmares anymore, for they had found a way to her even when her eyes were wide open?

After all, the memories of her past haunted her, and perhaps her current nightmares were no more than her body's, her psyche's, response to all the trauma, the grief, the loss, and how it caged her, how it tied her within its grip and didn't let go.

Antonia needed it all to make sense. If only she could talk to her mamá one last time. Instead, all she had left of her were . . .

The journals.

The charred journals with ripped-out pages that Antonia took with her the night they rushed out of the house. At first, she'd refused to read them, only skimming through parts, never fully paying attention to the words. But she'd held on to them, for they were one of the few things that connected her to her mamá. Not until recently had she gathered enough courage to face the pain that pressed into her at seeing Estela's words on a page, at the realization that these were the only things she had left from her.

Antonia thought about one of the pages she'd read over and over.

But as I write about this wondrous place, my home, my mind keeps drifting back to my querida Antonia. Mi Nona. She worries me the most. . . . Still, I wish I could put her emotions at ease, soothe her, console her.

What had worried her mamá? Antonia needed the rest of the pieces to put a picture together. Estela obviously sensed something wrong in Antonia, and the journal had been a gateway to her mamá's mind. Perhaps there could be other journals or other belongings of Estela's that Antonia could find answers in. If she could go back to the house, look to see if anything remained . . .

She forced the thought out of her mind and called out, "Carmela?"

The light no longer flickered.

"Nona, I'm here," came a voice from the end of the hallway.

Antonia started to the kitchen, the sound of her leather boots against the red tile echoing in the hallway. While the idea of possibly retrieving what was left of her mamá was tempting, she couldn't bear the thought of going back.

"You're early," Carmela, Antonia's longtime housekeeper and her child-hood tutor, said from behind the kitchen aisle. Her pinched expression was as familiar as the steel-gray hair parted severely in the center; her plaits, wound tightly around her head into a low bun, shone under the warm light. "Is everything all right?"

Antonia scoffed. Nothing ever escaped Carmela's intuition, especially not when it came to Antonia. Carmela was like a second mother after all. Now even more so.

Antonia nodded. "Yes. Catechesis. I'll tell you about it later." Fridays were the days she came home the latest. Catechesis lasted four hours, but today she'd been able to get through only the first one.

Carmela placed a silver platter of fresh-baked goods in front of Antonia. On it were cheese and guava pastries, almojábanas loaded with queso fresco, and Antonia's favorites: pan de bonos—tiny buns made with yucca flour and salty cheese.

"Eat up. Don't think I didn't notice that you went to work on an empty stomach this morning."

Antonia was thankful for Carmela's daily support, which nourished more than her body. Carmela had been with Antonia through thick and thin and knew her better than she knew herself. Carmela had started working for Antonia's parents when they got married. She had raised and home-schooled Antonia after the nuns decided, for some mysterious reason, that being her mamá's daughter made Antonia unworthy of a place in their institution. So Carmela taught Antonia everything she knew about life. She wouldn't have survived without Carmela.

"Thank you," Antonia said with a mouthful of fresh pastry in her mouth.

"Your father is getting ready for the opening."

Antonia stopped chewing and swallowed the last piece of her almo-jábana whole. "Of course he is. I can't believe I thought he'd forgotten about the party. . . ."

The invite had arrived three weeks ago, and her papá had immediately decided to go. Antonia was taken aback by his sudden change of mind. Her papá had refused to step inside the house since the moment they left, refused to even think about it, so much so that Antonia had handled all the paperwork regarding the house's rent and every single thing that came with it. So she struggled to understand why he was so determined to go back there after all these years, which was why Antonia was trying her hardest to change his mind. He'd come this far, she wouldn't let grief consume him once again. She'd even asked his physician, who'd advised her papá to stay away from the house, to intervene. After all, the memories and the pain that lived in that house were overwhelming for him.

But her father had ignored his doctor and her concerns. It was decided; he was going back to that house.

Carmela's expression faltered. "He'll never forget," she said. "We need to focus on getting *you* ready."

Antonia reached across the mahogany table for the aluminum coffee-pot and poured herself a cup. She took a sip; the hot liquid burned against her throat, awakening all her senses as she contemplated a return to her childhood home. She pulled out one of the wooden chairs at the kitchen table and sat.

In 1923, architect Ricardo Rubiano, Antonia's papá, finished building a sixteen-thousand-square-foot, five-story belle-epoque-style mansion on the outskirts of Bogotá. The house had been a gift for Antonia's mamá, a historian, a woman ahead of her time, who longed to live outside the big city in a fairy-tale, castle-esque-looking home. La Casona, as the locals called it, was unlike anything else the country had ever witnessed. Ostentatious, enormous, ambitious in its design, and built into the mountain itself, with 360-degree views of the Bogotá savanna, alongside a spectacular view of its natural neighbor, El Salto del Tequendama. The house offered a life away from the big city without giving up comfort and luxury. Large curtained windows, set in solid concrete walls, and burnt-red tiles on the roof. Natural hand-carved marble imported from Europe—from the Venus de Milo to more local deities such as Bachué and Bochica, the latter present in hand-painted murals, gilded carvings, and accents on the facade and the interiors.

La familia Rubiano became the envy of all. But a year after Antonia's mamá passed, and ten years after they'd moved in, la familia Rubiano had rushed out of the house without any intention of ever coming back.

Antonia's papá had given life to an isolated place, but that same place had taken life away from him. Away from his family.

"This *is* a bad idea." Antonia shook her head and drifted to her own thoughts.

The memories of Estela were too painful for Ricardo to bear. They were agonizing for Antonia as well, but she'd managed to keep her emotions at bay for the sake of them both. She ought to if she wanted to keep the semblance of her family together.

So far, Antonia had managed to keep them away from their former home for three years. They hadn't been there since Antonia had hauled her papá out in the middle of the night.

They'd been gone for good.

Or so Antonia thought.

Ricardo refused to let go of the five-story property and asked her not to sell it. Antonia assumed it was because that place had been built for her mamá, and even though he didn't want to step back inside, keeping it in the family felt like the thing he needed to do in memory of his deceased wife. So, several months ago, they rented the house out instead. León Rivera, one of the richest men in the city and her papá's best friend, became the new tenant of the house and, like that, it became a hotel.

But Antonia would've paid to forget about their time at the house; those memories her papá loved to reminisce about, she wished they would vanish. She couldn't bear the pain of having someone only through flash-backs. She wanted her mamá to be with her. Antonia needed her, and when Antonia wanted to go to her, the realization that Estela existed only in her faint recollections of the past killed her a little every time.

Out of all the memories, the one of their first night at the house pained her the most. It had been the promise of something good, of something better.

Antonia, her mamá, and her papá sitting snug by the fireplace, wrapped up in woolen blankets, crisp breeze seeping inside through the balcony, the roar of the waterfall the backdrop of their new beginning. The smell of roscón dulce and burnt arequipe, emanating from the kitchen, wafted in the air, tempting Antonia's nostrils and making her mouth water. Estela and Ricardo had been sipping on mulled wine from the cellar below, while Antonia kept her insides warm with hot chocolate con queso Carmela had made for her. Her papá had placed a big wooden box in front of her.

"This is for our Nona," he'd said softly, followed with a smile. Antonia exchanged glances briefly with her mamá. They'd just celebrated Antonia's thirteenth birthday right before moving out of Bogotá, and she wasn't ex-pecting any more gifts from her parents. So even though her eyelids were giving up on her, signaling that it had been a long day, she slid the top of the box to the side, the faint screech prickling at her ears. Inside were books, but not just any books, Antonia immediately recognized. It was a leath-erbound box set, ornate with golden carvings that read *Complete Brontë Collection*.

Antonia's heart skipped a beat, her chest filled with joy. "Papá…" Words evaded her—she'd devoured *Jane Eyre*, *Wuthering Heights*, and *Agnes Grey* over and over. To have a collection to add to her personal library in such gorgeous editions with deckle edges was a dream come true.

"How did you get this?"

"I had it shipped all the way across the Atlantic. We supposed it would be a nice thing for you to have now that we're here."

Carmela walked across the room that night carrying a silver platter with all the baked goods. Exhaustion still prickled at Antonia, but she knew she wouldn't be able to sleep. Seven books. All of them for her. New stories to be discovered, alongside the story that was just beginning for them too.

They were hopeful for what was to come, but that same hope would be snatched away from them several years after that.

"He is going. With or without you. It *is* better if you go." Carmela brought Antonia's attention back to their conversation. "Nothing will happen if you keep an eye on him."

"Dr. Ruíz told us to keep him away from that place. From all the memories. At least for the time being."

For the time being. The time being that felt like an eternity to Antonia. As long as the house was standing, her papá wouldn't get any better. And time waited for no one. Certainly not for Antonia.

Carmela nodded and stared at Antonia from the white marble counter. "It might be different this time," Carmela said, a trace of hope enveloping her tone. "Who knows, perhaps being there, at least for a little while, with the place looking different . . . perhaps he might realize that there's no one—nothing left to find there."

It *could* be different this time. Antonia wasn't a kid anymore; she wasn't the credulous prey she'd been growing up. The house would become no more than a steady revenue stream, and nothing else. If she could wait six months to save up her part, she'd never have to see the house or Bogotá ever again, aside from visits back home to see her beloved papá and Carmela. And a tiny part of her, even though she wouldn't admit it, wanted to go back. She wanted to see the house, to see if it was still standing while her world was crumbling, to see if it had changed below the hotel's new look. She wanted to find a thread of their past lives there, see if her mamá's scent still lingered in the air.

"It could serve us both, Nona," her papá began the day they received the invitation. "See the house again. Be there again. Realize that even though it hurts to be back, we've grown and we're better now. Perhaps closure is what we need. What *you* need, before you're able to get over what happened."

"Papá, no, I don't . . ." She didn't want to pick up the pieces that were left when they ran out. Perhaps the pieces weren't even there to begin with, not anymore. "Look at you. If you were better, you'd be doing the thing you loved most after Mamá—architecture. People ask all the time, and I have to keep lying. I can't tell the truth. I—" Antonia choked on her words. What else could she have possibly told him to convince him to drop the idea of visiting their former home?

"Aren't you even a bit curious? It's our house after all—"

"Yes, it's our house, but it's not a house anymore. It's a hotel. And it's no longer our home—" Antonia stopped herself from talking and kept her following thoughts to herself. Looking back, she wasn't sure the house was ever home to them.

Steps echoed through the halls, forcing Antonia out of her own head. She turned around in her seat to find her papá, his deep brown eyes a mirror of hers.

Antonia smiled. "Papá—you look incredible." And Ricardo did look good. As he stood, he appeared just like the man he'd been before his wife passed. Aside from the age marks, there was no trace of the person Antonia would see when she stared at him: a stranger, the shadow of who he once was. Right before her eyes, he had aged at least a few months each day, and even though he still looked old, now she could see the young and lively man within him, and it gave her hope.

Things *could* be different this time.

His usual pale olive skin took on a vibrant rosy hue under the warm light emanating from above. His black tuxedo brought something out of him, a pride and confidence that Antonia had for a long time been wishing to see resurface. His chestnut hair was slathered in hair wax, neatly pushed back.

She could feel her insides filling with a mix of hope and dread. She'd sacrifice by going back to the house if it meant seeing her papá this alive again. After all, it would only be for a few hours. It couldn't hurt, could it?

"Your mother must be really happy tonight."

His words made Antonia's skin feel slimy, and the hints of hope she'd found when she saw him vanished. *He thinks he's going to find her there.*

"No. She died there. Over four years ago. That place killed her—" Antonia didn't mean it literally. Houses don't kill people, people kill people. But it was Estela's fixation with that place that had pulled her down into the abyss like quicksand. Into an insidious and inescapable trap . . .

Antonia shook the thoughts from her mind and, with a deep breath, decided to approach Ricardo with a sense of calm rather than the sharp edge of confrontation. She was drained from the day at the escuela. Going back to her childhood home, if she was to return tonight, was a challenge that demanded every ounce of her remaining energy.

Tension warped around them and briefly kept them knee-deep in silence. The faucet dripped into the sink, the sound of each drop reverberating around the kitchen like a cymbal, yet no one moved, drank, or said another word.

Ricardo was the one to speak first. "Your mother was sick. She had the kind of illness that takes hold from within, the kind that is often overlooked by physicians. She gave up and—"

The words felt like a dozen bricks tumbling down on Antonia, and she couldn't get from underneath their weight. She'd heard that explanation before, and she'd forced herself to come to terms with it. But she still had days when she wondered how he could be so certain.

After all, Antonia hadn't asked more questions. Ricardo had told her that Estela had been acting strange that day, which Antonia had failed to notice, and that inevitably made her feel guilty. Next, Estela's body was flailing in the air. She was gone. *Dead.* Was there something Antonia could've done to prevent it? Could she have seen it coming? Could it be that Ricardo had been so sure because he was going through a similar illness too?

"Papá . . ." Antonia fought her tendency to talk back. She felt hollow. Two-dimensional. Useless. There was nothing she could do to help him.

"Nona, I know what you're going to say," he began. "Everything will be fine. It's just one small party. It is important for León—he's never given up on me, he's my friend, your uncle almost, and I want us to be there."

León had tried to help Ricardo out of the sadness that consumed him. Sometimes León would pick him up and leave with him for the day. Other days, when León couldn't convince him, León would stay at home with him giving him some company. While Antonia appreciated León's efforts, she still wished she could stay home.

"Your mother would've wanted it. That place was everything to her," her papá added.

The words punctured Antonia's chest. Nothing was ever just fine in that house. The place that meant everything to her mamá, even more than Antonia ever did, was the end of her. It became her tomb, her trap, her prison. One she could not escape alive.

"A small party?" Antonia said. "As if there ever was anything small and discreet about Doña Pereira's parties—"

"It's our house, Antonia. And we have to be there. *I* have to be there."

Antonia felt defeated. When would her papá realize her mamá wouldn't be there, waiting for him, a lingering shadow like the ones Antonia once . . . like the one she'd just . . . ?

Wait, what was she saying? Antonia didn't believe in hauntings, right?

But she couldn't deny the house had cast a shadow over their lives for years. Once an enchanting castle-like mansion, La Casona had later loomed eerily amid the dense shroud of moss and algae that clung to its weathered exterior. It seemed as though the mansion were rotting from the outside in, spreading a malevolent influence that tainted every living thing within its walls—mind, body, and soul.

They'd been isolated from everyone, from everything. At first, having Mamá, Papá, and Carmela had been enough. It was all Antonia thought she needed to be happy. Until they stopped leaving the house. It was as though it didn't want them to, as if the house's invisible grip dragged them deeper into a morass of despair. So the outings became reduced to less than a couple per month, and soon Antonia felt she was in some sort of confinement.

Recently, Antonia was beginning to think that the house was like an entity that followed them around. It was still with them, and no matter how much distance they tried to put between them and the place, it would always find a way to yank them back. Wouldn't let go. Not in the literal way, but in a way that's even worse. Even harder to get away from. It clouded their thoughts, their dreams. Their nightmares. But perhaps they were the ones at fault. After all, they were the ones who brought the house and the memories with them everywhere, not the house following them around like a sentient, living entity.

Perhaps it was people who haunted places, after all.

How could she expose them to their past again? That last night they were at the house, they barely got out alive. Antonia and Carmela had left to run errands in the city—they thought they'd spend the night in Bogotá, but they ended up coming back home earlier. It felt like any other night, the house was silent, the only sound coming from the falls just across. Exhaustion had consumed every inch of her body, and she went almost immediately to bed after Emiro dropped them off. But little did Antonia know her papá had already set a plan in motion.

The smell of smoke combined with the strangled screeches coming from outside had snatched her away from bed. Her hands scrambled to grab her belongings—her books, her journals. Her mamá's letters. *No. No. No.* All there had been left to do was run.

So she did.

She ran through her door and found Emiro sprinting toward her. He dragged her downstairs and eventually outside, where Carmela waited for

Antonia with Ricardo. She'd recognized it right then. The guilt overcoming his expression.

The memory of that night haunted her to this day. But with the recollection of the events came a flood of emotions. The main one being fear. Would Papá get confused again? Was he as far gone as her mamá was? And if so, was Antonia next? Were her nightmares the start, before delusion settled in?

It suddenly dawned on her: she might not want to go back, but she needed to if she wanted to put the pieces together. If the house was the cause of everything that transpired with their family, maybe it held other secrets yet to be revealed.

"Carmela is coming too." It came out as a knee-jerk thought because it was. If Antonia was to return, she would need backup.

A line etched between Carmela's brows. It was unfair, but there was no one Antonia trusted more than Carmela.

"I, um, yes?" Carmela managed.

"Thank you, you two, for doing this. I know it is not easy," her papá said, squeezing Antonia's hands inside his. His expression drifted, resettled. Antonia forced a smile. "Wherever she is, I am certain this will make her very proud and happy."

Something hardened inside Antonia. *No.* If the house hadn't killed her mamá, she'd be happy. If her obsession with the place hadn't pushed her to the edge, she'd be happy. If El Salto del Tequendama hadn't swallowed her whole, she'd be happy.

Happy and *alive.*

But the only place she was now was one she couldn't come back from. Death.

What was there left to be afraid of?

The house was featured in La Gaceta de Santa Fé.

"*Five stories tall, the mansion sits heavy and sprawling over the Andean grounds. Stone-walled like a fortress and majestic like its imposing neighbor, the Tequendama Falls.*

"*The first floor consists of two drawing rooms and architect Ricardo's studio. Two floors above is the main level, which features a kitchen, a spacious living room that can be converted into a ballroom, and an array of bedrooms and guest bedrooms. The two floors remaining, with the tower counting as its own floor, are dedicated for additional bedrooms, bathrooms, a library, and another study area for his daughter, Antonia.*"

The basement, the part they failed to mention, mostly because I didn't want to give them many details, was split into Ricardo's wine-and-beer cellar, with wooden barrels imported from Germany, and a room of my own. I longed to be down there while the house was being built; it already felt like my personal haven, with the water splashing against the windows and the waterfall even closer.

Everyone is starting to get settled inside, at last. Ricardo is isolating himself in his studio. He has unfinished businesses going on in the city that he must take care of. It's been a couple of weeks of going back and forth between the city and El Salto, to get everything in place. Still, cardboard boxes remain stacked high against the ceiling of several of our drawing rooms. The contents of the few that we've unpacked are already where they belong. These days I've come to realize that when a house lacks the warmth of a home, one becomes overly attached to material things. We give meaning to them, craving the feeling of comfort and safety, but they're all as empty as we are.

My room, from where I'm writing this entry, is ready. The altar has been installed; the handcrafted woodwork with gilded accents for the library was finished just a few days ago. Under the faint light of the iron sconces hanging from the walls, the carvings shimmer, revealing the most delicate and intricate serpent figures, as if they are slithering on the walls. Almost as if they've come to life. On the walls are also frescoes I spent the past months painting, the waterfall featured on multiple ones. But my personal favorite by far is the one that depicts a Muisca legend: Bochica, with the golden staff breaking the land, freeing it from the rainwaters.

Warmth settles in my chest, and for the first time I feel whole. Excited for the future in front of us. It's not long before our first gathering.

But as I write about this wonderous place, my home, my mind keeps drifting back to my querida Antonia. Mi Nona. She worries me the most. She's refused to sleep in the room we set up for her: first floor, by the balcony, a grandiose view of the waterfall across. Instead, she's requested the library for herself, three floors above. She says the sound of the water scares her, and I'm certain she hasn't even peeked at the falls. She's enclosed herself in her room, sometimes refusing to come out at all. I caught her glancing at my tunjos, stealing some when she thinks I'm not watching and gathering them in her dresser. Hiding them.

I let her. No need to trouble her any further.

Instead, I give her valerian root every evening, to see if that gets her to sleep, keep an eye on her.

But my attempts have failed. Antonia wakes up with shadows under her eyes. And sometimes she screams at night.

Ricardo said it's normal. It's her way of saying she misses our old home and wants to go back. And even though he's often quick to dismiss my concerns, perhaps he's right. Still, I wish I could put her emotions at ease, soothe her, console her. Ricardo says it's nothing but night terrors, that they'll subside . . . nothing she can't handle on her own. And after a while, Antonia agrees with him. I'm certain she's only trying to placate my inquietude. She's strong-willed, just like I am, so I don't push her, for there are other matters that also require my attention.

Amid these unsettling nights, Carmela has informed me that there have been occasional uninvited visitors. The place's history had always drawn them like flies. Townsfolk, mostly, driven by curiosity. But that doesn't concern me. We are here now, and I'm the protector of the place.

TRES

Antonia glanced at her papá, sitting comfortably in the front seat of the black Packard Eight.

The car moved along the darkened, muddy road, and soon they were immersed in the thick mist, curling in the air like funerary incense through the dense forest. A breeze sneaked into the car, its dry chill stinging Antonia's cheeks. Emiro leaned forward, peering through the windshield as his fingers fiddled with the radio, filling their ears with the latest from La Sonora Matancera.

Emiro turned on the fog lights and wipers before resuming his conversation with her papá.

Antonia's eyes went back to the half-open window. As they approached, El Salto del Tequendama opened to them like an invitation. Her chest heaved as she took in the striking waterfall. Even though it was almost completely hidden underneath the dense layer of haze, the thundering roar gave its presence away as the icy water crashed against the rocks at the bottom.

Antonia spotted her nogal. Her eighty-two-foot walnut tree—almost a half century old—stood across the field. The tree had been Antonia's haven for years—she'd devoured Gothic romances underneath its wide deep-green crown, collected its overripe fruit and brought it to her mamá in exchange for more Gothic novels. Estela painted clay vases and murals with the nogal's fruit juice, like the Muisca, the native people of this region, did. The only thing Antonia never did was climb it. She didn't even attempt it. She had an issue with heights, which she considered a joke, given that she lived on top of the Andean Hills.

But the land surrounding the tree proved much less fruitful. Estela had attempted to start her orchard right below it, with orchids, bromelias, along with fruits, but almost everything that stood close to it died while Antonia's nogal flourished, as though it consumed everything around it. So, her mamá's orchard had to be moved somewhere else. Antonia felt bad for the tree. It was condemned to a life in isolation—secluded from everything that wasn't as toxic as it was, something she was deeply familiar with.

The car came to a stop, ending her remembrance of her nogal, and, instantly, Antonia's suspicions materialized. From this far, the house stood unbothered by their presence, with an all-new white exterior, a sweeping driveway, manicured freshly cut lawns, towering concrete columns, intricate stone carvings, and regal symmetry that gave it an air of sophistication that it didn't have before, without giving up the original French style. The gates had been torn down for parking space, and the brick-colored tiles in the ceiling freshly painted bright orange.

More than a hotel, the estate had become a statement of wealth and power, and it was also a testament to Doña Pereira's extravagant tastes.

What a nice disguise it had on. It appeared innocent, defenseless. Welcoming even.

Something twisted within Antonia, and in it she recognized fear and hints of anger. While her life in Bogotá decayed, the house thrived as though it hadn't even missed them, missed her. As though it had been feeding off Antonia even from afar, sucking dry her hope and life energy, getting a new life of its own.

Antonia's papá gazed at her from the rear window. "We'll leave in a few hours," he said when Emiro killed the engine.

Antonia sighed, unable to hide her disappointment in being back.

Carmela leaned close to Antonia from the opposite end of the beige leather car seat. "We could always leave . . . ," she whispered against Antonia's ear.

Antonia shook her head. "No. You're right. Maybe things will be different this time around. It can be a quick visit, then we head back and move on with our lives. It doesn't have to be like last time." She drew out each word slowly, trying to ameliorate the situation. She couldn't leave because she'd seen things beyond her comprehension—things that lurked in the shadows, in every corner of the house, but she'd pushed those memories down so deep that she wondered if they were even real . . . until recently . . . with her nightmares.

Perhaps she'd been too young. Perhaps even if they'd been real, this time everything would be just fine. Or perhaps she needed to see it once again to make sense of everything. She had a sliver of hope that entering the house would allow her to find answers.

Antonia locked her gaze on the now five-story hotel as it rose before them. Just looking at it was enough to make her heart race. No disguise would ever be good enough to hide from her eyes what had been their former home. How her mamá had stood at its gate when Antonia first set foot in the house. The day they moved in had been joyful and filled with excitement for all of them.

"El Castillo de Bochica," Mamá had said, with a wide grin painted across her face. Antonia had never seen her as happy, as full of life. "It's a castle."

And it had been *hers*. Built into the mountain itself, the house mimicked the appearance of a fortress. A place that nothing could ever bring down. Came war, came a storm, it could stand against everything.

The only thing it couldn't manage was to keep her family whole.

Antonia turned her gaze away from the window, as to command the wave of pain overcoming her away. Her papá opened the door beside him; the first thing that hit them was the blast of frigid air, which snatched the breath from Antonia. Then came the smell, a sour marshy stench wafting in from the open door in the front seat, making her cough. The smell was familiar; the swampy stink had accompanied them during their last years at the house. It was so strong, it chased away every thought in Antonia's brain and left just one: fear.

Antonia waited as Ricardo struggled out, then took the hand he offered her as gracefully as she could and edged across the seat after him, closely followed by Carmela.

"Nona, you look ill," he said with a concerned expression.

"The drive. You know how dizzy it makes me," Antonia said dismissively.

Dusk was closing in and the chill was numbing, like a clammy shell that drew itself around their bones. Antonia wrapped her black sequin shawl over her pale, naked shoulders and leaned closer to her papá, enclosing her fingers around his arm like her life depended on it. So long as she kept him in sight, nothing could possibly go wrong.

And if it did, she'd fix it.

She always did.

The three of them stood on the gravel path that led to the house, framed by a lush green thicket. *Their house.* The high dark wooden door set deep in the walls, wide open.

As they strode toward the grand entrance, a sudden hush fell on the crowd around the main door. It didn't take long for Antonia to spot some familiar faces among the onlookers reveling inside.

A few dozen pairs of shining eyes swept over them, surveying, cool and assessing, as though eager to unveil the secrets that the Rubiano family kept. Secrets that could never see the light of day if Antonia wanted to keep their reputation intact and, most important, if she wanted to keep her job.

Antonia felt her insides knotting like a piece of string at the thought. No parent would want the daughter of a lunatic as the teacher to their kids, and the nuns wouldn't hesitate to fire her if they knew what she dealt with in the after hours. All people had to know was that the well-known architect Ricardo Rubiano was having a hard time dealing with his wife's passing, and his docile abnegated daughter and his housekeeper took good care of him.

"That smell has *really* gotten worse with time," Carmela said. "But the guests appear rather unbothered by it." She motioned to the sea of people making their way inside the hotel through the door. Although it was not customary for invitations to request special attire, least of all for a party on the outskirts of the city, tonight was an exception. The women wore knee-length, sack-like evening gowns and capes to protect them from the low temperatures, but especially from the eyes of nasty men who could see no woman's skin exposed without thinking it gave them the right to stare. The women's necks were adorned with esmeraldas boyacenses, precious green stones so valuable that they could've fed three generations of a family of ten. Men were dressed in black woolen suits with bow ties or long thin ties, and some wore black top hats and frock coats, like Antonia's papá, the mayor, and his cabinet.

"Their noses don't even twitch," Carmela added. "Do you think they smell it?"

A rancid taste lingered in Antonia's mouth, making her skin crawl. She swallowed. "Perhaps they don't care. They'd do anything to make it to the cover of tomorrow's issues of *La Nota* and *La Gaceta*, to be featured in the stories of the grand opening of El Refugio del Salto. Sewer smell and all." And it was true. Tonight's event was the highlight of the year. It was the time that a select and fortunate group of people (whom Antonia found profoundly unfortunate) got more than a quick tour around the palatial halls.

Antonia looked up again to see Doña Pereira waving at them from the parlor as they approached. Padre Juan stood beside her. Antonia cocked her head, and her lips slackened briefly. The last time she had seen the father had been over three years ago in this exact place. Doña Pereira had well intentionally brought him to take a look at Antonia's papá.

It had been a little less than a year since Ricardo's wife died, for God's sake. Sadness was the least he could feel. Holy water and prayers didn't fix him. Let alone an improvised exorcism by Padre Juan that further clouded his mind instead. Not long after the father allegedly exorcised the demons, her papá tried to burn down the house with Antonia and Carmela inside. If he wasn't possessed before, he certainly was after that.

Antonia stopped just before the threshold, as her eyes landed on the double-panel door. It stood open as a serene inviting presence illuminated by the soft glow of the fading sunlight outside.

Antonia's eyes flitted briefly between the door and the space behind her, as if suddenly weighing the decision to push forward or retreat.

A series of ornate, hand-carved moldings framed each panel, delicate and intricate, chiseled to achieve an elegant and timeless look. The door was flanked by large and robust wrought-iron hinges, with decorative scrolls and floral motifs that echoed the door's carved patterns.

The finishing touch, a brass knocker shaped like a sunburst, its rays extending outward, mirroring Muisca carvings inside the house.

Antonia took a deep breath, trying to gather the courage to step inside, to step into her past, but the heaviness of that decision seemed to press down on her.

Once she stepped foot inside, there was no turning back.

Antonia's hesitation vanished after a brief moment, and as she ventured through the door, her eyes swept over Padre Juan.

"Padre." She nodded at him. Antonia had never before seen the man without his cassock. He could almost have passed as a regular guest if it weren't for the purple monastic scapular hanging loose over his shoulders and the worn-out leatherbound Bible clasped firmly in his hand.

In the parlor, the space was bathed in a somber glow cast by the chandeliers hanging from the high, ornate ceiling. The crystal pendants, though brilliant, reflected only fragmented patterns of light, creating a play of shadows that danced across the checkered floors in unsettling, irregular movements. The walls, lined with dark, rich wood paneling, were decorated with tapestries depicting landscapes of the Bogotá savanna. The fabric seemed to pulse with a life of its own, the patterns shifting subtly, as if trying to tell her something. There was a tension to the room, as though it were holding its breath, waiting for something—something dark and unknown—to reveal itself.

No. She couldn't get caught up in her emotions, in the feeling of being back to what once was her home.

She needed her mind sharp, strong. She wasn't about to succumb to her past in there.

So, Antonia forced her focus back to Doña Pereira, snatching herself away from the hotel's new decor.

"Antonia, Ricardo . . ." Doña Pereira didn't acknowledge Carmela. Carmela's brown skin and steel-gray hair gave Doña Pereira enough reasons to find her presence undesirable, to refuse to let her stand anywhere close to her round, tanned face. "Welcome to El Refugio del Salto. We're honored to have you."

Upon closer look, Doña Pereira seemed to have rejuvenated a decade since Antonia had last seen her, which had been a little less than a year ago when renting out the place to León. Under layers of makeup, Doña Pereira's skin was firm, the wrinkles that framed her face were tamed, giving her a baby's complexion. Her sequin yellow dress sat tight on her body, her belly straining against its confines. Seeing Doña Pereira standing by the door like la patrona made Antonia's insides quiver. It was odd seeing the old lady call the place hers now. The last time, it had been Antonia standing by the door to begrudgingly welcome Doña Pereira inside.

Antonia's lips pressed in a slight grimace. "Thank you."

Doña Pereira was one of the few people who didn't share condolences every time she saw them, and Antonia appreciated that. Part of moving on after the death of a loved one is letting go, but the constant reminders of the person's absence made it harder to get over what had happened.

Antonia glanced at Padre Juan, her tone turning gay. "Padre, out of all the places I thought I'd run into a priest, the last of them was at a hotel opening party."

Padre Juan blinked nervously, then ducked his head as though avoiding Antonia's gaze as his cheeks turned light red.

He cleared his throat. "Hija mía, I simply came because Doña Pereira wanted me to bless the place. God knows this house has witnessed *tragedy after tragedy*, and we don't want any of that still lingering."

"Just like last time, huh?" Antonia paused, awaiting the padre's or Doña Pereira's reaction, but their expressions gave nothing away. Silence fell between them momentarily, but Antonia quickly resumed speaking. "Always a pleasure seeing you."

"He will always be welcomed in this place," Doña Pereira chimed in. "Just like he was when *you* lived here. . . . Besides, he is one of my closest friends."

Antonia's stomach hardened. "Yeah, I suppose," she said dismissively.

"Eleonora, thank you for the invitation. I can't think of better hands for the house." Antonia's papá's thin lips curled in a wide smile, his great round face glimmering with joy. Antonia stared at him as the words flew out of his mouth. He meant every one of them. "We're certainly pleased to be back for such a special occasion."

"Ricardo, the pleasure is all ours," Doña Pereira said slowly. "We've kept the essence of the house intact while also trying to make it look like the hotel the city deserves."

Antonia almost felt the air shift around them, toward Doña Pereira and her undeniable gravity.

Irritated, Antonia shifted her attention to the young man suddenly standing awkwardly to their side. He'd donned a fitted deep blue tailored suit, and his chest and shoulders pushing back against it made him look like the type that lifted heavy objects for a living. His brown almond-shaped eyes framed by bristly black eyebrows locked on Antonia's gaze.

He was rather handsome, no need for Antonia to look twice, and the thought sent a rush of heat through her cheeks. She immediately looked away, banishing her thoughts. She had no time for that now.

But Doña Pereira had noticed Antonia's blushing and turned to introduce the young man. "This is Alejandro Soler. He is a very fine reporter sent from *La Nota* to cover tonight's big event."

Antonia drew her eyes back to Alejandro. Of course. Doña Pereira would make sure the reporter met "the girl who survived the fire." She wanted every single detail captured and all over tomorrow's papers. The unfolded black compact camera hanging over Alejandro's chest was proof of that.

"Pleasure to meet you." He stretched out his hand to Antonia, his smoldering gaze drawing her eyes to his once again. Unlike Antonia's hand, his was warm and comforting to the touch, even with the cold weather enveloping them. She felt a jolt of electricity as he squeezed her fingers softly before putting his hand back inside his pocket.

"Alejo? Nice to see you." Recognition sparkled in Ricardo's eyes and Antonia readjusted her stance.

Antonia's expression was puzzled. How did her papá know him? If she'd met him before, she would certainly have recalled.

"The pleasure is all mine, Don Ricardo. I've always been fond of your work." Alejandro smiled, making his already chiseled cheekbones and jaw appear even sharper. He was probably only a few years older than Antonia.

"I thought you still worked at *Radio Noche*," her papá said.

Antonia's lips parted in surprise. The name *Radio Noche* elicited memories. Over the years, Estela had collected magazines, and Antonia was certain that she'd seen *Radio Noche*'s once or twice among her mamá's collection—that very magazine fed her fascination with El Salto del Tequendama. The obsession that ended up killing her.

Alejandro chuckled and then nodded. "I do, but working several jobs is a must. Being a reporter doesn't pay much after all."

A set of two familiar faces stepped through the crowd, briefly interrupting their conversation. León Rivera, Doña Pereira's only son and Antonia's papá's closest friend, stood in front of them with a welcoming smile, his wife, Lucía, accompanying him.

"It is a delight having you here." León wrapped his arms around Ricardo and offered Antonia and Carmela a kind smile.

"Antonia, Ricardo." Lucía smiled at them. She was dressed in a sapphire-blue satin gown, the neckline adorned with a delicate beading. Her brown hair was meticulously arranged in soft curls that framed her face and cascaded down her shoulders.

"Lucía," Antonia said, "you look ravishing."

She could see the woman's eyes brim with excitement. Doña Pereira wasn't one to hand out compliments, even less so her son, so Antonia thought Lucía would appreciate the gesture.

León spoke again: "You are our special guests—this night is yours as much as it is ours."

Antonia quickly realized by the sudden shift in Doña Pereira's face that León was not el patrón of the hotel, the old lady was.

Antonia felt sorry for him in that moment—empathy even. It had to be hard being his mother's son. Nothing was ever good enough, or enough at all for someone as ambitious as Doña Pereira. León was not the exception, and he was destined to live under her shadow.

But as empathetic as Antonia could feel toward León, she secretly admired Doña Pereira's strong will. Whatever she wanted, she had. Estela and Doña Pereira were alike in that sense. And Antonia would always admire courageousness and bravery and ambition in women. In a world such as this, that punished female ambition, Antonia was eager to find some inside her.

"Well, you know Papá, he wouldn't miss it for anything . . . *we* wouldn't miss it," Antonia quickly corrected between gritted teeth, swallowing her pride.

"Thank you," Ricardo said, and returned a smile.

"Why don't you take Ricardo to see the ballroom? I'm very interested in hearing what he has to say about our renovations. I very much appreciate his keen architectural eye."

León's face looked a bit strained as he agreed, but smiled in return. "Alejandro, Lucía, come with us," he called. "I'd love for you to catch Ricardo's wisdom."

Doña Pereira turned to face Antonia and continued, "It was such a pity that he couldn't help us with the renovations himself. I am certain the hotel would've turned out way better than it did."

Antonia shrugged. "Nonsense. You've done an outstanding job. I barely recognize our house anymore."

She lied. She could recognize this place from afar. The Muisca carvings, the checkered floors, the roaring symphony from outside, the frigid, stinky air filtering in even when every window was shut, the way the voices echoed as if the place were hollow, even though it never was. She could walk in blindfolded and still know exactly where in the house she stood.

But she wasn't about to engage in anything more than a civil conversation with Doña Pereira.

"That is because it is a house no more. It's a hotel, querida." Doña Pereira motioned them down the hallway and farther inside. "Tonight is going to be absolutely magical." Doña Pereira's confidence made Antonia's skin tingle. Magic was what Antonia would require if things went downhill. If Ricardo's thoughts and memories troubled him so badly and he started having second thoughts about keeping the house standing in its roots. Just like it had happened last time . . .

Antonia glanced at her papá, melting into the crowd, León trailing closely behind. So far, there was nothing to be worried about . . . even if they'd just arrived.

"The deeper we get inside, the worse the smell gets," Carmela, who had been walking the perimeter, said between pursed lips. Antonia nodded at Carmela and followed Doña Pereira.

As they moved through the long arched hallway, Antonia noticed Carmela was right. But she told herself the smell could be coming from the furnace, which hadn't been used in a while. El Castillo de Bochica had been closed for over three years after all.

Antonia let her eyes wander; being inside the hotel for the first time felt the same as coming back home after a long absence. The place had been her home for a decade, a small world unto itself. But the feeling sat uneasily, and she struggled to shake it away.

As she moved, the walls seemed to close in on her, as if the weight of her past were materializing into a suffocating sense of confinement suddenly constricting her chest.

Taking a few deep breaths, Antonia settled her racing heart and focused on what stood before her. Doña Pereira had meant it: they'd kept the essence of the place. But now, it felt alive and looked brighter than an opera house. Whereas before everything inside the house was barely discernible, the colors so muted and dull that they were almost gray, now everything seemed so clear and bright, almost as if the house itself were basking in the radiance of its new owners.

Dressed in all white, waiters and waitresses, holding crystal platters, danced their way through the sea of people crammed in the big hall. Stone archways, ornate with plaster Muisca snake cornices, her mamá's cornices, were enough to bring every eye upward, along with a few exposed beams, a personal touch from Doña Pereira, since they certainly weren't there before. At the end of the lobby, on the right side, a spiral wooden staircase twirled, leading the way up and down through multiple floors of the hotel.

Inside, boleros echoed within its walls, muffling almost every other sound.

As Antonia took everything in, her gaze caught on Alejandro in the ballroom across from her. He glided on the checkered floor with the compact device that seemed more like an extension of his arms, an entity of its own. Antonia followed his line of sight, catching him staring at the Muisca detailing.

"What do you think of the new insides, darling?" Doña Pereira's voice came from behind her, snatching her attention away from the young reporter.

But the question went ignored when her eyes landed on the wraparound balcony at the very end of the crowded ballroom that stretched almost from the front to the back of the main floor, the same place Estela had stood at day and night.

Antonia remembered her mamá peeking at the waterfall, as though making sure it was still there every morning and right before bed. Estela would stand and contemplate the beauty of El Salto del Tequendama for hours—sometimes she'd even paint her murals staring right into it. Antonia couldn't peer down at the precipice too close; her stomach would instantly heave, and she would beg her mamá to move away from the ledge.

Now, instead of Estela, it was the guests who stood there, sipping on sweet wine from the hotel's cellar, a handful of them regarding Antonia with curious smiles. A veil of fog swirled around them, as though a monster stretching its claws, preparing to grab its prey and never let go.

The enjoyment displayed on their faces was a stark contrast to what the house provided for Antonia: no shelter. All she found here were the remnants of memories she refused to keep, things a renovation couldn't take away: the sleepless nights, the things sneaking in the darkness, the sighting of ill-intentioned strangers who roamed the property at night and left a trail of objects scattered outside on the lawn. Eggs, cracked and whole, candle wax, coins, strips of cloth, pieces of photographs.

In the beginning, Ricardo would brush aside these activities, labeling them as the work of mischievous teens meant to cause fear and gossip in the local community. But later on, they became more vile—animal blood, empty black salt packets, sometimes they'd even find dead-animal burial sites and jars full of greenish bile. Antonia recognized the consistency of the ritual patterns and their recurring nature to view them as more than just vandalism. People were coming with a purpose.

"The place holds so much power and meaning to everyone that they come here to drain it of its magic," Estela would say. "It's always been a sacred place for los Muiscas. And with holiness comes evil too. The desire to corrupt the land. To take hold of it."

Soon after the disruptions began, Ricardo installed black iron gates outside to placate Antonia's uneasiness, but it didn't deter people from visiting the place. Sometimes Antonia could still hear them chanting in her sleep, the clatter of the leaves underneath their feet as they approached. . . .

The memories, Antonia realized, the good ones, she'd keep with her no matter where she was. She didn't need the house to feel the infinite love she felt for Estela. She didn't need the house to remember her face or her stories. Stories about los Muiscas and how Bochica had opened up a hole, a crater, El Salto del Tequendama, to save them from a flood.

"Bochica was their heroine," Estela had said. "They came here to worship her. To give thanks to her, for she gave them life when others threatened to take it away from them."

"Bochica *was* a woman?" Antonia had asked, her interest certainly spiked. She'd appreciate it if the protagonist of her mamá's stories, unlike most of the stories told to her throughout the years, was a woman just like her.

Estela nodded. "She is whatever you need her to be. And I guess it depends who you ask. History is, after all, written by men. I believe we can rewrite it. Nothing is ever set in stone."

Antonia cherished the days when her mamá told her stories. Tales about the heroines of the past were among Antonia's favorites, for oftentimes women were just the damsels in distress. However, regardless of what written history would say, all Antonia had to do was look to Estela for such inspiration. Antonia's real heroine had always been her mamá, even if later on she'd resented Estela's choice of Bochica and El Salto over her. It was that resentment that alienated Antonia, that caused her to stop listening to Estela's stories. Oh, how Antonia regretted having put an end to that special bond; she would give anything to listen to her mamá one last time.

At least Antonia still had Carmela; she was her heroine too.

The sound of drums and high-pitched guitars brought Antonia's mind back to the party, the beat getting louder the farther she explored.

As she stepped inside the ballroom, an unsettling feeling began welling inside her, the eerie sensation of being watched crawling up and scratching her neck. Her heart thumped so loud, she feared everyone around her could hear it. Reacting instinctively, Antonia turned around in alarm, her body moving faster than her thoughts. The vibrant, lively atmosphere of the room had vanished, replaced by the heavy, coppery scent of fresh blood. Goose bumps traveled through her as the sound of clashing water revealed that she was not in the room anymore but somewhere outside the hotel surrounded by . . .

Fear struck her, immobilizing her.

The humanlike creatures wore hoods, their white rags damp and covered in mud, and from their worn-out belts swung rusty flails as they sagged toward her. Faint moonlight shone from above, unearthing El Salto del Tequendama just across. Her whole body trembled and her thoughts were jumbled as she tried to make out how she'd transported herself by the waterfall.

She stumbled to get back on her feet, but the ground below her disappeared and now the water was reaching her waist. The waterfall stood even closer, as though Antonia had moved, or it had come at her like the rest of the creatures surrounding her.

The saliva in her mouth went dry as she realized she was trapped. She wouldn't be able to run. She felt stunned by the full force of their attention.

Suddenly, a set of bony hands wrapped around her neck from behind. She was paralyzed until a force, a grip she couldn't get herself out of, shoved her below the icy water and into its depths. Pain rippled through her as she strained upward.

What was happening? Was she going mad? Was her papá right in that she was as paranoid and sick as her mamá was?

Her nightmares. Her memories . . .

Figures full of hate had terrified her over the years in that house. She'd convinced herself she'd been too young to know better. Too naive. Gullible. Too sensitive to the old tales people would tell.

She couldn't deny them anymore. They were real. So she forced herself to look. But before she could take them in, in their entirety, the water and the filthy ghosts were gone. Her clothes were dry, as if she hadn't left the ballroom, as if it had all been in her head.

Antonia replayed the scene over and over in her mind until the rhythmic melody of drums and guitars along with the velvety voice of the lead singer blasting from the stage soothed Antonia's heart back to a regular pace. She was safe . . . for now.

Antonia scanned her surroundings. Everyone was dancing, completely absorbed in the festivities. And after what she'd just been through, the familiar figure she'd seen earlier at the house, a sudden thought struck Antonia. . . .

Without an ounce of hesitation in her body, she ran back to the lobby, squeezing between the sea of people swaying to the loud music, and sprinted up the spiral staircase to the fourth floor, scrambling to the hallway leading to her room. Perhaps entering what used to be a space of her own might help her clear her head, help her remember things, such as exactly how the nightmares had started. Even if the room didn't belong to her anymore.

Just as she was about to quicken her pace, footsteps, heavy and deliberate, grew louder and sharper behind her in the empty space, and a faint murmur of voices drifted up from below. Panic overcame her. Had someone followed her upstairs? Worse yet, she had no time to reach her bedroom. She couldn't risk being seen roaming the place alone. Doña Pereira would not want Antonia sneaking around. But she also couldn't run back. So, instead, she disappeared inside the first room to her right.

She closed the door behind her and pressed her ear against the thick wood to make sure whoever was coming wasn't getting any closer to her. But the steps, the echo of them that had lingered mere seconds ago, were gone, and the voices had blended into an indistinguishable hum.

Relieved, she stepped away from the door and took in the confines of the room she was in. It exuded opulence. Soft moonlight from outside filtered through ivory curtains, casting a gentle shadow on the floor. Nestled in a corner, a small writing desk with a leatherbound journal and a silver fountain pen. Next to it was a vase of fresh bromelias like the ones that used to bloom in her mamá's orchard, their scent mingling with the subtle hint of a half-burnt incense stick that was on one of the nightstands. The bed, with a gilt frame, dominated the center, its embroidered duvet a patchwork of burgundy and gold.

Her eyes continued their natural progression to the right, until they landed on the carved mahogany dresser with gold detailing standing against one wall. Beside it, a set of chestnut bookcases with a hand-painted landscape of the Bogotá savanna, lush and verdant grasslands with scattered trees that had been the primary home to the Muisca people prior to the Spanish colonization. Recognition immediately settled in Antonia. This furniture had belonged to Estela.

It wasn't long before Antonia found herself sweeping her fingers on the leather spines of the old books stacked on the shelves. The space around her filled with whispers of nostalgia as she collected fragments of her memory, fragments of the time Estela was still alive. To be able to find her mamá and find herself in a place that was long gone made her heart ache. Estela was dead, but in moments like this, Antonia couldn't help but think she was still alive somehow.

Antonia pulled out some of the books and fiddled with the yellowed papers mindlessly, as if she'd been locked inside the moment, trapped in memories of her own. This time she wasn't dreaming, she was traveling to her past while wide-awake.

As she pulled herself out of her stupor, diligently putting the books back inside the shelves in front of her, a folded piece of paper fell at her feet.

Opening it, Antonia immediately recognized Estela's handwriting. A glance at the date and the structure revealed it was from one of her mamá's journals. Without hesitation, she began to read.

Thud. Thud.

It came from the floors above. Then came a bang so loud the ceiling shook. Forceful, like a dozen giant rocks being slammed against the floor. I aimed my ears at the ceiling, listening, vigilant for more sounds to come. The light coming from my candle dimmed out, until there was nothing but moonlight sneaking in through the window across.

I gathered determination, jolted my body upward, and sprinted at the door, only for my hands to struggle to find the doorknob. My pulse throbbed in my ears faster and faster with every beat. But there was no door. There was no knob. I attempted to move to find my way out. Perhaps I ran in the wrong direction—it was so dark. How could I know? But my knees stiffened, and I could no longer move.

I breathed in shallow breaths and directed all my strength to my lower body. Still, I didn't move an inch. Yet a silent shriek managed to escape me. I screamed from the top of my lungs, except not even I could hear my own voice. Frustration gathered at the pit of my stomach.

What was happening?

Suddenly, the smell of sewage wafted in the air, landing on my tongue. My stomach twisted into knots. The scent overcame everything—clouding my thoughts.

Next, I caught a set of red eyes staring back at me. The features blurred out in the shadows that now almost completely covered my room. I gasped, audibly this time.

Someone locked me in here.

No. No. Who? The only person in the house was Ricardo. He knew I'd be in here. He wouldn't . . .

But I wasn't safe anymore. For something evil had been invited in after all.

Next thing I knew, a high-pitched scream pierced my eardrums.

Leave!

I can't say for certain it was a dream, as it felt so real. What I do know is that I need to run. I'm not going to die tonight.

Antonia stood there, her hands trembling as she stared at the words on the page in disbelief. She'd been certain Estela had gotten rid of the ripped-out journal entries . . . but Antonia had just found one! She'd left the party looking for answers about her nightmares and had discovered something entirely different. What did this revelation imply? Had her mamá fallen out of her own will after all? A rush of questions and uncertainty flooded Antonia's mind, each one more unsettling than the last, as she fought the tide of panic that threatened to overcome her.

Could there be more hidden entries around the house?

But however much Antonia longed to continue searching, an unnerving awareness gnawed at her. She knew her absence would soon be noticed.

Reluctantly, she decided to return to the party, already plotting her next escape.

There were more things to uncover, but time was slipping away like elusive shadows in the night.

CUATRO

A round Antonia, a heavy silence hung in the floors below, punctuated only by the occasional clink of glasses or the distant strains of La Sonora Matancera playing a muted, almost mournful tune. The laughter and chatter of the guests seemed muffled, swallowed by the oppressive stillness that pervaded the space as she marched down the spiral staircase.

On the main floor, Antonia snaked through the ballroom diligently, trying her best to fit in with the rest of the crowd, as if nothing had happened just mere minutes ago.

Antonia stretched her arm and snagged a drink from one of the waiter's platters. "Thanks," she mouthed at the tall lady, and emptied the little glass in one gulp. The whiskey left a burnt and metallic aftertaste in her mouth, but she didn't mind it. It was exactly what she needed to calm her nerves and the hundreds of questions running through her mind.

A few eyes swept over her, accusing, judging. Antonia could almost hear their voices in her head. Not very ladylike of her to drink Scotch, let alone publicly. Others shared their pitiful smiles.

It had been a few years since Estela passed and the family would still get the same reaction from people. But Antonia got the worst of it. They pitied her for having to deal with Ricardo, for devoting her youth to care for him and having to press pause on her life. As if those same people wouldn't judge her if she didn't. It was the duty of a benevolent and docile daughter to care for her father and for her future husband.

What they ignored was that it had in fact been her decision. She wanted to save Ricardo like she couldn't save Estela. If only she'd pushed harder, if only she'd insisted on leaving the house and taking them all with her, her mamá would be alive.

Antonia had yearned to see Europe—to see the places where her favorite Gothic novels took place. What if she'd insisted that her parents come with her before she left for Bogotá? The trip would've lasted at least three months—three months of a beautiful and idyllic summer in European lands.

She often blamed herself; she'd played a part in it too. And that tormented her. She didn't believe in ghosts, but she was certain that one could be haunted by the past. The haunting what-ifs. But after what she'd just discovered, were there others she should be pointing the finger at?

Antonia banished the thoughts briefly, and a wave of relief engulfed her when she spotted Carmela a mere few steps from her among the crowd, her braided updo too familiar for Antonia to miss.

Carmela squished her eyebrows together and made her way to Antonia.

"What on earth happened to you—?" She grabbed Antonia's arm and pushed her away from the crowd and back to the hallway. Carmela motioned at Antonia's face and handed her a napkin. "Where were you?" she asked, her tone low and mindful of their surroundings. "I thought you wanted us both to keep an eye on your father? Yet you vanish for like half an hour and come back looking as if you've been on an expedition in the wilderness."

Antonia patted down the beads of sweat accumulating on her forehead and fumbled to pin back the loose strands of hair gathering at the sides of her face.

"It's . . . um—I've been dancing. I mean, I thought, 'Why be miserable when I can enjoy myself instead?' It's been a long while since I've attended any party. I thought I'd make the best of it—"

Carmela stared at her in disbelief. "Uh-huh, right. And just so you know, you missed Doña Pereira's toast. She gathered all guests here like her flock, and we had to listen to her talk for five minutes that felt like an agonizing nightmare."

"A toast?" Antonia scoffed. "Of course."

"She wouldn't miss the opportunity to brag about her big accomplishment. How she was able to rebuild this place, to give it the life it always deserved, and so on. . . . Anyway, I take it you are enjoying the party, then? With all the dancing?" Carmela asked, bringing their conversation back to Antonia's vanishing.

She wasn't enjoying it, but Carmela didn't have to know why.

"How? It's like everywhere I look, there's someone's scrutinizing gaze all over me. If I got a peso for every single hypocritical 'I'm so sorry for your loss' that I got, I'd already have a fortune," Antonia muttered.

"The people who share their condolences with you every time they see you are the same people who called your mother names, who called her—"

"Yes," Antonia hurried on to stop Carmela from pouring out the words from her mouth. "Yes, you're right."

La bruja.

The rumors about Estela being a witch began after she died. If El Castillo de Bochica was haunted, there for sure had to be a witch involved. It was a good-night story essentially. Fuel for kids' nightmares. And the ghost of her mamá happened to fit right in.

Antonia had never concerned herself with what people said about Estela, let alone after her death, but now, she couldn't shake the questions that started to plague her. Why and how had Estela died? What truly happened in the house? Before, Antonia thought her mamá's obsession with the house and El Salto had been the reason. Now, however, she wasn't so sure.

Antonia leaned on Carmela. "I need to see it. El Salto . . ."

The place where Antonia had last seen Estela, the place where she'd died could be the place to start seeking explanations.

As if conjured by her thoughts, images flashed through Antonia's mind—Estela leaning, her hands locked around the iron barrel, her back at Antonia, Ricardo just across from her. The waters had been slamming fiercely against the rocks, but her papá had been louder, angrier. Rain poured as the skies turned gray. Antonia had walked closer, Ricardo had advanced a step or two.

But something had distracted Antonia . . . hadn't it? She could've sworn she'd taken her eyes off her parents for just a second. Next thing she knew, Ricardo was so close to Estela, he could've grabbed her if she were to fall. . . .

Antonia had been there when the police found her body. They'd labeled it as an unfortunate accident at first, then, after several hours, it was clear they thought of it as a suicide. But as troubled as Estela was, as much as the house had effects on them all, killing herself, ending her life, wasn't something Antonia had feared her mamá would do. She was her heroine; she had more agency than that.

"No, she'd never kill herself, Papá—" Antonia had cried when she heard the police's statements. "If she hated this place, if she wanted to leave, she would've left. But she'd never put an end to her life. . . ."

"There's no way for us to know that." Ricardo wrapped his arms around Antonia and pulled her closer. She gulped down a few breaths, struggling to fill her lungs with air.

"You know I'm right," she told him at last. "She loved us. She would've never—"

Words had evaded Antonia, mostly because she knew Ricardo wouldn't agree with her. He'd oftentimes been dismissive about Antonia's concerns.

"Antonia, stop," he said, his jaw tight. Exasperation clouded his expression, as though he wanted her to shut her mouth. "This hurts us both, in ways I can't explain. But she's gone. We need to accept that. She jumped out of her own free will. No one pushed her—"

Pushed her . . .

Antonia pondered those last words. She hadn't considered it a murder. The thought . . . the possibility hadn't even crossed her mind. Did he think that? Did he have reasons to believe she'd been—

Someone locked me in here. No. No. Who? The only person in the house was Ricardo. He knew I'd be in here. He wouldn't . . .

Ricardo? Her papá? That couldn't be. Especially not when he had also been there just like Antonia. He wouldn't have done it. And if he would, he wouldn't have in plain sight.

But what if he thought no one was looking?

Antonia tried to shake the thought from her mind right as Carmela's voice landed in her ear, bringing her back to the party. "Nona, we needn't go out there. Let's go look for your father instead. . . ."

Antonia pushed past Carmela, then darted through the hallway toward the ballroom's balcony, almost too aggressively. Antonia wanted answers, and she would dig underneath the very foundation of the house if she had to in order to get them.

But before she could reach the balcony, Estela's Muisca mural brought her to a full stop. It remained intact. Without even noticing, Antonia found herself standing right in front of it, tracing her fingers around the figure.

The walls were so cold, they stole heat from her warm fingers. The colors shone as though they'd recently been painted—not ten years ago. "The mist. It looks so dense, so real, but so delicate, like a veil." Antonia studied the painting. She'd seen her mamá work on it, but she couldn't figure out how she'd achieved such detail. It seemed as though the Muisca men were swallowed by the mist, but then they rose back up as the largest birds in the world. Their plumage all black except for a frill of white feathers at the base of the neck and large white bands on the wings. All those details were as close to the real thing as they could be, and when the cóndores flew, they appeared to leap off the painting and into the real world.

Legend said the Muisca would jump off El Salto del Tequendama in an attempt to escape the Spanish colonizers. Jumping freed them from a life of misery and abuse. Once they jumped, they turned into majestic Andean cóndores and gained the real freedom promised by their goddess Bochica. They saw the light; they saw pquihiza.

But Bochica hadn't given her mamá wings. Instead, she'd handed her death.

Wasn't Bochica supposed to have saved her? After years of Estela's worship, of building an altar, because the house was nothing if not an altar, a shrine, she couldn't save Estela?

Staring at these cóndores, Antonia couldn't help but think back to the days prior to their moving into El Castillo de Bochica. Estela would spend her days mostly reading and painting. She walked around the lush meadowlike garden that framed their house, adorned with bloom orchids and wild encenillos, their verdant leaves hosts of birds that nested atop.

Antonia watched in awe as the birds perched on the windswept branches. Noticing her daughter's fascination, Mamá would tell her about murmuration—the mesmerizing dance of massive flocks of starlings. Mamá described how thousands of birds filled the sky, swirling and swooping in ever-changing shapes. Each starling, mirroring the movements of its neighbors, created stunning patterns that shifted and flowed like living waves.

"It's a shared purpose," Estela had said, gazing at the view above them. "Profound trust and admiration for each other."

Antonia had stared at the almost divine spectacle—one moment it was moving shapes swaying in the evening sky, and the next an ominous sphere, like the moon hanging over a marsh.

Antonia's lips had stretched in a gaping grin, her eyebrows arched to the sky. Her mamá squeezed her arms around her, and Antonia breathed slower, her body melting into Estela's embrace, as if every muscle lost its tension.

Estela would also point out how the wildest and strangest birds thrived. How even the quirkiest groups stuck together when they flew south. A family, like their own. She always made sure Antonia felt safe, seen, loved.

But Antonia's outings with Estela had almost entirely stopped when they moved to El Castillo de Bochica. Ricardo, in a grand gesture, and in full proof that he was incapable of saying no to Estela, proved his uttermost devotion and infinite love by building his wife a dream home. Antonia didn't believe something could ever top such a declaration. For a while, it had set her expectations above and beyond every realistic relationship she could find for herself. But then she realized that love so unmeasurable was bad, for it could kill.

When they moved in, Antonia watched Estela fall in love with the place every day. Doña Pereira fed her obsession, visiting almost daily and passing it on to her like a legacy. Almost like evangelization. Doña Pereira would talk about Bochica and how to look beyond the "superficial film of reality," whatever that meant. She would always remind Antonia that Estela was a bird—a bird needed wings to fly as high as cóndores . . . cageless, free.

Then came the history books, the magazines, the old leatherbound behemoths written in Chibcha—the Muisca's native language, a language Doña Pereira and Antonia's mamá understood and spoke fluently—the mysteries that surrounded the falls, and *Radio Noche*.

Things took a turn for the worse once Estela's infatuation with los Muiscas and El Salto del Tequendama reached a point of no return. It started two years prior to her death, with changes so gradual they were almost imperceptible at first—like a pot slowly simmering before it boils over. Estela's mood swings became erratic, and she increasingly retreated to her hidden sanctuary, spending hours upon hours inside. There would even be days when Antonia wouldn't see her at all. The sanctuary was off-limits, and while Antonia initially saw it as Estela's study, just as her papá had his, she began to wonder if Estela was hiding from something, or someone. Perhaps even from the company of her own family. But if so, why?

It got so bad a year prior to her death that Estela would only come out of her sanctuary to go on days-long adventures at the bequest of Ricardo. The few times Ricardo was successful at prying her away from El Salto, she was revitalized, and things went back to normal for a few days. Light and excitement gleamed in her eyes. She'd work on her orchard and ask for Antonia's help. She'd have every meal with them, she'd spend hours talking Gothic novels with Antonia in Antonia's room, and if Antonia was lucky, they'd talk boys. Estela would make pastries with Carmela. And she'd lie by the fire with her husband. Brief moments that Antonia wished could last forever, when Estela's life wasn't all about the house, El Salto, or los Muiscas.

But the effect only lasted a few days. Exhaustion would soon wash over her mamá's face. Her eyes became distant, almost vacant. When she stayed at the house, she'd roam around like a ghost, journal in hand, jotting down thoughts rapidly as though she feared they'd escape her if she didn't get them out of her head. She'd eat one meal a day at most, and that only happened when Carmela and Antonia begged her. Her hair turned into a bird's nest, her white dresses covered in dirt and grime, as though she'd spend her days at the orchard, or doing lawn work, even though she never left her room.

Antonia started to miss Estela being around. She started to envy the lives of people with conventional families, even if she wasn't keen on many social conventions to begin with. What did Antonia have? Carmela, of course. But as much as she adored Carmela and didn't know what she would've done without her, Antonia also wanted her mamá there. Especially at night, when the nightmares crept in.

"Nona? Hello? Are you listening to me?" Carmela's question broke through Antonia's stupor.

"What? No, sorry. I got lost in Mamá's mural. What were you saying?"

"For you not to run away from me anymore. I'm old, my legs don't work like they used to. I can't be chasing after you like I did when you were a little girl."

"I'm sorry, Carmela. I just . . . I have to see it," Antonia insisted.

"Are you sure you want to do this?"

Antonia nodded. She had truly planned to listen to Carmela and avoid the place where Estela died, but she quickly found herself there. Even though she wouldn't dare say it aloud, part of her hope was that she'd find her mamá as she always used to all those years ago, or at least understand what she was thinking. Was she calling to Bochica for help? Was she running away and stopped here for guidance when someone caught her unaware? Perhaps Ricardo was right: Antonia had unfinished business, she needed closure, and that was why she couldn't move on. Perhaps she had to exhume the bones of her past after all to cast away her nightmares.

Antonia locked her gaze on the falls, almost completely hidden behind the layers of thick fog dancing in its waters. Droplets pelted her arms and face. Her heart sped up. Antonia adjusted her posture, drawing her shoulders back, as Estela used to do. She was ready to hear whatever message the falls had for her.

"I never understood why she was so fascinated with this. It's a damned place," Antonia whispered to herself, then grabbed onto the iron banisters firmly, almost as if her life depended on it. The drenched and chilly iron against her skin nearly burned, but she didn't let go. The cry of the falls swallowed even the sounds of owls, and those of every other bird who dared defy the wintry night.

The same way it had done to Estela.

A chaotic swarm of memories instantly rushed through Antonia's mind. Just like last time, Ricardo was standing a few inches away from her mamá, arms outstretched, as if trying to restrain her, to secure her. Estela was leaning dangerously close to the edge, peering over the precipice.

This time, though, Antonia remembered what had been the cause of her distraction, the reason she'd abandoned the sight for the briefest of moments: the sound of a loud clunk echoing throughout the open space.

When she turned to see Estela again, she wasn't there anymore. . . .

Antonia yelled and yelled until her throat grew ragged. She'd run to where her mamá had stood, Ricardo and Carmela dragging Antonia backward, fearing she'd be the next to fall.

And just as quickly as it arrived, the memory ended.

She felt frustrated. Why were things coming back to her in bits and pieces? And why were they always different from the last?

"Nona, I think you've seen enough. We should go inside." Carmela was back to being by her side, Carmela's eyes drawn to the stuffed ballroom. "We can't leave your father unattended for long."

"Do you think she really fell—or jumped?" Antonia caught a glimpse of Carmela's pinched brows from the corner of her eye. "Do you think someone pushed her? Do you think, Papá . . ."

"Nona, we shouldn't do this here."

"I'm serious, Carmela," Antonia pressed.

"I don't think she fell. And I also don't think . . . *anyone* pushed her."

Antonia held Carmela's gaze. If she knew, she would tell Antonia, wouldn't she? Of course she would. Carmela wouldn't hide anything from her.

Tears threatened to escape Antonia's eyes, but she managed to hold them back. This was not the place nor the time for a scene, especially since everyone was so ready to pity them. She was probably already drawing even more people's eyes toward her just by standing at the site of Estela's doom. And that was already way more attention than Antonia had wanted on her and her family tonight. If it were up to her, people would've never known about Estela's tragic death.

Unfortunately for her, she couldn't do anything to stop the truth from coming out. The news took off a few weeks after the tragedy; before then, they had tried to keep it as low profile as possible. Living in the middle of nowhere made it easier, at least at first. But then the news leaked, perhaps from locals who roamed the place regularly and noticed Antonia's mamá's absence from the balcony, though at first Antonia thought it had been the police. Antonia's family had to recover the body, but no one could attempt it other than the police and their rescue team. Soon the news spread like wildfire. Nothing stopped people from drawing all sorts of conclusions. *The house is haunted and evil spirits got to her. She didn't fall by accident, she jumped willingly. She was one of those tormented women in a Brontë book, the house and the isolation were the real death of her. Madness runs in her blood, the girl must have it too. Her husband had enough of her nonsense and pushed her to get rid of her for good. Who would blame him?*

The latter accusation left a sour taste in her mouth. She noticed her heartbeat slugging as her limbs went numb. A morbid thought began to take form.

Ricardo had been so close to Estela. Why hadn't he stopped her from falling?

Tears flowed down Antonia's face. She didn't stop them this time.

CINCO

t the bar, a dozen conversations were happening at once, told in loud
voices, all of them competing with the boleros dominating the atmosphere. Antonia wound her way through the warm bodies, almost as easily as the smoke being blown in the air. She cursed herself for letting her
memories get to her and tried to shake off the feeling that had come over
her while she was on the balcony. But something inside her had shifted. She
couldn't get the thoughts about Estela being murdered out of her head. Let
alone when she'd decided her suspect was Ricardo. Was he capable of it?
Was his love so intoxicating that he could've killed her?

Antonia rested her body against the black marble counter and locked
eyes with the middle-aged bartender on the other side. Much like the other
waiters, he wore an all-white suit, his straight brown hair carefully pulled
back in a long braid, giving him an aggressive, yet soft, look.

Through the white floor-to-ceiling windows framing half of the room,
there came an illusory calmness about El Salto del Tequendama when she
watched it from afar. She sat behind the counter and hummed an old ro-
mantic bolero. "Something strong. The strongest thing you have."

He stared at her briefly with upturned deep brown eyes. Antonia
stared back, trying to see through his blank expression, but it gave her

no hints. She turned away from him and back to the view through the window.

"Rough day?" he asked playfully as he placed a tiny glass in front of her. He turned around and grabbed an almost-empty bottle.

Antonia struggled to read the golden label, but she didn't much care what it was. She simply needed a drink, then she'd go back upstairs to meet Carmela and Ricardo. As much as she wanted answers, perhaps it was best if she didn't get them, as she feared they'd be way more sinister than she could handle. Wasn't the truth scary oftentimes?

"More like rough years."

She drank. The warmth and dryness of the liquid masking, at least for a bit, the dread simmering in her blood. Second time today she'd relied on alcohol for some relief from her thoughts.

"Good. Very strong. I'd like another one." She slid the now-empty glass toward him across the counter.

The man glanced briefly at the little cup, then back up to Antonia, raising a fine brow at her. "Are you alone, miss?"

Antonia was left puzzled by his question.

"A señorita like you shouldn't be drinking by herself. It's not recommended."

She lifted her hand to cut him off and chimed in, "Well, it's good that I'm no señorita." She managed a crooked smile. The last thing she needed was the bartender scrutinizing her.

The corner of his mouth twisted upward in a shy grin, and he dutifully filled her glass again. As she watched him, she suddenly felt something, *someone*, melting his or her body against hers from behind.

Antonia jolted to the side and locked gazes with Alejandro. His brown eyes appeared darker under the dimness of the room. He leaned forward to grab her back. He was so close that she could smell his scent over the strong cigar stench. She stumbled to straighten in place, then remained motionless.

"We met before . . . at the door?" he said softly, but loud enough for her to listen over the people's chatter and the rhythmic boleros blasting from every corner.

Antonia wouldn't forget such a face. "I know."

"Antonia, right?"

"Listen, I'm . . . I want to be alone." She didn't want to come off as rude, but all she needed was to be by herself.

He exuded an aura of confidence; his big, almost inquisitive eyes didn't leave hers. "Let's start again," Alejandro offered, and a smile slipped off the corner of his mouth. "I'm Alejandro Soler."

Antonia raised her brows high. "I know who you are. We met at the door."

"I just—"

Antonia stared and flushed briefly. Under different circumstances, Antonia would certainly allow him to court her. And if it came to flirting, she'd flirt right back. But her flirting skills were rusty, and tonight wouldn't be the night to start again.

"Right," he said at the lack of response from her, and that she was still standing in front of him. "Nice to meet you. Again. I'm a reporter for *Radio Noche*, both their local station and their magazine. Maybe you've heard of us . . . ?"

"I'm familiar," Antonia said stoutly. "What I don't know is what *you* want with me," she added with exaggerated patience.

Alejandro brushed his tousled hair back, but strands of wavy hair objected, framing his face and giving him a softer look.

"I want to interview you."

"Me? Why?" Upon closer inspection, Antonia realized there was indeed something familiar about Alejandro. Back at the door, she hadn't recognized him, and she still didn't, but there was something in him that she now swore she'd seen before. She couldn't shake the feeling off, and the way he stared back at her made her believe . . . no, made her positive they knew each other. Or at least that she'd seen him somewhere before.

Alejandro crossed his arms over his chest, and his corded muscles stretched underneath the fabric of his white shirt. He shrugged as though it were obvious. "You lived here. My boss is obsessed with this place and all the stories that surround it . . . you know? The deaths, the hauntings—" He pressed a golden fountain pen against his chin.

Antonia shook her head. She had nothing to say in that matter. And even if she did, she wouldn't dare reveal a single thing.

She didn't wish to feed people's curiosity—enough things had already been said about the waterfall and her family. But Antonia was certain that all sorts of rumors still traveled back and forth between Bogotá and El Salto, from the Muisca myth to when Antonia's papá had chosen this place to build a mansion unlike anything the country had ever seen. According to the locals, El Salto was haunted, and therefore the mansion overlooking it was equally doomed.

She remembered the last gossip from months before Estela died. It was close to dawn—the whispers that buzzed in Estela's wake like a trail of flies around a corpse and those hungry pointed looks. Police officers swarmed at the gates, taking statements. A couple had disappeared—according to witnesses, they'd last been seen by the falls. Their car remained abandoned a few feet away.

"You must have seen something—heard something?" one of the officers had asked Estela.

"We were all asleep," she'd replied between her teeth. "You come banging at our doors like we could possibly have something to do with these people's deaths—"

"We didn't say they were dead, ma'am."

"I trust you to know better than that. There's no need to give their families false hopes."

The officer remained silent as he scribbled something on a worn leather pad.

Did Estela know more than she was willing to tell the police?

"Now, if we see anything, I'll call you myself."

And Estela called them exactly three days after, when two more people disappeared. That time it had been Antonia who'd seen them jump.

No use thinking about those things now.

"I have nothing to say," she said at last to Alejandro.

"Listen," he continued in a more soothing tone, almost shyly, "all I want to know is if you have any stories."

Did *he* believe in these old horror tales? Did being a ghost hunter require you to believe that demons really haunted the living? Perhaps not. Being a priest didn't require you to believe in God, you only needed to sound like it.

"I don't."

His lips parted in surprise, as though Antonia were saying something that made absolutely no sense. "What? I don't believe you—"

How dare he speak with the confidence that only a witness, like her, would have? Whatever happened in this place, he was *not* around to see it, *to live through it.*

"Do you want a story? Guess what? Ghosts are *not* real, and you, as the young intelligent man I want to think you are, shouldn't believe in said things."

Antonia should've known from the second she saw his badge hanging over his neck where this was all going. If she had, she wouldn't have wasted any time talking to him. Antonia had not come to the house to relive all those years, to talk about what had happened with some stranger. She was certain that her answers would be entirely different to the story Alejandro wanted to hear anyway.

Alejandro gave Antonia a questioning look. "So you're saying you've *never* seen anything? Heard anything?"

Antonia didn't attempt to respond. She wouldn't. *She couldn't.*

"*Smelled* anything?"

Her muscles quivered at his emphasis on that word. Did *he* smell it too?

She opened her mouth to ask but stopped herself. Asking him meant that she'd be acknowledging it, and she wasn't certain she could. Not after everything she'd already dealt with today.

Though to herself, she couldn't deny the foul smell. It permeated every single corner of their home and was exacerbated the closer you got to the base of the house. Sometimes Antonia had even dreamed of it. It seeped into her brain so much that when she was not in the house, she missed it. Then there was that one time, when no one was watching her, Antonia had come so close to the waterfall, it was as though the smell were a trail, pulling her all the way down deep to the falls.

"Listen, I really don't understand where you're going with this, but I have nothing for you." She spun on her heels, and as she made her way outside the lounge, she stopped and turned to face him again. He stood motionless right behind her, as though he knew she'd come back. "And don't go looking for answers elsewhere. Leave my papá alone. He shouldn't be talking about these *things*. . . . It's not good for him."

Antonia then turned and melted back into the crowd, but not before snatching a glass of wine off a waiter's tray and downing it. As she walked away, a feeling of unease washed over her, crawling up her back, burrowing in her stomach. The house still managed to make her feel sick and uneasy, snagging peace from her. Four years had gone by since her mamá's death and Antonia had managed to survive. She didn't want to be swamped by grief or bitterness for the rest of her life. She only yearned to leave it all behind, to pretend like it had never happened.

Antonia wouldn't let the house shut its gates on her.

She wouldn't let it consume her. She wouldn't stay, none of them would.

It was time to leave, journals and answers be damned.

⊷ ⤙ ⤚ ⊶

Antonia stood in the courtyard with the Andean Hills sprawled in the distance. She was glad to see her walnut tree, something that was a part of her, still standing strong. It was another of the things that hadn't changed, despite Doña Pereira's efforts.

She breathed in deeply, filling her flattened lungs with crisp air. The thickets should have been shades of emerald at this point in October, but the scarce vegetation that grew in the outer courtyard was as brown as the earth and dotted the lawn that led back to the house. Now, as she faced the hotel, gray under the too-dark, almost blue sky, a feral feeling seized her.

Leave.

Antonia briefly stiffened. But she refused to let herself give in and banished the feeling. It was just her mind playing tricks on her. It was foolish. She'd been taken aback by Alejandro, that's all it was. And that was no reason to let fear take hold of her.

Outside, it was silent, her footsteps the only sound as she reached a set of low, broad cement steps leading up to the front door. She stepped onto the first step, then froze, a shocked gasp escaping her.

A dead, two-headed, long black-and-brown snake was splayed before her, half of its body grotesquely distorted into a bow-like knot, squeezing its guts out. Its heads twisted at an angle, eyes wide and glossy, almost human-like, frozen in a terror-stricken expression.

Flies and moths buzzed frantically above the corpse, and Antonia had to fight back her urge to puke.

"Wha—" she began in a weak cry of surprise before something—*someone*—yanked her back from the steps.

Doña Pereira's light laugh lilted over her head. She was directly behind Antonia, then at once at her elbow. Antonia cast her a sideways glance, catching Padre Juan standing beside her.

"The cóndores did it—those damned flying beasts," Doña Pereira said gaily, as if explaining away a troublesome kid.

Antonia wasn't certain this had been the work of nature, for she didn't believe nature to be evil. If this was the game of predator and prey, as Doña Pereira had suggested, why would the latter be left behind in such a state? Antonia was no fool. She'd seen these things before. Usually the doings of a human.

"Ricardo looks better. He has light in him that I hadn't seen since, you know—"

"Mamá killed herself?" Antonia supposed that was what Doña Pereira was going to say. She just filled in the gaps for her.

"It was hard for him—confronting her death. She looked just fine to me that day. . . ."

Had Doña Pereira been there too?

Doña Pereira probably noticed the shift in Antonia's expression and hurried on before Antonia could speak a word. "I don't think we'll ever recover. It was such a huge loss." Doña Pereira patted a hand over her heart.

The gesture drew Antonia's brown eyes to Doña Pereira's thick gold necklace, glowing under the faint warm lights coming from the hotel, as the old lady whispered into Padre Juan's ear. Antonia then spotted the big gold pendant sitting on Doña Pereira's chest—a carved humanlike face decorated with tiny black crystals. There were tiny red stones to mimic eyes and flattened lips. Why did it look so familiar? She didn't have time to try to remember. . . .

"I-I need to go look for Papá," Antonia managed, overwhelmed by her thoughts.

Excusing herself, Antonia rushed up the stairs that led back to the main floor directly from the courtyard. It was the same she used whenever she'd helped her mamá out by the orchard or read her books under her nogal. Whispers and mumbles scratched at her eardrums as she struggled to keep her legs moving. Was someone following her around? There was no way it was Doña Pereira, she couldn't possibly be that fast.

Antonia turned. Then, as if by impulse, she pressed her ear to the whitewashed wall and whispered, "Hello?"

The reply was so loud, it shoved her backward.

LEAVE.

A whine escaped her. It would've been a scream if she could've delivered enough air from her lungs, but her breathing was quick and shallow. Something moved in the darkness of the narrow stairwell. She could feel her limbs tremble, and thoughts scrambled in her head as she staggered to her feet.

The house awakened something in her, a feeling she'd been able to control enough to hide. Despite this, she felt in her gut that if she tried to leave now, the house would allow her to escape. Perhaps it wasn't the house she should fear, but the people that were in it. She just needed to find out exactly who that was.

SEIS

⟡———▪—▪———⟡

Antonia wasn't ready to face her papá. Dread and uncertainty were unsettling her. What if Ricardo had something to do with Estela's murder? Even if Antonia had seen her mamá moments before she fell off the balcony, she hated that she couldn't even trust her own memories. That they didn't shed a clue for her.

No matter how much Antonia yearned to depart the house, she knew uncovering the remaining journal entries was essential to unraveling the truth. She longed to absolve someone from her scrutiny, most fervently her papá. That is, of course, if there were any entries left to be found. Antonia was hopeful there were.

So, instead of heading back to the party, she walked in the opposite direction. A few people were scattered around the hallway, most of them too drunk or too distracted to even glance her way. She cringed at each creak on the wooden steps, but it didn't sway her determination to make it upstairs.

Halfway up, a shadow flickered at the corner of her vision, penetrating red eyes settling on her every move. Antonia froze, and as she stood there, she caught a woody accent lingering in the space. Incense? A shiver made the hairs on the back of her neck stand on end, then cascaded down her backbone. She suddenly knew exactly where to go. Antonia's reading room—Estela would always burn sage and incense whenever Antonia was in her study and complained about the smell from outside.

The sound of Aurelio Rocha's deep voice snapped her back to the present as it reverberated on the ceilings of the third floor. The music was loud enough she could make out the lyrics.

El dolor de tu partida me estremece.
(The pain of your departure shakes me.)

She continued up the stairs slowly, nervously. With each step, the song got louder, competing with her thundering heart.

Intento encontrarte tantas veces.
(I try to find you so many times.)

Uncertain what she was going to find, if she'd find anything at all, she managed to hurl herself up another set of stairs and through the floor's main hall. The floor beneath her feet was covered in a wine-red carpet, and the four wooden doors, two on each side, were clad in white. When she opened the door to what used to be her reading spot, which had now been turned into room 421, the song practically boomed out of the room.

Inside, it was pitch-black. The kind of darkness that gave her a pause. Goose bumps formed on her exposed skin.

She stepped into the room, hugging herself with her shawl for some warmth. She flicked the switch by the door, and light flooded the room at last. Across from where she stood was a bed with handmade carved wood, white bedding with embroidered golden flowers, and a nightstand on each side. On the left side of the room was a vanity, a silver platter resting on it, with tiny glass bottles all with labels that read EL REFUGIO DEL SALTO. On the right, her eyes caught a glimpse of an armoire. Antonia recognized both, as they belonged to her family. The carved detailing on top of the armoire was hard to miss. On it were cóndores, the legendary bird of the Andean Hills, the gold handles on each door, and its light brown and blue color. There was some light decay on the wood, perhaps due to humidity, but its sumptuosity remained.

She positioned herself in front of it, then wrapped her fingers on the golden handle, pulling it open slowly, followed by a faint creak. Inside, where Antonia's old books and journals used to be, were empty cardboard boxes and old jars. Antonia crouched to see if anything else was on the cabinets underneath, but aside from a layer of dust, there was nothing to see. She'd been hoping this armoire would hold another puzzle piece, just as the hand-painted shelves had, but she felt defeated when no such thing appeared.

As she shut the door a little too forcefully, the sound of musical notes broke the silence. She yanked the handle and felt farther inside, and there it was. She'd nearly missed it: a hand-cranked, engraved music box with silver details that her mamá had gotten for her. She slid the lid up. Antonia's name was carved on it, alongside the date: November 18, 1922, two months before they moved in. Tucked in a corner, a ragged piece of paper was folded into thirds.

The page made a crackling noise when Antonia attempted to smooth it out against the wood, like the crunch of leaves on the courtyard outside.

Antonia recognized her handwriting even though she did not recall writing it herself, let alone putting it inside. This certainly was unexpected and not the type of note she'd been hoping to find. It wasn't Spanish or English or any of the languages she spoke fluently.

It was Chibcha, she realized, rattled, a language she was familiar with thanks to her mamá but couldn't possibly speak, let alone write.

Perhaps Carmela knew what this was. Maybe they'd had a Chibcha lesson at some point. But Antonia quickly scratched the idea; she didn't recall a lesson, not one that was extensive enough for her to be able to read or write Chibcha.

Antonia would have to find a dictionary, something to help her translate whatever this was. With shaking hands, she folded the paper back and slid it inside her pocket. Then she started to the door and traversed back to the main floor.

◆— — —◆

In the ballroom, the party continued full swing. Antonia had lost track of time. How long had they been here? Two or three hours at most?

Ricardo's eyes caught hers. Carmela stood beside him vigilantly. The tension was palpable around them, but Antonia refused to look away. Had he lied to her all this time? She'd done everything right, she'd been the benevolent and caring daughter, she'd sacrificed her dreams, her life, for him. Refusing to leave him alone in his ailing. They'd survived because of her, and he'd squandered it like an ill-raised kid. He'd torn their family to pieces. He hadn't saved Estela; instead, he'd built her a burial site.

Antonia wished so much to confront Ricardo with her questions, but the party was not the place to start. She'd discovered enough here. It was time to go.

"Papá, I think we ought to leave," she said once she approached, hoping he wouldn't fight her this time.

He waved her off in a dismissive gesture that Antonia had seen before one too many times.

. . . He's often quick to dismiss my concerns.

He'd dismissed Estela's too. Had he grown tired of her? Of succumbing to her every wish, and that led him to . . .

"Not yet." His response awakened her from the depths of her thoughts, now tainted with anger, heartbreak. "Emiro is outside, you can tell him to take you back to the city if that is what you wish. I'm staying."

"Listen to Antonia, Don Ricardo. It's getting late and you know how tricky the road back is," Carmela pressed. "It'll probably start raining in no time."

He shook his head. "I am staying."

"And I suppose you're spending the night?" Antonia muttered. "Do you recall what happened the last time we were here?"

Ricardo's voice grew louder this time. "You took me away in the cruelest way."

Cruel? *She'd saved him.* She'd saved him when she should've let go of him long ago. She'd saved him even though it meant not saving herself. What on earth was he talking about?

In his defense, he couldn't have known. . . . Or could he? That Carmela and Antonia were inside the night of the fire? They'd left him alone at the house. Big mistake, yes, but they'd had affairs Antonia needed to deal with in the city, and he'd been too fragile to even put him through the legal matters. He'd begged to stay at home, and Antonia had trusted that nothing worse could possibly happen after her mamá's death. What could be worse than having someone wrenched from one's life forever? Without warning. Without the chance to say goodbye.

Death was inescapable. Death was certain. But it wasn't less painful. It wasn't less cruel. It was always a tragedy.

But she was tired of justifying his actions. Of forgiving him, of loving him unconditionally. Where had it gotten her? Nowhere. At times she wished she hadn't saved him. She wished she didn't take care of him like she did. At least she would've been free from the weight, from such a responsibility. It pained her to allow herself to turn to those thoughts, but she couldn't help seeing him in a new light.

"This place changes you. You're not the same person when you're here. And you know that. Papá, please. Must I remind you?" Antonia pleaded. The sooner she could get him out of the house, the sooner she could have him answer all of her questions.

"Antonia, I know what happened. But you have to understand, Nona . . . I felt guilty, for bringing you and your mother here. I thought by tearing down these walls we would stop suffering. You must believe me when I say

I didn't know you and Carmela were inside. How much longer am I going to have to stand you making me feel guilty over it?" His voice lowered this time, and his hand wrapped tightly, too tightly, around Antonia's shoulder, ushering her away from the euphoric crowd.

His voice took on a darker, almost menacing edge. "All of that's over now. I know you think I'm sick, but I am not. Stop it."

How could she trust him after what she'd just read? Estela had been locked inside her room. Ricardo had been the only one inside the house. That night . . . the night of her mamá's death . . . he was so close to her. Ricardo could've saved Estela, grabbed her.

Or he could've pushed her. . . .

"Papá, I . . . I know she was murdered," she snapped, the words escaping her mouth before she could stop them.

No, no, no! This isn't how I am supposed to confront him. What if someone overhears us?

She watched as all color drained from his face, leaving nothing but a blank expression.

Ricardo turned away abruptly, running a hand through his hair, exasperated. "Goddamn it, Antonia, you're chasing shadows." His expression hardened when he faced her again, his eyes darkened and cold. "*Who* would've murdered her? *We* were there. Eleonora was there—you were crying, yelling. Your mother was fragile, sickened."

The words resounded in Antonia's brain like a barrage of gongs, sending a tremor down to her feet. Yes. They'd been there. But Antonia could've sworn it had only been her and her papá. Doña Pereira had mentioned to Antonia that she'd seen Estela the day she . . . died. Had she meant being next to them all along? Wasn't it Carmela and Ricardo who'd rushed toward Antonia? Why couldn't she remember it clearly? Why was her mind playing tricks on her?

"Let's just . . . You're acting just like her, Nona. With this paranoia . . ." His voice lowered, softened, but his words stung just as much.

Was Antonia as sick as Estela had allegedly been before the fall?

"I said I'm not leaving. You can either stay with me or leave without me," he added.

"Fine," she managed, but she didn't mean it. Nothing was ever fine. Not ever since they'd moved to the place, or even after having left. Antonia had always blamed this house, El Salto del Tequendama even, but whom could she blame now that they'd left? Perhaps her papá was right: sickness ran in her family, in the blood that traversed every inch of her body, spoiling every corner like a plague.

Antonia's eyes widened suddenly, and in an instant, she felt the walls closing in on her, the sounds around her muffling. She couldn't move. She couldn't see. She couldn't hear. She couldn't breathe. Her only thought was a single word repeating endlessly.

LEAVE. LEAVE. LEAVE.

Antonia had seen several dead bodies. The first one when she was fourteen: a young man fell off the ledge of El Salto after staring down at it for too long. Antonia had been the only witness, or so she thought. From her bedroom window, with a 180-degree view of the majestic waterfall, much to Antonia's regret she'd seen the body fall in seconds.

When, after weeks of failed attempts, the rescue team managed to retrieve the body, Antonia had sneaked outside to see it. The man's eyes remained open as though he hadn't died from the fall but from shock. His skin had turned deep blue, almost a dark shade of gray, and across his body, barely covered in what remained of his rags, were open wounds. But not regular wounds; it was more as though his body were eating itself from the inside out, and it was all completely exposed to the daylight. Estela had told her it had been an accident, and Antonia had believed her for several years, until the bodies began to pile up, and the *accidents* became regular events. To this day, sometimes Antonia still sprung out of bed in the middle of the night and saw the man's green eyes staring back at her.

The second dead body she'd seen had been her mamá's. She'd . . . What? Jumped . . . ? Been pushed from her balcony? Antonia didn't know anymore.

It didn't take the police as long to retrieve Estela's body, a few days at most, but Antonia's sense of time had been warped. It had felt as if time were going too slow and too fast simultaneously. But she would be lying if she didn't admit the wait gave her a sliver of hope. It allowed her to cling to the possibility of a miraculous return. What if the police found her mamá alive and breathing? What if the fall had done not much other than knock her unconscious, caused some scratches and bruising? What if there was still something to be done because her mamá wasn't gone yet?

Her thoughts were a small consolation as the inevitability of a goodbye loomed over her. Antonia had stared at El Salto from the balcony, refusing to move an inch, despite the officer's request, despite Carmela's and her papá's insistence.

But her hope was a fragile thread, and part of her knew that Estela was gone. There was no way she'd survived the fall—hitting herself against the rocky slope.

When they brought her body up, Antonia felt as though she had gone through Estela's death all over again. It was as though her brain lived and relived that moment.

Grief hit her like bricks, and it took her some time to emerge back to the surface.

"No, no, no," she'd cried on Carmela's shoulder. Her knees had turned to gelatin, barely keeping her from collapsing against the floor.

Antonia had not been ready to say goodbye to Estela. She didn't want to ever say goodbye to her. And she had not wanted to see her, to remember her like that unmoving, wet, bruised-up corpse.

But Doña Pereira had forced Antonia to look at her mamá's dead body.

She said Antonia owed it to Estela, and it was the only way, according to the old señora, to say goodbye to the ones one truly loved.

Antonia foolishly had wished it to be the last dead body she'd ever see. And it *had* been ... until tonight.

Tonight, another one lay sprawled in one of the lounges on the fourth floor.

Antonia had rushed up the stairs when pounding and shouting came from above. A man's voice, but not just that of any man ... her papá?

Her chest hitched as she struggled for air; her only thought had been: *Papá, please be okay. . . . Papá, please be okay. . . . Papá, please . . .*

She'd felt no strength in her hollow bones, but she seized the handle of the studio door with shaky hands, almost tripping over the rug.

The sight was a heavy blow to her gut. She clamped a hand on her mouth to stop herself from screaming. Next to the body lay Ricardo. He began to speak, pointing to the other man, but even with Antonia slouched farther over him, she couldn't make out what he was saying.

Antonia turned her attention to the man sprawled on his back. Tainting her nostrils was the strong metallic scent from the bloody fluids pooled at his sides. His eyes bulged out, and his mouth was drawn down in a grimace of pain. The remainder of his features were mangled. His belly was slashed open as if a wild animal had gone berserk on it with its claws. Its insides spilling out and twisted at the most grotesque misshapen angles.

Antonia drew back, and her breath burst in and out, failing to still her racing heart.

She recognized him—he'd been talking to Ricardo in the ballroom just an hour or two ago. He was the mayor's chief of staff, Carlos López.

What was happening? Antonia felt slumped, defeated. She couldn't think. She couldn't breathe. She couldn't . . .

The corpse's hand shot out and seized Antonia's wrist, pulling her back to the scene before her. The man's eyes quickly rolled down and fixed on her, his mouth twisting itself into a sneer. When he spoke, his voice seemed to creep out of the wound in his throat:

"It begins again."

This wasn't happening. This couldn't be happening!

"Hey, Antonia," a disembodied voice said.

Antonia recognized it. Alejandro stood somewhere to her left.

"Antonia, the police are coming for your father."

Antonia leaned over Ricardo, reaching out to touch him. His breath was shallow, and he was drenched in blood.

"Papá," she whispered against his ear. "Papá, wake up, please." She placed one hand behind Ricardo's neck. Instantly, it was soaked in blood. Was it his own?

He opened his eyes, but instead of relief, she felt horror. Those were *not* his eyes. His pupils were reddened, and also deep, sunken, like a void. Empty.

A gasp escaped her. "Pa?" Her voice trembled. "Pl-please."

Alejandro approached from behind and spoke with urgency. "Antonia, we need to get him out. The police are coming for him—we need to take him somewhere—"

But Antonia was unable to move a muscle. Paralysis gripped her, rendering her incapable of processing Alejandro's words.

"Antonia, listen to me—this man died here, and your father is the only witness." Alejandro drew each word out slowly. "Are you understanding what I'm saying? Whoever did this will blame him for it. It's not looking good for him."

"You don't understand. I need to know what happened. He needs to tell me what's going on. . . . Papá, what happened?" she pleaded from on top of him, but his eyes were shut once again. "Papá, please, say something. *Do* something."

His lips barely moved, and when his voice came out, it was shrill. "Nona . . ."

Antonia opened her mouth to respond, but a deep voice from behind her took her aback.

"Señorita Rubiano, come with me, please."

Antonia's body quivered as she stumbled to get back on her feet. Alejandro stretched a hand to her, helping her up. Men dressed in all white placed a stretcher next to her papá. They carried him on it, his hands slumping at each side. One of them grabbed his wrists twice to check his pulse. He was so out of it, he didn't notice anything. And if he did, he gave no signs.

Antonia stared ahead blankly, oblivious of her surroundings, lost in the commotion.

León, unnoticed, approached from behind, his footsteps muffled by the chatter of the crowd outside. His tone, gentle yet urgent, broke through her daze. "Antonia."

She turned to face him.

"What is happening?" she cried out to him in desperation. "What—"

León stretched his arms toward her, placing a hand on each of her shoulders. "Nona, I—"

"What . . . did he—?" Antonia couldn't coherently stitch two words together.

"They need to take him. I'll be with him." León gently squeezed her shoulder. "I won't leave him alone, but we need to go."

His words failed to soothe her, to bring her mind to ease. Her thoughts, her feelings, were lost.

Antonia began to cry. It wasn't out of sadness, it was fear. Fear for what she was about to confront.

"What happened?" she pressed again. She stared at León, his expression blank. She wanted to scream and shake him vigorously until he gave her a response, yet she was devoid of any remaining strength to do so.

When León let go of her, the police officers took it as a sign to proceed and quickly strung ropes across the studio, to mark out the scene.

Antonia remained immobilized.

Murderer. A single word echoed inside the thick walls, scratching at her ears. *Murderer.*

Antonia didn't need to question whom it was referring to. She knew the answer.

The realization choked the breath from her body and short-circuited her mind. What had once been whole shattered the moment Estela died, and tonight it felt like the tiny pieces Antonia had been able to pick up over the years had fallen and crashed all over again. Ricardo tried hard to make her believe this narrative that Estela was ill and had jumped, putting an end to her pain. But she'd seen him there, so close to her. And Estela's notes about him, in the journals. How he locked her up inside her own room. He'd always been a loving man; when had it all changed? Did it happen as her mamá started to change too? What if he'd had enough of los Muiscas, of the isolation, of her?

What if Ricardo was so sick, like he claimed Estela was, and it made him kill this man tonight . . . ?

Antonia felt adrift, and within her was emptiness. Life itself had forced her to confront her past, her present, what she thought was the truth about Estela's death, about Ricardo. . . .

But now was not the time to give up, to succumb to fear, to pain. Determined, Antonia gathered the necessary strength to haul herself out of the room and into the hallway. She had to find Carmela, she needed to go back to the city.

People pressed against the staircase, all of them struggling to take a look upstairs. Antonia caught Doña Pereira and Padre Juan as they attempted diligently to usher all the guests out. They all came looking for ghosts, and instead, they found murder.

Alejandro placed his arms gently around Antonia to keep her steady and upright. For a moment, she welcomed his embrace, but when she saw Carmela hurrying toward her, Antonia rushed to her for comfort instead.

"Nona, what happened? We need to help him. We need to think—" Carmela pulled Antonia into her arms.

"It begins again," Antonia mumbled, repeating the dead man's words, unable to stop herself.

"We have to go, Antonia," Alejandro said, ignoring her last words.

Yes, she had to leave. Whatever was the root cause, whether it was her nightmares, the sinister things that lurked in the shadows that had belonged to the realm of dreams and were now permeating her reality, some twisted joke, or that her papá was truly capable of these things, she needed to put an end to it all.

Antonia let Alejandro lead her outside the main door.

"Léon Rivera left with him," he began. "You need to go back to the city and be with your father. But here, take this. Use it if you need it." He handed her a napkin with a number scribbled on it. "If you need anything, don't hesitate to reach out. Seriously, anytime. For whatever."

Alejandro walked her to where Emiro waited for her and Carmela and opened the door to the car for her.

"Thank you. For this," she said, before she slid inside.

She wasn't ready to give up her story yet—perhaps she never would be—but maybe Alejandro would be one of the few people who would listen and understand. He didn't owe her anything, yet he was willing to help. He'd warned her about the police coming for her papá. He didn't judge. Didn't ask questions. After years of shutting her emotions down, of bottling everything up, the idea of being listened to felt like the thing she desperately needed.

"Trust *no one*, Antonia," he added, as she watched him through the window streaked with raindrops, the sky above them turning a deep gray, signaling a storm was about to begin.

SIETE

———————

It was almost dawn when Antonia arrived in Bogotá, and she had sobbed the entire time, until she thought her ribs would crack. Alejandro's last words had left her scrambled. *Trust no one, Antonia.* A hint of warning had underscored the softness of his voice, an ache building slowly inside her chest.

The usual three-hour trip from El Salto to the city had been longer. Gusty winds and heavy rain lashed the road back home, making it almost impossible to drive. But this was not the reason why the trip felt particularly long and excruciating for Antonia. It was what awaited her back in Bogotá.

And Antonia wasn't sure she'd survive it this time.

Back in the city, as soon as sunshine shone over the cobbled streets, Antonia asked Emiro to take her to see Ricardo. Even though León had assured her that he would take care of everything, she felt like it was on her to handle things. Wasn't that what she'd been doing for the past three years? Taking care of him?

She knew the prison was a dangerous place—especially now with a deadly plague rolling, packed dungeons would provide the ideal conditions for a virus to spread. If her papá was getting out of jail, he needed it to be fast, before physical illness took hold of him.

In the car, Emiro nodded from his seat and started the engine. "Señorita, get him out. There's no way he can be a murderer. He's the best man I know, and he doesn't deserve to be in such a place."

Antonia watched Emiro as he adjusted in his seat.

The idea of pitying herself made her cringe, but sometimes she wished someone would consider what she wanted as well. She didn't deserve to play parent to her papá. She was tired. And if her suspicions were right, Ricardo deserved no less than prison for himself.

"I'll see what I can do." Her voice came out cold, vacant. But she couldn't help it. If he was truly a murderer, there was no way she'd save him this time. Even if it cost her losing the last remnants of her family.

"Señorita Nona, everyone was talking about him earlier today at the plaza."

Emiro's words took her aback.

"What do you mean everyone?" Antonia asked. Rumors, the bad ones, had a quicker way of spreading around. "Who knows?"

"Señorita, it happened late enough that it couldn't make it to the papers, but everyone is talking about it. The guests must have spread the news. The grand opening of the hotel turned murder party is what they're saying."

If her family was once again the source of dirty rumors, there was nothing Antonia could do to save their reputation this time. But moreover, if rumors reached the escuela's gates and Madre Asunción noticed her absence, which she probably would, Antonia would lose her job for good.

Antonia couldn't let things get any more out of control than they already were.

"Emiro, not a single word to anyone about what happened yesterday. You *do not* speak to anyone that's not me or Carmela about it, do you understand?" Her voice was commanding and stout.

"Of course, señorita. You can count on me."

They drove the rest of the way in silence. When they arrived, Antonia bolted out of the car to stand before the gates of the local prison. The centuries-old structure stood tall in front of her. The wind remained damp and cold from last night's thunderstorm, numbing Antonia from the outside in. The brown stone of the prison's square structure contrasted against the unusual backdrop of clear skies. The smell of tobacco and pooled rainwater tainted the air.

"Señorita Rubiano?" A warden at the tall iron gate recognized her. The first thing she noticed about the man was his size. His frame cast a shadow over hers as he looked down at her.

Antonia's expression was strained. "I'm here to see Ricardo Rubiano. He was brought here last night. . . ."

"That's impossible, I'm afraid. This is no time for visits, and the only person allowed to see him is his lawyer, Mr. Rivera."

Antonia clenched her fists at her sides. "You do *not* get to tell me if I can or cannot see him. I'm his daughter, and I will see him. If I have to burn this place to the ground, I'll do it."

The warden stared down at her with suspicion, then marched inside without another word. Antonia's gaze followed him dubiously.

The man returned shortly after, closely tailed by León Rivera. Antonia felt a tingle of relief, and the tenseness, at least for a moment, melted away.

"Nona." León opened his arms wide in an inviting gesture, but she remained still as he got closer. "I was about to go find you at home."

"I need to see him," Antonia said stoutly.

"Nona, this is no place for you. Let me handle it, okay?"

Antonia's blood boiled. If there was something she despised more than anything else, it was to be undermined, for being too young, for having a dead mother, for being a woman. He insisted on treating her like a child, and Antonia wouldn't let him. Not this time.

León ushered her farther outside, and she followed reluctantly. When he spoke, his voice was loud over the cars' claxons and the passersby's chatter.

"Let *me* take care of this, Nona. Your father doesn't want you to see him like this, let alone in such an awful place. . . . A señorita does not belong here."

Where did señoritas belong? At home, dutifully performing chores and being proper?

No. Antonia didn't want to be a señorita. She'd been the perfect daughter, and where had that gotten her? She'd had enough of that life.

"If he doesn't want to see me, he's going to have to say it to my face." Antonia stood her ground.

The way León stared at Antonia was revolting. She'd seen that pitiful look before.

"I am not leaving until I see him."

"Nona . . ."

"I've seen him at his worst. I've been with him"—Antonia cleared her throat—"always."

"Nona, sorry, but you have no business here. You are not a lawyer; you also don't have a man or a husband to take care of you yet. You legally aren't authorized to be in a place like this without a responsible man by your side."

The edge in León's voice laid clear how little he cared for her thoughts on the matter, or on anything else. And suddenly that feeling of relief at seeing him turned into spite.

"*I'll* take full responsibility," Antonia replied.

León began to show his loss of patience. "While your father is behind bars, it is on me to take care of you—"

"I am here to see him," Antonia interrupted. "Besides, taking care of me is not your responsibility, getting him out is."

"Antonia," he insisted, grabbing her by the arm, "you are going to make this harder than it needs to be. We'll find a way to get him out of this, but your being here won't help. At all."

Antonia struggled out of his grip. "Your presence isn't helping either.

He's still in prison as far as I'm concerned. Perhaps I should busy myself looking for a more apt lawyer?"

"It's not that easy," León muttered. "His head is clouded with explanations that don't make sense. People don't need a motive to kill someone. It could've been unintentional. Someone was killed in the most vicious way. There's no way it had been an accident. He's sick, and we both know that. The house stirs up a lot of memories inside him."

Antonia couldn't say she didn't agree with León, because she did. But she wouldn't admit it out loud, especially not to León. She needed to hear the truth come out of Ricardo's mouth.

"And yet *you* insisted on having him at the party. . . ." Antonia marched quickly past León, walking through the big main gates.

Antonia wouldn't let anyone get in the way of finding out the truth.

⊷ ⟶ ⊶

Inside, the prison was devoid of color. The stone walls painted in gray many years ago carried the burden of memories of convicts who'd scratched at the walls.

What little oxygen managed to find its way inside and failed to escape was overtaken by the smell of bodily fluids and decay. The inmates were crammed in their cells so tight they constantly touched one another. The only sound other than men banging rhythmically on the walls was the one from what Antonia gathered were torture rooms. The screams were layered one on top of the other, a deafening gruesome choir of pain.

The ward was no brighter than the gathering gloom of dusk, even this early in the morning. As she looked up as she walked, one of the kerosene lamps flickered as many moths fluttered around it.

Antonia's presence didn't go unnoticed. A few pairs of inmates pressed against the rusty iron bars, gave her lewd looks, and hollered salacious comments at her.

"Looking for a gentleman, dolly? You certainly got it. Come closer. I got a piece for you."

"Ha! Only harlots come to prisons alone. I know what she's looking for."

"You're a dish, my dish."

Antonia averted her gaze and tried to hide between the folds of her clothing, walking faster. The guard escorting her didn't make her feel safe either, but all Antonia wanted was to see Ricardo.

Even though the ward was massive, Antonia felt the walls and low ceiling closing in. Her blood was pulsing in her wrists, throbbing in her neck like a severe migraine. In the distance was the sound of water dripping from an old dingy pipe splashing into a puddle on the floor. León had arranged for Ricardo to be put in a safer place—somewhere he would at least have a cell of his own—but soon, León's influences would be of no use. If they convicted Ricardo, he was forever doomed.

Isn't that what a murderer deserves?

An ache spread through her at the sight of him. "Papá," she managed. "It's me."

In the silence, he sat back, his gaze distant and fractured as if trying to look at many things at once. The prison cell was barely six feet by four, a hollow cube-like stone structure. The bed was a plank of wood on legs, no mattress, no cushioning, and only one thin, worn-out blanket covered with speckles of what Antonia thought were old bloodstains.

He glanced back at her, his eyes vacant, unlike Antonia had seen them before. Briefly, the bitterness in her face faded to weary sadness.

His hair was scruffy, and he looked more tired than Antonia had ever seen him. Heavy shadows accented the gauntness of his face, giving a certain grimness to his expression, as though he had wilted overnight.

"I didn't kill him." He reached for her hand, and his touch was as cold as the iron bars locking him in.

Antonia recoiled, composing herself. "Papá, I need you to tell me the truth about what happened. All of it," she said, determined. Her suspicions were like needles jabbing at her skin. What if he confirmed her theory? Was she ready to face the truth?

Ricardo raised his eyes, looking somewhere else, someplace Antonia couldn't see without turning around. Disappointment was written all over his face.

"It's the house . . . it's the—" he uttered in a ragged voice.

"Stop," she said, cutting him off. The wounds inflicted to the chief of staff made it hard to blame it on a house. Ricardo must've seen something. Heard things. Felt things. He was the only witness. "Stop it," she insisted. "You were there. What happened to *you*? You were lying on the floor next to a corpse. A dead man, Papá."

How had it gone from their being guests at the opening of a hotel to his being imprisoned for murder? And to her believing that he could've killed Estela as well.

He leaned closer, and when he spoke, it was in a low whisper. "Antonia, we made a mistake. The hotel needs to be shut down, or else more deaths will follow. We should've never rented out the place. People must be kept away from it. Don't you understand? We were never meant to be there. I should've listened to her sooner."

Her eyes widened in alarm. *Listened to her? Who? What is he talking about?*

Antonia drew in a sharp breath, and she could hear the slow, dragging beat of her heart as she scrambled to stay focused. She needed information from him, and she wouldn't leave until she got it.

"Papá, what happened last night? I don't want to ask again, so please answer me," she pressed, as though she hadn't listened to what he'd just said, even though his words still rumbled in her head.

"I need you to believe what I'm saying," Ricardo let out with an unnerving directness.

"I can't if you don't tell me what happened—"

His hands clawed at the iron bars, shaking them, as though he might wrench them from their moorings and lunge at Antonia. The metal groaned under the pressure of his grip, a sinister echo of his own anger. "The house, for God's sake, Antonia. The house happened. The land. What else can I say?"

Antonia's breath quickened, and she took a step back. Her shoes scraped against the gritty floor. "Papá," she managed. Her own composure a fragile shield against Ricardo's fury. "The judge will expect you to give a more coherent statement—"

And Antonia was expecting him to at least tell *her* the truth. After all, he owed it to her.

Ricardo's hands let go of the iron bars, and he now stood still in a rigid posture, his face soaked in sweat. "There is *evil* inside the house. Estela knew it too. That's how she ended up dead."

"What *happened* the morning she passed?"

Ricardo's face contorted into a snarl. His eyes darted restlessly as though unable to settle on anything, as if searching for an escape from his confinement, and perhaps even his own tormented mind. "She was ill. She was tormented. She had no choice but to—"

"Papá, stop! Tell me the truth. I know you locked her up in her sanctuary," Antonia said accusingly. She wouldn't reveal that she'd read Estela's journals, but he would certainly wonder how she knew that. "And then I saw you *there*. You were furious, and she was standing on the ledge. You could've held on to her, prevented her fall," Antonia growled. "You could've saved her—"

His eyebrows squished momentarily, and a low, guttural chuckle slipped through his dry lips. "Antonia—that's not . . . you were . . . You think *I* did it? You really think *I* killed her when all *I* did was *love* her?" His voice raised in harsh, bitter tones, each word dripping with more irritation than the last. "I devoted myself to her like I've never done to anything, to anyone. You're confused. You're hurting."

Something snapped inside Antonia as the words landed on her ears. *Confused? Hurting?* How could he be so dismissive? What was he attempting to cover up?

Antonia frowned with anger. She wouldn't let him brush everything under the rug this time.

"No, Papá. Stop trying to treat me like I'm Mamá. I know things now. And if you don't want to tell me about her, about that night, then at least tell me what happened yesterday. I swear that if you don't, I won't get you out of here."

A gloom overcame her, and she felt layers of unsettling emotions. Could she let him rot in prison? Did she have enough strength within her to witness him like this? But she couldn't pretend that there wasn't something wrong with him. Not anymore.

He crumpled on his bed, looking crushed, hollow. "I can't tell you any more than that because I was *not* there when it happened," he blurted out. "We found the chief of staff dead. . . ."

"We . . . ?" Antonia perked up. "What do you mean *we*?" Hadn't he been alone?

"Yes. We—Alejandro, the reporter, and I . . . he wanted an interview, and I—"

"Alejandro?" *Oh my God.* Antonia felt her insides knotting. "Then why didn't he say a word when the police were taking you away?" *Why would Alejandro keep his mouth shut?*

"He is a young reporter, Antonia. The police wouldn't have believed him, they would've blamed him too. He would be as screwed as I am, and we wouldn't have anyone to help us."

Antonia cocked her head, confused. "I don't understand. . . ."

Ricardo rose to his feet again and locked eyes with Antonia. "I'd agreed to meet him on the fourth floor for the interview. Somewhere we could chat, where it wasn't too loud. When we both got there, the door was locked, but we heard voices, murmurs, inside, so we knocked. A few times. The room quieted for a few moments, and we were ready to leave, but we heard something—*someone*—scream. It got louder, wilder, less screaming and more screeching, shrieking. Animal-like sounds."

Horror settled over Antonia slowly with each word Ricardo uttered, and something inside her told her that worse was yet to come.

He squeezed her hand inside his and pulled her closer.

"Alejandro left to check on other rooms, and I stayed to try to get the door to open. I pushed hard against it a few times, and it finally flew open, revealing what was inside—" He paused.

"How did you end up covered in . . . blood?" Antonia's mind was spinning. There was something macabre about his voice. "How did *you* end up *here?*"

Antonia had already accumulated enough disbelief when it came to her papá's words. How could she consider believing him this time?

He shook his head. "I don't remember. I woke up in your arms and everything else is blurred in my head."

Her hand slipped from his, and her eyes widened in alarm. Antonia couldn't decide if the sudden panic that seized her throat would make her vomit or cry. "I need you to remember. You must."

"Antonia," he growled. "Something happened in that studio. And it had nothing to do with me. I'm telling you the truth!"

"Papá, you have to understand that a prosecutor will find this very hard to believe. . . ."

He held her gaze. A flicker of disappointment was in his eyes, but Antonia didn't have it in her to let guilt consume her. "I think *you* find it rather hard to believe as well."

"It's not about that. . . ." But it was about that. She knew there had to be more to the story, she just wasn't exactly sure what that was. And whether he would be the one to deliver the information, or if she was the one in charge of finding out herself.

"Well, I don't know what you want to hear, but this is the only truth."

There was resigned sadness in her eyes. Whatever, whomever, he was covering up for, he wouldn't tell her.

Steps came from behind, and the clang of a hanging key chain followed. "Visit is over," the same guard who'd accompanied her moments ago announced.

Antonia struggled to lean back against the cell, but the man's grip was tight against her shoulder. "I'll see you soon, Papá."

Now it was Antonia's turn to lie, especially if her suspicions turned out to be true. Antonia wasn't sure she would care to see him again if they were.

OCHO

M adre Asunción sat on her throne-like chair. Her deep-set eyes followed Antonia as she strode inside through the mahogany doors. Madre Asunción's office was adorned with paintings of saints and an imposing altar at the end of the broad room, carved and gilded during the Spanish conquest. Faint incense wafted, along with the toasty aroma of cigars, the smoke making its way toward the faux-Michelangelo-wallpapered ceiling.

Antonia shifted her weight, feeling suddenly pinned under Madre Asunción's scrutinizing stare.

Thoughts of Ricardo in prison still crowded Antonia's mind. The possibility of his being convicted, of his being dragged away forever, of her losing him too, made her dizzy and her heart ache, an intense pain she hadn't felt since Estela's death. But what truly terrified her was the possibility that he'd been her mamá's killer.

Antonia focused on Madre Asunción, on what she came here to do. Antonia knew that she had to justify her absence to the nun before losing her job was added to her list of concerns.

The old lady motioned for her to sit.

Antonia pulled out an ornate gold stool, with a scarlet velvety fabric covering the cushion. The room felt almost like it didn't belong in the escuela. Its sumptuosity contrasted against the weathered, dull, and bleak surroundings.

"I—I wanted to excuse myself for not being able to meet my weekly schedule." Antonia didn't normally work on weekends, but she often took on more lessons in an attempt to make some extra pesos. "See, we've been having some issues at home and my papá . . ."

Madre Asunción's eyes slid across the narrow cedar table and landed on Antonia, their black so deep, it was almost dark blue. "Issues?" she said flatly. The cigar curled between her cigar-stained bony fingers pressed against the crystal ashtray. "Don Ricardo is in prison charged with murder. I wouldn't call that 'having some *issues*.'" Madre Asunción paused momentarily. "In all honesty, Miss Rubiano, I think that is good enough of an excuse not to show up to work."

Madre Asunción's words struck the air off-key, distant and slightly dissonant. Had Antonia misheard? Was she imagining it? She was certain she'd heard the old nun say those things, but Antonia hadn't expected Madre Asunción to be understanding. Perhaps it was due to how frantic the last twenty-four hours had been that her brain was blurry, almost unable to process any information effectively.

"Pardon me, what?"

Madre Asunción gave Antonia a swift, frank look. "Yes. We know about your father, and I figured that was why you missed work earlier this morning. In all honesty, I wouldn't have been here if I were in your position. . . . I wouldn't want anyone to see me go through such a shameful situation. I would hide under a rock. What this means for your reputation. Poor thing, my heart shatters for you," she said snidely. "But you have been a model of a daughter. Perhaps one day you'll make a stellar wife and mother yourself."

Humiliation tainted Antonia's cheeks. She felt her guts knotting like pieces of wool, but she wouldn't let herself succumb to Madre Asunción's words.

"I'll get back to my regular schedule next week, I promise," she said, forcing a brightness into her voice that rang hollow in the closeness of the room. "And I'll keep taking on more lessons if necessary."

Madre Asunción's face shifted, resettled. The tension in the room was now palpable, and she seemed to have cut through it when she spoke again. "Actually, we've gotten several dozens of calls from concerned parents. . . ."

Antonia lifted her head, her eyes fixed on the old nun. She opened her mouth to speak, but Madre Asunción spoke first.

"Rumors spread quickly, especially in wealthy circles, as you might be familiar with, and they wonder if you're the right person to teach their girls."

Antonia bit her tongue, the image of Madre Asunción at the end of the slope going blurry as tears threatened to come out. Madre Asunción was right. If Antonia was in their position, she would be concerned too. But her papá hadn't been convicted yet. No one had proved that he was guilty as charged.

"He is *none* of those things," Antonia said at last. She needed to lie through her teeth if need be to keep this job.

The expression on the nun's face shifted immediately, from serene to irritated, but Antonia didn't hold back. "You *know* him. You've pretended to be his friend, our family's friend, for years . . . but I'm sure that was only because of the very generous donations he selflessly gave to you and the congregation. I now know exactly where these donations went. . . ." She gestured around. The old bitch had to know that Antonia knew about it.

Madre Asunción cast her a sideways glance, disbelieving. "I am simply telling you what the parents are complaining about," she said harshly. "Whether or not Don Ricardo is guilty, I don't know. The only one who can judge him is our Lord. Your father seems like a completely fine man, *troubled*—understandably so—but fine. I can't blame him. But perhaps he lost his mind after all. He married your mother; look how that ended up for both of you. You both are paying the cost of her sins."

The words stung Antonia and took her aback. The nuns had never agreed with Estela's lifestyle. With her beliefs. In Madre Asunción's eyes, Estela was nothing else but a heretic. One that deserved to be burnt at the stake, though sadly for Antonia, society had different ways of retaliating nowadays. None involved fire, but they burned equally, if not more. Her mamá was doomed to an eternity in hell, while every member of the Rubiano family had been condemned to a living purgatory. What Antonia never understood was how someone like Doña Pereira, who was not the epitome of a good Christian at all, could manage to have, as her right hand, someone who belonged to Madre Asunción's congregation, someone like Padre Juan.

"It matters not what I think. These concerned parents won't stop until you're out of here and as far away as possible from their children. Tell me, Antonia, what am I supposed to do?"

Antonia bolted out of her chair, loathing itching against her skin as she looked down at Madre Asunción. "Fire me. I resign if that is what you need me to do." Antonia momentarily regretted having said it. She was willing to put up with Madre Asunción if that would assure her that she'd have the life she had yearned for, for so long, a free one.

But right now, more than ever, she felt trapped, trying to save her family. Her papá again.

Madre Asunción was still for a minute, then she said quite firmly, "I could fire you at their request, but I cannot afford to lose you right now. You're one of our best tutors, even when I don't condone your ways of teaching.

"You will remain with us. But I need you to handle your *issues* before this escalates any further. If you agree to do that, then you can stay, and I'll handle the parents," Madre Asunción said sharply. "Hire a good lawyer and do *not* talk to the press. People will gossip," she added reassuringly. "Pay them if you need to shut them up. It is not only your job or your future that are at stake, it is also your reputation."

As much as Antonia didn't want to agree with the nun, she was right. Antonia's future was at stake. If Madre Asunción was willing to let Antonia stay, she wouldn't refuse. She had more pressing issues to deal with.

"I will fix it," Antonia said, although she was getting tired of making promises she wasn't sure she would be able to keep. She'd promised to keep her family safe, that leaving El Castillo de Bochica would put an end to their misery, that her papá would be fine. But here she was. She often thought of their decade at the house as a long dream, a dusky haze, one that consumed her. But the dream soon became an ongoing nightmare that threatened to bring her down for good. It didn't rest, it didn't relent. And now it had become her reality.

As much as she longed for an escape, she'd proved she couldn't run away. Not without putting up a fight.

She'd cross the gates once more, even if her survival was put at risk.

—————

León Rivera stood outside the escuela's iron gates. Antonia stared at him from the slope as she strode down the gravel path, framed by delicate-bloomed bromelias and lush thickets that contrasted against the backdrop of weathered ancient nogales leaning into the muted late-afternoon sunrays and into the dirt road.

"I can drive you home if you want," he offered.

The last thing Antonia wanted was León's company.

She shook her head. "What are you doing here?" She didn't stop, simply walked forward.

He didn't stand still. "Carmela told me you'd be here after seeing your father. Since you were so upset earlier, I thought we could talk in a more civilized manner now that you're calmer. I need you to listen to me."

Listen? She'd done enough of that already.

Antonia didn't turn to face him.

"Nona, I've been worried sick since we last spoke . . . about you, about your father. I want to help. I need you to promise me you won't do anything to meddle your way into this. Things are very delicate, and we need to go about things the right way. Ricardo has gone through some very tumultuous times. First when Estela died, then when he tried to . . ." León trailed off.

Destroy the thing that he believed was causing his family despair? Antonia had been there, she needn't a reminder.

Antonia's first instinct was to defend Ricardo, but unlike with Madre Asunción, with León she didn't need to pretend. And there was certainly much to agree with in what had come out of León's mouth. Ricardo was unstable, perhaps he was capable of acts of violence that Antonia simply hadn't realized until now.

"I do not need the reminders."

"What I'm proposing is . . ." León hesitated. "You declare him mentally impaired. That way, we're able to get him out of prison and put somewhere else safe, a facility . . ."

Antonia hadn't considered the possibility, and León was right in that it could secure her papá a way out of prison. Even if it didn't mean he would be free, he'd at least be in a better and safer place.

But if he was found guilty, would she be content with the injustice Ricardo had committed? Did he not deserve a life sentence? Wasn't prison the place where murderers belonged? Where her mamá's killer should be?

An uneasy feeling settled over her. "Somewhere safe? What, a mental institution instead?"

Another form of prison. A prison for his soul. Perhaps a murderer was deserving of such a place as well.

"Antonia, you've been at that place. I've managed to find him a relatively safe and good cell, one where he's less exposed to others, to the plagues and illness . . . but when a judge sentences him, I won't be able to protect him anymore. From then on, he's on his own, and you've seen how horrible the conditions are. This is the only solution."

Antonia took in a hot, impatient breath. "Do *you* believe he did it?"

"Look, Antonia, things are complicated right now, so what I think or don't is not enough to get him out. There's too much press involved—someone from the local government was killed. The community is putting a lot of pressure into solving things."

"Answer the question, León. Do you think he did it?"

"Nona, who knows. I wasn't there. Sure, he seemed well enough last night at the party. He talked to the investors, coffee people who're looking to expand their business. They had an amazing conversation. It seemed as though he was back. As himself, his past self. He even gave Alejandro an interview."

Antonia's eyebrows drew together at his last statement. "How do you know about the interview?"

"Well, I talked to Alejandro, questioned him rather. I wanted to see what he knew . . . you know, to help your father out, a potential witness." León was blabbering now. He seemed nervous, unsettled. "He told me he was there on the fourth floor with him, and he left your father briefly to check on the room next door, to find help, not even five minutes had passed, and next thing he knew, Ricardo was lying on the floor next to a corpse. So we can't use him as a witness—your father was completely alone, and that incriminates him further."

Wait. Five minutes? The man had been mangled, dismembered almost. There's no way her papá could've done that much damage in less than five minutes.

Was he innocent after all? Had he simply been at the wrong place at the wrong time, or did someone, the real killer, frame him?

"He's innocent," she said in a low voice, when her thoughts escaped her. "He didn't do it."

"Antonia—" León looked confused.

"No, you know he couldn't have. You saw the body. It's not possible for him to kill someone in that short amount of time. The man was double his size. And there was no way Alejandro wouldn't have noticed, wouldn't have heard things if he was near."

But another thought hit her. It had all happened on the fourth floor. Antonia had been there, twice. While everyone danced and drank, Antonia had been upstairs trying to get to her room. She'd heard voices, steps approaching her.

Could it be that while she was hiding, while she was seeking answers, murder was occurring just next door?

"Antonia . . ." León pulled her back, startling her from her daze. His jaw sharp and clenched. "His trial was scheduled for Tuesday. That's less than four days from today. It's not the standard, but there's extra pressure on this one. Even if we believe him to be innocent, all evidence incriminates him—people saw him lying next to the corpse, covered in blood, and we don't have time to find all the evidence or come up with a better solution."

Antonia's heart sank. She wanted to speak, but the words lodged in her throat. There had to be something they could do. She needed to find a way to get Ricardo out. But if he hadn't done it, what truly happened that night? Was the truth hiding somewhere within the hotel's walls?

"That's the only option we have right now."

"No, *you* could literally save him. This is no time for you to stab him in the back. An asylum? You can get him out."

"I don't have the time to find strong enough evidence, neither do you. But this plan . . . it buys us time. It could be just for a while . . . until we sort things out," León offered. "Antonia, it's the only way I can get him out of there."

"No. I will not agree to any of this until it is really the only choice left. I will find a way out. I know he didn't do it. You know it too."

She felt a stab of guilt gnawing at her, for thinking Ricardo capable of killing that man. But what about her mamá . . . what if he was guilty of killing her?

When León spoke again, his tone was suddenly softer. "Think about it." He grinned. "At the end of the day, we both want what's best for him. There's more to this than time working against us. You know he'd be better off at a mental institution, at least for a while. They'll take better care of him than you ever will. He really could get better."

She stared briefly at León, then drifted back to her thoughts. What if León's plan was really the only way out for her papá? What if, come the time of his trial, she had no evidence, nothing that could prove him innocent. Would she let him rot in prison? That would be sentencing him to the death penalty. He wouldn't survive it, no one did.

But would any of them survive at all if she couldn't get the house to spill its secrets?

NUEVE

ntonia stormed inside her house, and she felt like she could breathe again. Her conversation with León had left her drained. Something about his behavior, his reluctance, made her not want to trust him. But he'd given her an ultimatum: if by early Tuesday she didn't have evidence strong enough to make a case in defense of Ricardo, she had to agree to his offer. But all she had right now were Ricardo's words. Words that a prosecutor or a judge wouldn't believe either.

The words of a lunatic, a sibilant voice echoed in her mind.

But León had spilled out all the proof she could possibly need to believe her papá. Perhaps he was simply a victim of bad luck, circumstantial evidence. Or, something way more sinister. Someone wanted to put the blame on him, someone had framed him. Regardless, she needed to come up with a plan if she wanted to uncover what was happening.

Antonia slouched over the mahogany kitchen table and dipped a piece of roscón de arequipe into freshly brewed coffee. The sweetness of the cake-like bread along with the dense layers of the arequipe spread banished the bitter taste she'd carried in her mouth all day.

Antonia filled in Carmela on everything that had happened.

"I just have this feeling that León is hiding something. I'm trying to make sense of it, but I can't."

Carmela stared at her from a corner as Antonia gulped down the last of her coffee. She motioned for more.

"No more coffee for you, miss. There is not enough coffee to keep you awake at this point. You *need* to rest, Antonia."

"Ay, Carme, please. If coffee won't keep me up, all this shit will."

Carmela raised her brows high, then dutifully leaned against the table and poured Antonia the remainder of the coffee inside the pot.

Antonia smiled as she watched the steaming liquid stream over her cup. She drank it and perked back up. She had no time for lounging around, so she placed her hand inside the right pocket of her jacket and wrapped her fingers around the already-wrinkly napkin inside it. She lifted from her chair, walked to the gray telephone hanging against the blue azulejos underneath the kitchen cabinet. Her fingers circled around the metal dialer, then she pressed the handset against her ear.

Carmela regarded her with curious eyes from the corner, but Antonia gave her no hints.

Alejandro's voice was crisp, sharp, and bright as it flowed from the telephone.

Antonia swallowed. "Alejandro? It's Antonia Rubiano."

"Antonia, my God. How is your father doing? Is he okay?"

"Not at all, I'm afraid. But I can't go into details right now. Listen, I need your help. . . ." Alejandro remained silent, so she continued speaking. "I know you were with him." Her confession must have triggered something in him, and Antonia felt as though she could almost see his reaction.

"Antonia, I—"

"You don't need to explain anything. Whatever your reasons were to remain silent last night, I don't need them. Not now. What I do need is your help, and I need it fast."

"Antonia, I don't know if I can get involved in anything to do with what happened yesterday or your father. My job is at stake. If I meddle in a case like this, if someone even suspects me, my career could be gone forever."

"I understand, but I need—"

"Hold on, let me finish. I just need you to understand what's at stake for me. But there *is* something I'm willing to do it for."

Antonia gritted her teeth. Of course. She should've started there. "How much?"

He scoffed. "A story. I went to the opening party looking for one. I need something good enough to pitch to my boss. Less urban legends and gossip, chismes won't do it for him. I need more of the *real* stuff. Something good. I need *your* story—"

Her story? She didn't even know it. Not with the certainty that being the protagonist should give her. All she had were flashes of memories, scattered and jumbled images of El Salto and her former home that threatened to consume her if she dared give herself to them. Within them was the truth about her nightmares, about Estela. There were plenty of blank spaces too, spots she'd tried to fill in. She had some of her mamá's journals—the things she'd said in them that contradicted the stories Antonia had been telling herself for the past three years. And perhaps it was all because of Antonia's grief. Didn't one's brain make up stories to shield one from pain?

Trust no one, Antonia, Alejandro had said. But she now doubted she could trust herself.

"Fine, I'll do it," she agreed at last. There was no way Alejandro would know she'd lied.

"Are you sure?"

"Yes. I'm willing to do anything to help him."

Alejandro was so desperate for a story that any anecdote she'd give him would probably be enough. Her story, however, the real one, was locked away in her brain, in a place so deep that she struggled to reach it.

"If Papá didn't kill that man," she continued, "any ideas what might've happened?"

"Oh, many. I think we stumbled into a blood ritual."

"What do you mean?"

"It's no secret that the land where the mansion stands has been used for all kinds of . . . practices. Rituals, sacrifices, juju, the good and the bad ones . . ." He paused. "The land is sacred for the Muiscas, but everyone else has been using it for other reasons. Muisca or not, people believe there's something . . . special. Something worth draining energy from, if you will."

Alejandro was right. She'd seen people sneak inside. The house, when it got built and they moved in, didn't deter people from visiting and leaving their tracks scattered all across their land.

But a ritual? Some sort of rite? In the middle of an opening party?

How Alejandro knew all of this, she didn't know. But perhaps there was more information that he was holding on to.

Antonia didn't have any other choice than to go back. All her answers were within those walls: the rest of Estela's journals, the proof of Ricardo's innocence, what really happened to her mamá . . .

Antonia's thoughts went back to the notes jotted down in the Muisca language. One of the latest pieces of the puzzle she'd found while roaming around the house, but she still couldn't figure out if it was relevant.

"Do you speak Chibcha?" she asked.

"No, but I can read it."

That should be enough for Antonia to find out what she'd written on that scrap of paper.

"Why?"

"I'll explain later. . . . Listen, I'm getting us both inside the hotel."

"What?"

"I have a plan. For the plan to work, we need to go back there. It's the only way."

The clock was already ticking against her, so they needed to be fast.

Thankfully, Antonia was good at thinking on her feet. "There's a Brujas party tonight—"

"The Halloween party?"

"Yes. But we're not going. At least not as ourselves."

"I'm lost. . . ."

Antonia huffed, "It's the perfect time for a good disguise." She watched as Carmela's deep brown eyes widened with fear. Antonia swallowed, waiting for a response on the other end of the line, wishing that her own idea wouldn't be the end of her this time.

Alejandro laughed with his deep vibrant voice before he said, "You're good."

The corner of her lips turned slightly upward. "I am."

"Also, modest."

"*Not* a single ounce." She didn't know if it was excitement or fear coursing through her body in that instant. Perhaps a combination of both. "Alejandro, I'm trusting you."

"We're going to get him out." He emphasized each word, and something about his tone was reassuring.

"I'll see you at my house by the end of the afternoon. Not a single word to anyone, especially not your boss."

Alejandro agreed before she hung up the phone.

Fear was written all over Carmela's face, and a faint crack crept through her voice. "Nona, what are *you* going to do?"

"Turns out that to get Papá out of hell, *I* must go through it first."

But would the cost be too high in the end?

DIEZ

In most cases, Antonia didn't remember her dreams—her nightmares had lately been mere fragments of a full picture—but today she had.

In it, ghastly wind moved right through her as she stood on the balcony, chilling her bones to the cold of splintering ice. Inside the house, fog seeped in, curling its wisps around her. The need to run started her forward, but the sudden sharp pang all over her body put an end to her will to run. Her heart pounded in her chest, the blood pumping through her veins almost visible through her skin.

She stared in horror—the yellow wall in front of her was stained with splashes of blood. The ironlike scent lingered in the empty hallway. She felt an urge to puke, but it quickly vanished when the thud of soles echoed from behind her. Panic. Terror. She turned on her heels and let out a blood-curdling screech as she came face-to-face with the most horrifying thing she'd ever seen.

Its figure was gaunt, a mere skeleton cloaked in rags of what was once a gray robe. The creature's almost skinless frame seemed to squirm as though the very darkness around it were alive. Two glowing red eyes pierced through Antonia with unnerving precision, preventing her from daring to look away. Below, a jagged slit stretched across its face, crudely sewn together with thick black stitches. Each muffled movement of the mouth was accompanied by a disturbing rustle, like fabric being torn, but it didn't open fully, only revealing a glimpse of a darkened, void-like interior.

A twisted, gnarled mass of bristly, blackened strands that appeared to writhe and shift with life of their own framed its head. The hairs seemed to twitch and tremble like tendrils of shadows reaching out for any stray glimmer of light.

With a scream caught in her throat and her silk robe drenched in sweat, Antonia bolted upright in bed, disoriented.

It was just a dream. But the dream made her jolt in recognition. She had seen that nightmarish image somewhere in real life, recently. And she needed to know why.

She lay restless in Ricardo's bed. She knew she had to get up and start getting ready for their drive ahead, but the white sheets tickling her nose with her papá's nutty lotion were bringing her a certain comfort. Everything was quiet. The only sound that of her own breathing.

She drew her eyes to the pinewood vanity table across the room. On it, a set of Estela's tunjos. Antonia locked her eyes and her focus on them for a moment, straining to find some connection to them beyond her mamá's words. Tunjos were part of the Muisca tradition—the tiny figurines were used for various purposes, from rituals to offerings. Estela had collected hundreds of them. Most of them were locked away at the house, in her room.

Antonia's eyes then darted to the round mirror framed in gold. The table no longer held Estela's necessities; instead, gold ornate frames were stacked on it. Pictures of the three of them together: the first time at the house; her mamá standing on her balcony, wearing her favorite red suede dress; Antonia's papá laying the first layer of paint on the ground floor. In all of them, their faces were adorned with the widest of grins; they all looked happy. And for a while, they had been. Their time at the house, the first several years, had not been the torment it eventually turned into. But eventually, their pictures became misleading. They lacked the nuance of real emotions, and most of them, if not all, were heavily staged. Like the one taken a year prior to Estela's death.

Estela had just gotten word that her cousin Celeste and her kid had died in a tragic accident. They'd visited that same day, hours earlier, and little did Estela know it would be the last time she saw them. That just several hours after that, they'd both be dead. The baby was barely a couple months old, and Celeste had lost her husband months before her daughter was born.

Pain had engulfed Estela after hearing the news, her face overcome with sadness as tears flowed incessantly down her cheeks. Papá had said it'd been a tragic loss, that "those things happen," but the words failed to soothe her, if they were meant to console her at all. Aside from sadness, Antonia had caught a trace of fear in her mamá's eyes too, like anxiety was gnawing at her from within.

Ricardo had insisted that they take pictures regardless, for the holidays were just around the corner. And in it they looked like a happy family of three—a facade of contentment.

There was a knock on the door, accompanied by the creak of its rusty hinges. Carmela poked her head in.

"Nona, may I?"

Antonia nodded and motioned her to step in. The smell of chocolate caliente invaded Antonia's nostrils immediately. Carmela held a silver platter with hot chocolate, cheese, and freshly baked tiny buns. She slid it carefully across the bed to Antonia, who sat up straight against the wooden bed frame, still tangled in Ricardo's white blankets. A loose lock of brown hair flopped over her tiny forehead before she pinned it back with a plastic clip.

"I couldn't take my afternoon nap, couldn't fall asleep," Carmela said. Her under eye was coated in gray, and her usual sleek braids hung loose on the top of her head.

"I was able to briefly, though I kept dozing in and out of sleep." Antonia lifted her gaze off the steaming chocolate.

"Have you been having nightmares again?"

Antonia nodded. "I saw a . . . Never mind. I was just noticing Mamá's tunjos before you came in, and it made me think of something I saw last night—Doña Pereira's necklace. Did you see it?"

Antonia couldn't help but wonder if the sight of the pendant had permeated her nightmares.

Carmela hesitated, as though the words were piling up inside her mouth, but she couldn't let them out. "A svetyba."

"A svetyba, a demon entity according to Muisca tradition," her mamá had told Antonia even before they moved into the mansion. They sat by the fireplace, each with a book in hand, while a storm blasted outside. "Bochica is light, she was the moon goddess. But where there's light, there's also always darkness. A svetyba is that."

"But Bochica protects us from svet—" Antonia's voice was shrill. She'd been eight years old at the time. Her doubting whether Bochica or the evil entity was real was out of the question back then.

Estela reached for Antonia's hands hidden under the woolen covers. Estela's features shimmered in the warm glow of the candle's light. A tiny smile formed on her lips, her head cocked to the side. "I won't ever let anything hurt you, Nona," she'd said, reassuringly. "A svetyba can't come into this house. Or our family. Svetybas are evil, but they only come when called upon. They need to be summoned, and it's bad people who summon bad things, right?"

"Why?" Antonia pressed.

Estela let out a breath and leaned her back against the velvet couch. "They think the svetyba can bring them joy, good fortune, essentially all they've ever wanted. But there's always a price to pay."

Antonia considered her mamá's last words for a moment as she sipped her hot chocolate. Perhaps Bochica and the svetyba were both the same. After all, they all promised to bring good things to their people.

The recollection of that night still lingered in her brain, and with it, fear stroked her. If Doña Pereira had adored Bochica as much as Estela had, wasn't wearing a necklace with a svetyba a form of sacrilege? A form of betrayal for their goddess?

Antonia stiffened and forced herself back to the present. "Yes, I . . ." Even though she tried to convince herself that it probably meant nothing, and that the stories she'd heard over the years were getting to her, there was something about it that she couldn't overlook. "Do you think that's odd?"

Carmela's features went blank. She dropped her eyes down at her lap, before locking them on Antonia again. "She's an evil woman. If anything, the pendant suits her," Carmela said at last. "Although, I don't think there's something more to it than vanity. She's ostentatious and oftentimes tacky. Perhaps she appreciates the looks of it, she has poor taste after all."

"But that thing—" Antonia began, but stopped herself just as quickly. She knew Doña Pereira used to wear the same pendant as her mamá, the one with a Muisca serpent. It now belonged to Antonia, and even though she didn't wear it, she kept it.

"I think you should stop thinking about Doña Pereira and those things," Carmela added.

Antonia poured herself more hot chocolate, dropped some pieces of unsalted cheese in it, and stirred. Under different circumstances, Carmela would be right. But the past days, hours even, had been a whirlwind. Antonia's memories, her newly found discoveries, had become a blur. She couldn't dismiss them like she'd done in the past. Answers could, after all, be anywhere. Even within her.

"Can you go see him later today? I don't want to run into León, and I also don't want Papá to feel like we've forgotten about him." Antonia lifted the cup to her mouth—the hot steam rising from it felt good against her face.

"He won't. But, yes, I'll go visit him later."

Antonia set her chocolate down on the platter again. "Thank you." She smiled. "As soon as Alejandro gets here, we'll leave."

Carmela nodded. "It is rather odd seeing you and Alejandro together. After all this time."

Antonia arched an eyebrow. "What do you mean seeing us together again?"

"You probably don't remember, you were a little girl. But you two already knew each other. His mother and Doña Estela were very close, up until his mother died."

That explains why her papá had recognized Alejandro at the opening party.

"Alejandro spent a lot of time with us when you were both little," Carmela continued. "But when he lost his mother, he moved to Tunja with one of his aunts, and we stopped seeing him. There was no reason for him to come back to visit, and who can blame him?"

Antonia cocked her head. "I . . . don't remember. I knew there was something familiar about him when I saw him at the party, but I couldn't point out what it was."

Questions curled in her chest like weeds, their roots finding firm placement in Antonia's ribs, but she had more important things to deal with than to dig up Alejandro's past.

"Nona, please take care of yourself." Carmela patted Antonia's hand with the absent-minded affection of a mother. And she was like a mother to Antonia after all. But a hint of warning traced underneath the softness of Carmela's voice. She needn't say the words; Antonia knew what her gesture meant.

"I'll be safe. I have a plan, and it will work," Antonia reassured, hoping to convince herself more than she could convince Carmela. "But no one can know that we're there. Especially not Doña Pereira and León. If we somehow ruin the plan, Papá won't ever get out of prison."

"Of course, Nona. I won't say a word. But tell me more about this plan of yours."

"Carmela, if I told you, you'd just worry. But I promise to call if things don't go according to plan."

"Nona—"

"Carmela, I truly promise, okay? I'll be safe. Alejandro will be there. And if you really want to help, perhaps you can by telling me what you would say were Mamá's most precious belongings." The question came out as a knee-jerk thought, and Antonia was uncertain if something would come out of it. But Carmela knew Estela really well, perhaps she could point Antonia in a better direction.

Carmela frowned, then released her eyebrows and softened her expression. "Well, everything in her sanctuary. Her books, her journals. Her tunjos especially..." She pointed at the ones on the vanity in front of them. "Why?"

"It's nothing. I just wish she were here. I miss her dearly, you know? I'm thinking about bringing back home all of her things. It's where they should be."

Carmela gave Antonia a questioning look, but remained quiet, then picked up the silver platter and walked out the door.

When Antonia no longer heard the sound of Carmela's footsteps, she threw the white covers to the side and leaped from the bed. The cold floor greeted her bare feet as she advanced toward the vanity. In front of her, one of the gold-and-copper figurines the size of an infant's fist glimmered with a faint, ethereal glow. She picked it up and was able to wiggle the tunjo around her fingers, trying to figure out if there could be answers within them. Estela had mentioned that Antonia used to steal them from her, so maybe there had been a different reason for that other than Antonia's wanting to play with them. After all, they were considered to be vessels of belief and power.

The one in Antonia's hands was a shaman, his face etched with serenity. She picked up another one—the urgency of the moment propelling her to action—a regal bird with wings spread wide as though it might take flight at any moment. A cóndor, her mamá's favorite.

The one she grabbed after that was bigger. Antonia examined it closely, her fingers sliding over traces of dust and wear. It was a frog, crouched in a moment of poised stillness, and between its feet was a vase, in it a piece of paper rolled up in a scroll.

Something lit up inside Antonia; perhaps the tunjos held more than just power.

I miss the days when Antonia and I sat under her precious walnut tree, and I would teach her all about the Muiscas. The last time we did this, Antonia had worn a knee-length, thick linen gown. Its hue the many pinks of a rose garden, much like mine, contrasting against her fair complexion. Her brown hair tied up in a ponytail—a few wavy strands framed the sides of her face.

"I prayed to Bachué for a girl," I'd said. "And she gave me the most perfect daughter." I handed her a book all about Bachué, Chia, and Huitaca, three of the most legendary Muisca deities. All of them female. Antonia fancied that about the Muisca culture. Their societies were in most cases egalitarian, women as involved in most, if not all, important matters. And I proudly told her that even after the Spanish colonization, societies had remained as such.

When I spoke about Bachué, she listened intently. Bachué was the so-called mother of humanity and the goddess of fertility. It was said that after she accomplished her mission—to populate the world—she retreated back to her sacred lagoon in a serpent form. With that, I finally gave Antonia a golden necklace with a pendant on it. A form of protection to some, but it could be used in many other ways as well.

Then we went on to Chía, our moon goddess, and Huitaca, the goddess of sexual liberation, strong-willed, who'd rebelled against Bochica. Antonia listened, but a faint sensation prickled the nape of my neck.

Something within Antonia was pushing back.

I reached for her hand, squeezed it. "There are pieces of all three in you, Nona. Don't ever forget that."

But are there really? Her behavior the past weeks has made me doubt if Antonia will ever be ready.

She's been acting willful and defiant, a total contrast of that day. Whenever she hears me speak about the Muisca tradition, she parrots back all the facts. Sometimes she even goes as far as waking me up in the middle of the night dressed as a Muisca warrior. She's gotten too comfortable making a mockery out of me, out of my beliefs. I fear I'm los-

*ing control of her, just as much as she's losing control over herself. And I fear that once she
loses it, we won't be able to bring her back.*

It may be too late.

Has she already called in the darkness?

For darkness spreads. It sickens, rots. It dooms.

*We'd tried a cleansing ritual a few months ago at the base of El Salto. A way to soothe
her intense emotions. Cold water, especially that flowing in a sacred place, does wonders
to the body, and the spirit. A two-minute immersion was all she needed. She needed to let
it all go, flow away from her.*

*Taking her down there had not been easy. But she eventually relented, begrudgingly
agreeing to visit the base of the waterfall with Eleonora and me.*

*I pressed her head down and into the water with my own hands. She squirmed, strug-
gling to come back to the surface, and although we were on the shallow side of the base of
the waterfall, I could see fear in her eyes when she finally emerged.*

*I sometimes wonder if I made the right choice. If I was in the right to bring her here to
help her fulfill her destiny.*

*Another cleansing is due. I need to dig a little bit deeper. She needs to understand
what's at stake.*

⊲⊶ — ⊷⊳

Antonia balled her fists, crumpling the paper in her grip. Her breath
hitched, each inhalation ragged and shallow at the weight of Estela's words.

And I fear that once she loses it, we won't be able to bring her back.

It may be too late.

Has she already called in the darkness?

She clutched her hands at her temples, as if trying to steady the world,
her world, which had suddenly tilted off its axis.

What exactly was her mamá seeing in her . . . ?

What had she "called in"?

Antonia's face drained of color, and her lips parted in a silent desperate cry.

A svetyba.

The reddened eyes she'd seen outside her house. The same eyes that haunted, infected her dreams. The creature she'd seen earlier today . . .

Panic coursed through her, a torrent of guilt and disbelief flooding her thoughts. Estela believed there was darkness inside Antonia, and perhaps she was right after all. Perhaps Antonia had lost control and invited evil to the house.

Could she have had something to do with her family's demise? With her mamá's death? Could it be that all this time, all she'd done was point fingers at others, accusingly, judgingly, in an attempt to shield herself from the truth because she knew she wouldn't like it? Were her current nightmares simply there to force her to confront the truth?

No. No. No.

She'd never . . . She'd seen Estela mere steps away. She fell of her own volition. Even if she hadn't, Antonia was certain she hadn't been the one to push her off the balcony.

Right?

Her face contorted with anguish, and she stumbled back to the edge of the bed, trying to regain composure. She forced herself to focus. She was going to the hotel. If she was guilty in some way, if she was being haunted by a svetyba, if she had invited one in, she needed to get to her mamá's sanctuary. Not only would she face the truth down there, but she would also find a way to get rid of it. The darkness. There had to be a way to get rid of it, right? Unless it was already too late.

ONCE

———————

It took four hours to drive to El Salto del Tequendama. When Alejandro helped Antonia out of the car, she was struck by how crowded the grand entrance was, as though a man hadn't been killed in the hotel just last night.

Antonia had set up everything for her and Alejandro: they'd pass as newlyweds in town for the ultimate luxury experience, a night at the most sumptuous and expensive hotel to ever exist in Colombia.

She'd packed a suitcase with expensive knee-length, low-waisted beaded dresses she hadn't worn once, along with a pair of Ricardo's finest suits that would fit Alejandro like a velvet glove. Antonia had also brought a pair of carnival masks for them—gray, ornate with copper details—that covered half of their faces. It was a costume party after all, and for them, even more so. She couldn't afford to be recognized, and in case Doña Pereira or León stumbled by, she was certain they'd be safer under the masks' cover.

"So, we're Lina and Manuel Ospina." He said the names slowly, as if trying not to mess up, then turned to Antonia, offering her his right arm.

She paused briefly, but then carefully wrapped her fingers around the thick of his biceps, stretching against his black suit.

"Yes," she said. "I don't think anyone will ask, though; as long as we keep a low profile, we'll be fine."

"Just wanted to make sure before I messed up." He scoffed, "When I thought that we were disguising ourselves, I didn't think we were *literally* disguising ourselves. Especially not as a filthy rich couple."

Antonia raised a brow at him.

"I mean, I'm the one putting on the look. You're a born aristocrat. The role will come naturally."

His eyes traveled up and down her body, sending a wave of heat through her cheeks. There was his smoldering look again, locking her focus on him, refusing to let her go. And she hadn't been wrong: her papá's frock fit him as though it had been tailored for him. His broad shoulders bulged underneath the thick fabric. Alejandro didn't appear extremely muscular, but his tall frame made him stand out in a crowd. And there was the way he handled himself, with confidence, charm, and a slight seductive air, one of a Casanova.

"You look really good. With your costume and all."

Now, fire rushed through her entire body. She wouldn't say it out loud, but she enjoyed his attention on her. Antonia felt like a different person in her black beaded dress with a drop waist and uneven fringed hem. Spending the past few years caring for her papá and being the head of her disjointed family, she rarely had time for parties anymore. Working for the nuns, even less so. And she missed it. She liked exposing a bit of her skin to the cold temperatures of the city.

"If the ghost hunting doesn't work out, you could try becoming a buffoon." She laughed. "It's a Halloween party, remember? *Of course* we're wearing costumes." Her arms crossed over her chest. "I thought you were supposed to be an expert in this kind of festivity. . . ."

"I'm more interested in the day after, in el Día de los Muertos. But you rich people would do whatever for the sake of partying, won't you?"

Antonia shifted around in a mocking gesture.

"I could've gotten press passes for us, you know?" he teased.

"And *I* got us both one of the best suites," she clapped back. She adjusted the fantasy mask resting over half her face.

Alejandro drew his eyes to hers. "Let's go. If we stand here any longer like marble statues, people will be staring at us soon."

There were many places a person with money could spend the night. El Refugio del Salto wasn't one of those. The hotel provided luxurious accommodation for those lucky and fast enough to book a room.

Antonia wrapped her silken shawl over her shoulders and locked her arm around Alejandro's as they crossed the arched threshold into the hotel, which was finely decorated with black and white roses, as though they were stepping into a funeral and not a party. There were six long, narrow cedar tables to accommodate the guests, each of them crowded with an assortment of platters and dishes: auyama soup, cordero stew with braised beef and pork belly, potato and yucca roast, merengón de piña, and bocadillo bites for those with a sweet tooth and a love for guava.

A sea of partygoers swept their eyes over them and greeted them as they moved to the rhythm of the latest hits. The enthusiastic crowd was relentless: half of them had chosen elegance and glamour over the real Día de las Brujas spirit, the other half had gone wild with the attire. One costume caught her attention immediately: La Llorona. Although not a tale that had originated in Bogotá, but rather on the Caribbean coast up north, its growing popularity made it hard not to know what it was. The hallway with serpentlike Muisca carvings cast a shadow over the woman, making her look almost sinister as she danced in place.

A loose veil hung from the woman's forehead, and her disheveled black hair fell over her waist. Her lips were slathered in red lipstick, her undereye shadow a thick black charcoal color, making her eyes appear sunken. Her shoulders were exposed, and her torso was tightly enveloped in beige rags sewed in place with wool to make a faux corset, her lower body hidden behind a long white silk skirt. Her darkened feet peeked through the light fabric. In her arms, she held a bluish baby-like doll that appeared almost as full as a newborn, its arms aloft as if dreaming or cuddling its mother. The woman slid her pinkie into its open hand, and for a moment Antonia swore she'd seen its fingers curl around it.

Antonia staggered backward. The baby's lips twisted apart as its round face warped and changed. Its red eyes gaped wider, and its tiny mouth twisted into a sneer.

Antonia's skin paled, and a warbling voice resounded in her ears.

WELCOME HOME.

Antonia, shaking, pressed her hands to her face, squeezing her eyes shut. There was a tinge of familiarity in the scene. . . . *A svetyba!*

I fear I'm losing control of her, just as much as she's losing control over herself.

Antonia couldn't help but wonder once again if her mamá was right about something dark living within Antonia.

It's just a Halloween party—it's just a costume. Snap out of it!

She snatched a few long breaths, attempting to push all thoughts aside. She couldn't lose control of herself.

Alejandro retrieved her attention with a soft but firm pull. Antonia was immediately grateful. "Are you okay?"

Am I okay? It had been a while since she'd last been okay.

He stared at her pointedly, a frown creasing the seal between his thick dark brows.

"Yes," she managed. "I . . . still can't believe we're here," she said instead, leaning closer to Alejandro. Her gaze drifted back to where La Llorona had stood moments ago, but the woman had vanished from sight.

Was she losing her grip of reality at last?

⊹•— ⊷ —•⊹

The ripe odor appeared to have gotten stronger since she'd been at the hotel a little over twenty-four hours ago, especially within its walls.

Antonia scanned the room as they stood in the lobby. Several servants wandered by, making sure drinks didn't run low. Doña Pereira had turned

Muisca natives into goods at the disposal of mean members of Bogotá's so-cialites. Men and women wore fique tunics, tightly tied up at the shoulders, made with thick yellow-mustard cotton fabrics, embellished with embroi-dered orange stripes along the waist and hems. On their foreheads lay flam-boyant feathers beaded around their heads, matching the colors of a rainbow. Their arms and necks were adorned with faux-gilded bracelets and necklaces.

But Doña Pereira was sickened with the same air of superiority, one Antonia had sometimes questioned in Estela.

"You might need a drink. It's going to be a long night," Alejandro said.

"I'd love to, darling," Antonia teased, a smirk forming in the corner of her mouth.

He grinned before dragging her past the lobby and up the staircase, where a bar was placed before the fourth floor.

At the bar, Alejandro ordered two shots of aguardiente and two shots of lemon juice. Antonia sat back against the marble counter, humming the old bolero playing in the ballroom, the fringed hem of her dress moving delicately along with the wind seeping in through the half-open floor-to-ceiling windows.

A high-pitched, disembodied voice came from Antonia's right side, snatching Antonia's attention. "Antonia? You've changed so much since I last saw you."

Antonia caught a middle-aged woman's gaze, her curly black hair se-curely pinned up with silver combs adorned with small pearls that caught the warm light hitting from above. She wore a fitted, burgundy, knee-length dress, adorned with floral embroidery at the sleeves, and her head tilted slightly to the side. Even though she wore no mask, Antonia couldn't recognize her.

"I'm afraid you're mistaking me for someone else. I'm Lina," Antonia said, smiling.

Alejandro's arm now rested around her shoulders, and up until then, she hadn't even noticed.

The woman's scarlet red lips twisted upward. "I swear. You look so much like her."

Antonia's heart sank. If this woman spoke to others, they were ruined. "I'm not who you think I am. I'm sorry again."

The lady smiled and excused herself. But even though she had left, she kept sneaking glances at them over her shoulder every time she had a chance.

Antonia began to panic. She couldn't let anything ruin her plan. But she also couldn't draw any unnecessary attention toward them. So she forced herself to let it go and downed her drink. "Thank you for coming with me, really."

"You know, you're really not the woman I expected you to be. . . ."

Antonia had heard those words before, and even though she and Alejandro were not on a date, they stung for a bit. But she had to bite back.

"Boring? Submissive? The woman who does nothing else but care for her papá? Disappointed much?" In many ways that was the woman Antonia thought she'd become. But there was herself, the real one, she thought, itching to be free. Perhaps being here was no more than her attempt to gain her freedom back.

He smiled. "Not at all. I find you're rather fascinating." He leaned against her ear. His breath, tainted with aguardiente, brushed against her neck, causing her to shiver. "I want to know you. Truly see you. See what's under that mask."

She'd locked her gaze on his, and she couldn't look away. Antonia could feel her entire body becoming increasingly hot as he shortened the distance between them once again. Was Alejandro flirting with her? Guilt began to form inside her.

"I lied," she blurted without thinking twice. "I said I'd give you my story, but I can't . . . ," Antonia said softly, and she felt herself starting to open to him. "Turns out, most of my memories are jumbled inside my head, and they don't make much sense. I'm trying to put the pieces together, but somehow they don't fit with each other anymore."

Alejandro chugged down another shot, as if buying himself more time before he spoke.

With her sudden confession, Antonia could've just ruined her chances of his helping her, and she would understand if he wanted to back out of her plan.

"I'd say those broken memories are an integral part of the story." The easiness of his voice felt like lace caressing her ears, his kindness a warm embrace.

"I'm glad you said that because I need you to help me with something, something that might help with my memories. I need you to translate something for me." Antonia pulled out a folded scrap of paper from her coat and handed it to him. She was ready to set her plan in motion: they'd go to their suite on the fourth floor, and from there sneak to her mamá's sanctuary. There was no place else as safe as Estela's precious room, and Antonia was certain the answers to everything would be down there. But for now, they had to wait until the party settled a little longer.

Alejandro's eyes swept over the note. Once, twice. Three times. His lips pursed, and Antonia watched as the muscles in his neck clenched and unclenched.

"This is . . . ?"

"I wrote it," Antonia confessed. "But I can't speak, let alone write, Chibcha."

He'd believe her, wouldn't he?

"*You . . . wrote* it."

"Yes, and I have no idea what it says, but I need to know. Something tells me that—"

"Where did you even find this?"

"Where I found it doesn't matter. It's old. I know I wrote it because it's my handwriting. I don't exactly remember when, but it might've been six years ago. I just don't know how. And here's the thing—this is exactly what I've been concerned about. There're blanks inside my head. And the ones I can recall, I don't even know if I can trust. . . ."

"This is an ancient prayer. A calling . . . A *summons*. You could've copied it from somewhere. It doesn't need to have any meaning at all. . . . Notes scribbled down on paper don't have any power. I mean, in order to summon something, you'd probably need to perform a ritual of some sort."

No. To summon evil into her own life? Antonia's mind was reeling.

At the lack of Antonia's response, Alejandro opened his mouth as if to say something. Antonia's focus drifted back to him, and she quickly added, "You're right. I must've jotted it down from one of Mamá's books. . . . I need another drink," she said in hopes that her brain would clear. But it was too muddled still.

Alejandro gestured at a waiter, and one of them diligently came toward them. Alejandro snagged two drinks from his platter and placed one in Antonia's free hand.

She took a sip, then asked, "How much do you know about the svetybas?"

Alejandro's eyes widened at the sudden change of subject. "Those things—"

"Svetybas." Antonia pressed her lips against his ear and felt him flinch a little. "Saying the name won't curse you."

"Svetybas were . . . *are* one of the most feared creatures, not only to the Muiscas but also to several other native communities spread over the Colombian Andean Mountain range. It's the antithesis of what Bochica was to them. Seeing it is bad news—it's a symbol of a curse or a deal with a Devil entity.

"They're not like other evil things suggested in Catholic and Christian tradition. They don't take hold of a body. Instead, it takes hold of a place or torments one person. It will haunt you, all of you. During the day, at night. You're not safe even when you're asleep. It's the opposite of the pquihiza, of light. It can be called upon via a blood ritual, a sacrifice, but in most cases, you must offer a soul in exchange for a favor."

You're not safe even when you're asleep.

"If you somehow get involved with a svetyba, you're no longer seeing the light. You're cursed. Sometimes forever."

Antonia gasped. She'd read her mamá's own words, how her cleansing hadn't worked on Antonia. And now, a svetyba seemed to be following her around, lurking in the shadows of her every waking moment, clawing its way into her nightmares ... perhaps not for the first time. But why? Or better yet, what if it truly had been Antonia who'd summoned it? ... What if that had been the thing that killed her mamá ...?

According to Estela, Antonia was confrontational, strong-willed, defiant, and troubled. She'd gathered Estela's tunjos in her room when she thought her mamá wasn't watching. Could that be why she wrote down the summons? And her papá ... Antonia killing her mamá could give Ricardo a reason to try to cover up the truth by burning down the house. *To protect her.*

No. To turn against Mamá? No. It didn't make sense.

Antonia would've never hurt her, would she?

"I ..." She leaned forward and lowered her voice. "I think I might've summoned one." Antonia heard the words spill from her mouth, but they were dissonant, as though they weren't coming from her but someone else.

Alejandro raised his eyebrows high.

"I think it's all connected to what's been happening. At least with Mamá and the house."

"Hold on—I'm lost. How?"

"I'm not sure yet." How could she be? If svetybas had something to do with this, if she allowed herself to believe in it again, wouldn't she hand it power to destroy her, to consume her?

"I've been reading Mamá's journals and having nightmares again. Memories of the day she died, especially after coming back to the house, have returned. Papá refuses to tell me what truly happened to her, and I have this growing suspicion that she didn't jump, that she was murdered. I don't know how this connects with what happened the night of the opening, and I need to find out if I want to get him out of jail, but I swear, I have this feeling inside me ... that somehow everything is connected."

And that I'm right at the center of it.

Antonia waited for Alejandro to say something, but she knew he'd need a moment to digest what she'd just said. So she gestured at the young man standing on the other side of the counter. He nodded and slid another aguardiente shot.

"Alejandro, what a surprise," a high-pitched voice came from behind them, instantly putting a pause to their conversation. Antonia flinched and flipped her head to the side. A petite, light-haired woman, dressed in a sack-like yellow dress, not much older than Antonia, was making her way to them.

"Oh fuck," Antonia whispered harshly.

But before the woman could reach them, Alejandro pulled Antonia into his embrace and pressed his lips firmly against hers. His mouth was soft and warm, tainted with the faint scent of alcohol.

The gesture took Antonia aback. It had been a while since she'd last been kissed.

As she heard the woman let out a huff of disappointment and begin to retreat, Antonia reluctantly pulled away, immediately regretting the action, especially with the lingering scent of him still enveloping her.

"What was *that* about?"

"The kiss? I didn't mean to—"

"No, not the kiss." Although perhaps she meant that too. "I mean, her. Who is she? What if she goes around telling that you're here?"

"She's just—we used to, you know? I-I wouldn't worry about her." He forced the words out as Antonia followed the line of his gaze before it landed on the tall arched doorway.

Antonia's face flushed, her veins visibly throbbing in her neck.

Doña Pereira stood just below.

DOCE

They steered clear of Doña Pereira's path, determined to stay out of the old lady's field of vision. The last thing they needed was to get caught, especially by her. So when she crossed the threshold into the bar, they were already out and down the spiral staircase and headed to the big ballroom balcony overlooking the waterfall.

Antonia's brown hair fluttered in the evening breeze. Light rain fell from the deep gray evening sky as she wrapped her fingers around the iron bars. "I thought she wouldn't be here."

Alejandro was down to his last smoke. Antonia took a drag, then handed the cigarette back to him. She shifted her weight, feeling suddenly pinned under his eyes.

"Do you think she saw us?" he asked at last.

"No, I don't think she did." There was more hope than certainty in her response. There was no way Doña Pereira would believe that Antonia came for the party, especially not as Ricardo was rotting in jail.

Antonia's thoughts went back to her papá for a moment. The memory of him behind bars sent her for a loop. Tonight needed to work out. And her plan needed to be set in motion.

"Doña Pereira's presence complicates matters. We need to make sure to steer clear of her if we're going to find the evidence to set Papá free."

"Any updates on your father's case?"

"None, except that his best friend wants me to lock him up in an asylum. Not to mention he won't help, even though he knows there's no way he could've done it."

Alejandro's jaw was sharp and clenched. "Your father's not crazy," he said in an exasperated voice. "He didn't kill that man."

Alejandro was right. Ricardo couldn't have done it. Logistically, it didn't make sense. Her papá was haunted by regret and grief, and that had taken a toll on his mental health. But that didn't make him a lunatic, even less a murderer. And when it came to Estela, Antonia had already positioned herself as the prime suspect of her own theories.

"I know that, but I only have days to prove his innocence, or else I'm afraid I'll end up saying yes to his offer. . . ."

"He questioned me, came asking me if I'd seen or heard anything. If I knew anything that could help him, he seemed concerned. . . . I told him the truth."

"I know, he told me."

"But I don't see how putting him in a mental facility is a better option." Alejandro's gaze traveled somewhere else. It was as though he weren't looking at something on this plane anymore, but rather seeing something he really had to focus on.

Antonia fought against the urge to whirl around and instead spoke again. "Prisons are plagued with diseases. I'd rather have him somewhere I could go visit, a place where I wouldn't constantly worry about whether he made it through the night or not—"

"So you *are* considering it?"

"I don't . . . No; at least not yet," she spat out. "That's why I'm here with you. I want him out. I have a plan, remember?"

"I have one too," Alejandro said, with no trace of hesitation. "We just need to wait for the right moment. It's too early still."

"As long as it happens tonight. I never thought my papá and I would step foot here again. But then we came back for the opening night, and I came here defenseless, thinking it would be different. Look how that turned out," she scoffed. "This time I came prepared, and I won't let this sneaky little bitch of a house . . . whatever lives in it, whatever *I* might've brought inside, ruin our lives anymore."

"I have to say I'm not surprised. Your father has told me how stubborn you are. I didn't expect any less from you."

Antonia smiled. His words had a way of soothing her. His playfulness obliged her racing heart to beat at a slower rate.

"I don't stop until I get what I want."

"I *like* a woman who knows and gets whatever it is that she wants."

Antonia's cheeks flushed a soft shade of pink as his words sank in. In a world that trashed women's ambitions, it was refreshing to have someone appreciate the will inside her.

She felt grateful for Alejandro's presence, not only because he'd agreed to help her but also because she was actually . . . starting to fancy him being around her. Even if it was brief, and under the grimiest of circumstances, selfishly, she wanted to have him with her.

A tinge of curiosity spread through her. Could he be feeling the same about her? It couldn't be a simple story he was after. There had to be more. At least she hoped it was more.

"What are you doing here? Really," she asked him, ushering him inside. "I mean, you say you want to help Papá, and I believe you . . . but why? You didn't have to. You said it yourself, your job could be at stake. . . ."

Was she selfish or delusional enough to believe Alejandro was here for her?

"I already told you. A story. I want my boss to take me seriously. My stories to be taken seriously. I've been at the station since I was twenty-two, it's been six years of long nights, hard work. I'd like a promotion, to have my own column. I want my articles to be under my name."

He was ambitious just like her. Antonia appreciated that. Even though she felt a little deflated at his response. Maybe the feeling was one-sided after all. Perhaps what she was reading as flirting was simply friendliness.

"But if I'm even more specific . . . I got a story assigned when your mother died," he said.

Died. That hadn't been the word the police officers had used to describe what had happened. Or perhaps they'd known she'd been killed, but Antonia's papá had enough influence and money to cover it up. Especially if Antonia was to blame.

"It was right after I'd gotten my first official position at the station. I was thrilled—I knew this was a big one. My one chance. We knew her death hadn't been accidental. . . ." He paused when Antonia's eyes caught his. "We knew there was something else to it, but we never got the chance to prove it, and I guess that still bugs me to this day. I was hoping I could find some answers with you and Ricardo."

Antonia could feel her insides knotting, her rib cage shrinking against her lungs, and for a moment, she struggled to breathe. For months after Estela's passing, Antonia had wished for something that could've explained what had happened, something that could bring her mamá back. She'd longed for hope. But all of it, along with her tears, had gone to waste. Soon, instead of dealing with her grief, Antonia forced herself to understand it would've happened anyway.

But the explanation that had once been enough failed to soothe her. Especially if underneath this new light of information she'd gathered in the past days, Antonia played a huge part in everything that transpired.

Only her mama's journals could explain what exactly happened, or at least let Antonia rebuild the truth from scratch. After having found a couple pages, Antonia knew Estela hadn't gotten rid of them. Antonia wasn't sure why . . . but that didn't matter. She would find them. She needed that clarity. She could no longer make herself believe in words that were far from the truth.

"Maybe you're right. Maybe I *can* help. My mamá's room. Her sanctuary," Antonia began. "Well, down there is where all the answers are. Her journals, she kept many of those, but when we left, I barely was able to secure one with a few pages in it. It's the most important place in this house, the most special one. If you're right that it hadn't been an accident, and if my suspicions about the svetybas having something to do with all of this are correct, the proof will be down there."

Antonia had always been curious about the room. She'd sneaked downstairs during late nights, hoping to get a glimpse of what went on inside. It was Estela's safest place, the place where she gathered with her closest friends. Her haven. Something that was only cemented further in Antonia's mind when Carmela told Antonia about Estela's sanctuary holding everything dear to her.

Not until after Estela died did Antonia get to step foot inside. Doña Pereira told her that if she really wanted to learn who her mamá was, she had to go there. Antonia had been too scared to find that Estela was someone else entirely, so she'd resisted the idea until Carmela and she went looking around for paperwork.

"Alejandro, this, to me, goes further than proving my papá's innocence. Selfishly, I also want to absolve myself. I want to know that what happened to our family, to Mamá, was not my fault. I want to prove to myself that I didn't do it, directly or indirectly. That I didn't bring the haunting, the svetyba, to this house. I want to lift the guilt off my chest before it takes hold of me. And if it turns out I'm guilty, I want to deal with that too.

"There's your haunting story. That's what haunts me. The guilt. The what-if. What if I'm the reason my own mother is dead?"

⊲⊳─ ─⊲⊳

Antonia and Alejandro left the now-crowded lounge, traversing through the main hallway to the ballroom. Gusts of wind coming in through the open doors that led to the balcony rattled Antonia's hair and stung her chest.

Alejandro sighed and rubbed his chin. "We ought to move around. Dance or something. If not, we're going to raise unnecessary suspicions."

Antonia eyed him briefly. "Or perhaps *you* simply want to dance with me?"

He shrugged, painting creases over his white shirt. "That too."

Antonia understood they had more urgent matters than to partake in this activity, but boleros were her favorite music to sing and dance to. And, surprisingly, she found herself wanting to dance, particularly with him. This newfound realization startled her; just a few days ago, such a thought would have been unthinkable. She had never relied on a man before, but she couldn't deny that his presence was becoming a welcome distraction. Besides, she *was* itching to relieve her fears, her worries, if only for a few moments. It couldn't be that bad if she gave in to her desires for one song.

"Can I have this dance?" Alejandro reached for her hand as she hoped he would. She nodded and clasped her fingers around his, the same warmth emanating from them as on the first night they met and shook hands.

Alejandro escorted her swiftly to the dance floor, then pulled her closer toward him, pressing his body gently against hers, and she softened into him. He rested his left hand on the small of her back, guiding her with a delicate firmness. Antonia leaned into him, her breath mingling with his as they glided across the floor to the sultry rhythm of the bolero, their gazes locked in an intimate, unspoken dialogue.

A tingling heat spread through her body, making her pulse quicken with every step. The atmosphere cracked with covert desire, and Antonia recognized the sense of closeness and intimacy that went beyond physical contact, as though they'd danced before.

Each step and spin drew them closer, the music weaving undeniable chemistry between them.

Antonia felt his breath caressing the side of her neck. Each exhalation amplified Antonia's heartbeat. She shut her eyes and, for a moment, allowed herself to get lost in the melody, in the softness of the tunes of the guitar, followed by the deep voice of the lead singer.

"You're quite a dancer." Alejandro's rusty voice brushed against her ear, sending a shiver down her spine.

"I did artistic dance until I was eighteen. It's a vain-people thing," Antonia said mockingly. Their eyes met once again, igniting a thrilling mix of intrigue and connection that heightened Antonia's senses.

She was acutely aware of her body pressing into his, of how each movement of their bodies shared a synchronic precision, as though they belonged to the same duet. Antonia's left hand rested lightly on his shoulder, her fingertips grazing the nape of his neck, stirring a flutter of anticipation in her stomach.

"I think you liked kissing me," she said softly against his ear. "More than you're willing to admit."

"Did *you*?"

Within her was a heady blend of nervousness and yearning to savor each second of their shared intimacy, making Antonia feel alive.

She held his gaze in hers. "I wanted to kiss you right then."

"I told you; I like women who take what they want."

Antonia swallowed.

Alejandro scoffed and whispered something to her, but his words got lost, for she was no longer listening.

Someone caught her gaze in the middle of the dancing crowd. Next to the band, a figure stood still, its emaciated fingers clenched on a faux scythe covered in rust and red stains. *Blood!* Antonia trembled at the sight. The creature's mangled face was loosely covered with a veil. It had reddened sunken holes instead of eyes, and a long, ragged beard poured from a pointy chin. Blood-like liquid squirted from it as though the creature were choking on its own insides.

Antonia clamped her hand to her mouth to stop herself from gagging and bit back a shriek that cut through her vocal cords.

Under her feet, the floor trembled, as though the thick cement base of the house wavered in place.

Alejandro, and every other guest, had vanished, his grip no longer guiding her through the dance floor. Nothing but El Salto del Tequendama roaring outside and the house, *her* house, remained.

She couldn't move. She felt stunned by the svetyba's attention as it approached. Its feet slugged across the floor, leaving a trail of greenish slime and dirt just behind.

RUN!

She staggered backward, struggling to remain standing. Sweat trickled at her nape, and she felt her knees weaken.

But right before she stumbled to the floor, Alejandro's arms tightened around her waist. And soon, she was back on the dance floor. Everything as lively as it'd been moments ago.

"What the—are you okay?" he asked.

Antonia's eyes bulged in fear.

She shook her head frantically. "No, no, it's, that thing—" Her voice trembled. Her eyes surveyed the spot where she'd seen it just moments ago.

Alejandro instantly whirled around, following her line of sight, a questioning look on his face. *"What?"*

"I-I think I need some air," Antonia managed to say before taking off through the ballroom once more, Alejandro following closely behind.

That thing, the costume, the rags, the scythe . . . it had seemed so real. *It had been real.*

And there was nowhere else to run.

"What was that about?" Alejandro asked once they were back outside, a hint of worry in his voice.

Antonia's hand slipped out of his. "What?"

"What? What do you mean what?" he blurted, ushering her away from onlookers and smokers piling up against the balcony's railings. "You were paralyzed, and then you looked like you were going to fall headfirst on the ground, like you were about to faint. C'mon, you can't tell me nothing happened. What did you see?"

A svetyba, a voice whispered from within her.

This hadn't been a hallucination, even though she'd like to believe otherwise. Things were slowly starting to fall into place.

It had started several years after they first moved in. Antonia would wake up in the middle of the night, sweating, screaming, yelling for help. Even though possessed with fear, she'd run all across the house to her parents' bedroom in alarm, seeking company and consolation, something that could get her to sleep peacefully. She'd tell them a mean thing was chasing after her, holding a scythe, with a dark robe that almost covered its face and red eyes looking back at her.

At first, her parents seemed concerned enough, letting her sleep in their room, Estela singing her to sleep. Eventually, Ricardo gradually began to offer excuses for her nightmares, suggesting it was an act of rebellion in order to move back to Bogotá, trying to convince her that it was all in her head, probably from all the Gothic novels she read.

"It's nothing, Nona. You've been reading too many English Gothics lately. Be a good girl and go to bed. Everything will be fine, I promise."

Like that, Antonia was forced back to her bedroom, tears pooling in her eyes.

Carmela and Estela were no help either. Carmela would ask Antonia to pray and would occasionally sleep with her. Her mamá would listen to her silently, stare at her for a while, press her lips against Antonia's forehead, then simply tuck her underneath the covers again.

"Nothing is ever going to happen to you," Estela would say.

Nothing worked. Antonia only felt safe when she was awake. And it wasn't long after, perhaps because of the lack of sleep, she'd started seeing, feeling the presence when the sun was still out, when Antonia was wide-awake.

And just like that . . . everything that could go wrong with her, with them, went fatally wrong.

Antonia drew herself out of her memories. "Nothing." She didn't have time to share the details with him, even though she felt, deep inside her, that out of all people, he would listen, he wouldn't judge her, and he would believe her.

Alejandro's eyes swept over her, assessing, as though he knew there was more to it, but he let it go and, instead, said, "Doña Pereira left the ballroom."

Antonia shrugged and tucked loose strands of light brown hair behind her ears. "Well, that's better for us. . . ."

"No, that's our sign. The plan is on. Mine at least."

He stepped right in front of her, his body almost entirely blocking her from sight. He looked over his shoulder twice, then thrust his right hand into his pocket, pulling out a pocketknife. The blade was steel coated with gold plating, intricately engraved with circles and radiating lines that depicted the sun god worshipped by the Muiscas. Farther along the blade, the carvings rendered figures and ceremonial objects including the traditional Muisca balsa, a gold raft, and the ceremonial tunjos. The light reflecting off the raised elements brought the tapestry of carvings to life.

Antonia stepped closer. "What is this?" she asked, shoving the pocketknife to one side.

Alejandro clasped his hand firmly against it. "This is the murder weapon. Not the real one, but a look-alike."

Antonia snatched a few long breaths. "Why do you have it—how?"

"The police have the real one. Or at least they should. It was at the murder scene that night. I photographed it."

"How? And what about this one then?"

"It's a long story, but there are several of these out there. With the same handle, the same carving. Antonia"—he reached for her hand this time—"this is one of the keys to your father's freedom."

With that, Alejandro escorted her toward the courtyard.

<hr />

The lawn was empty, except for the owls that rested on the treetops of the wild encenillos and nogales. The breeze rattled the branches, accompanying the explosive crash of cascading water. Alejandro dragged her farther into the woods, not far enough that they were outside the vast property, but far enough that the house was merely an imposing backdrop. Before long, El Salto del Tequendama was a few yards away from where they stood.

Antonia's footsteps were firm against the muddy trail of beads of grass, and when a faint chant became clearer, Alejandro motioned her to bend behind a lush thicket as they peeked at the scene beyond. A dozen people gathered, their backs to them, their voices meeting in a low chant. The only light was coming from black candles and swarmed in a circle around them. They wore black coats, so long that the fabric dragged against the damp grass as they moved in place, their heads hidden behind pointy hoods.

Antonia became petrified when the people spread apart, revealing a stake-like wooden structure erected just before them. Someone—a very dead someone, completely stripped of any clothing—hung upside down from the top. Their head was drenched in blood gushing from their throat.

Antonia let out a soft, shocked grunt and turned to Alejandro, who didn't appear any less horrified than she was.

The singing grew louder, the minor key almost sinister, as Antonia surveyed the somber scene.

"What is this?"

Alejandro remained silent, his focus on the events unfolding across from them, as though he too was struggling to turn away.

"A ritual? A sacrifice? A cult?"

Her mouth went dry at the mention of the word. *A cult? A murdering* cult?

Before she allowed herself to get lost in her scrambled thoughts, Alejandro spoke. "Look. *Closer.*"

Antonia did as Alejandro said, careful not to let herself be seen through the thick bushes. Her eyes drifted to the top of the wooden stake structure, the tip carved in gold with the same spiral, snakelike figures of the murder weapon.

Sweat coated her back, the air around them suddenly too hot, too dense for her to breathe. Antonia stared down at her lap, her hands trembling with fear.

Beside her, Alejandro snatched his camera out of the inner part of his coat. He pointed the lens at the crowd beyond, carefully hiding it within the bushes in front of them.

The caroling became louder and harsher, drawing her attention.

"Svetyba ic phiz aka za huichy. Svetyba ic phiz aka za huichy. Svetyba ic phiz aka za huichy." Antonia couldn't understand the chanting, but she recognized the language. It was Chibcha, the Muisca tongue. But she could make out one word perfectly. *Svetyba.* The demon.

A night like this was the perfect scenario for a reaping . . . the night of the opening party had been the perfect scenario too.

A whine escaped her.

Was a svetyba being summoned?

Antonia strained to take a closer look and spotted another figure approaching the swarm, its silhouette enveloped with a black tunic almost like the one that the other participants wore. Antonia strained her eyes some more, trembling with effort, to see in the dim light. That's when she realized who it was: Doña Pereira. The old lady moved her mouth, but her words were too low for Antonia to hear from where they hid. In her right hand, Doña Pereira held a scythe, its blade almost shiny. She swung it firmly beside the corpse, close, but not close enough to cut, almost like she wanted to pose a threat.

Antonia could feel her muscles cramping, her joints stiffening, as though pinned in place. The sight made her want to scream, to turn away from it, but she couldn't. Nor could Alejandro.

She watched as Doña Pereira leaned even closer to the corpse. A *female.* This time, Doña Pereira didn't contemplate; she swung the blade, the steel cutting cleanly through the neck. Soon, the body was nothing more than a headless figure, completely drained of its blood. Doña Pereira retrieved the head and threw it like a fireball down the waterfall.

TRECE

⊰⊱———————●━●━━●———————⊰⊱

Antonia remained still as the flock of people followed Doña Pereira and melted back into the deep forest. The sound of Antonia's heart throbbing in her ears briefly drowned out the jeering crowd.

"Svetyba ic phiz aka za huichy. Svetyba ic phiz aka za huichy. Svetyba ic phiz aka za huichy."

Soon the forest swallowed the chanting, and the only melody left was that of the nogales thrashing to the rhythm of the wind.

Antonia looked at Alejandro, silent, kneeling beside her, his eyes following the line of people vanishing through the forest. Antonia collapsed onto the high grass, spent, pain carving through her belly. Her hands shook as she pressed them to her face, squeezing her eyes shut, as if the darkness were enough to keep the sights of what they had just witnessed at bay. But it all came flooding back.

A woman had just been killed. Doña Pereira had fucking cut her head off.

Antonia struggled to breathe.

Doña Pereira worshipped svetyba. Doña Pereira had the world at her feet. She was free.

Wasn't that what Antonia wanted too?

Am I like her? I may not have summoned the svetyba, but do I have the darkness inside me to take someone's life? If it means I can do as I please?

Antonia lay stunned on the ground, overcome by the savagery she'd just witnessed and all it implied.

Antonia thought power was about making choices of her own. Of escaping familial responsibilities, societal expectations, writing her own story. But perhaps real power demanded more. What if it meant forcing people to follow, to listen, to be steered? Or else?

"You do understand what this means, don't you?" Alejandro questioned.

Yes. The reality had struck her the minute she saw Doña Pereira pull out the blade. "She had something to do with the murders. Her pendant. *This*. It is no coincidence."

Alejandro nodded. "Somehow this is way darker than all the possibilities that had been rattling in my head."

Words evaded Antonia as the weight of betrayal settled over her shoulders. "Why would she do this? Incriminating and framing my papá? He didn't do anything, and she knows."

"Your father doesn't need framing—he was there. He was found with blood all over his clothes. . . . It was merely coincidental, and it worked for them."

Antonia had always had reservations about Doña Pereira, about her ambition, which at times Antonia secretly admired but had never said it out loud. Antonia knew Doña Pereira to be obsessed with El Salto and the Muisca culture, but a cold-blooded murderer? Was Doña Pereira, the woman who'd raised Estela, part of a murderous cult? And who had truly been Antonia's mamá? Had she been part of this cult too?

"Antonia . . . ?"

"They *want* to incriminate him." The certainty sank inside her. Ricardo's imprisonment had all been part of a plan. "What I don't get is why do it at the hotel. They could buy an entire city if they wanted to. They're filthy rich. . . ."

"It's not about the hotel, it's about the land." Alejandro's voice was stout as he held her gaze.

Antonia's hands clutched at the fabric of her dress as if trying to prepare herself for the revelations that were about to come.

"I think it's time you knew more about your mother."

Antonia's eyes widened, pleading for clarity amid the diabolical storm they'd just witnessed. "Know what? What are you getting at?"

"She undertook a huge responsibility. She was a protector of the place. Not the house but El Salto itself."

Antonia's face grew paler, her lips trembling as she tried to process the information Alejandro had thrust upon her. The protector? Antonia had known about Estela's obsession, but, frankly, she'd never thought it went any further than that.

Her thoughts churned with disbelief and dread as she struggled to put the pieces together. Her mamá had talked about this in one of her journals, hadn't she? She'd mentioned Antonia having to undertake a responsibility.

I sometimes wonder if I made the right choice. If I was in the right to bring her here to help her fulfill her destiny.

Antonia paced, seeking something, anything to anchor her in the chaos of her thoughts and emotions.

"Responsibility?"

Alejandro looked contrite, as though he was holding something back. "Yes, like she promised to take care of the land, but it eventually began to be too polluted . . . and her efforts might've not been enough."

Antonia's breath quickened, each inhale a shaky attempt to steady herself.

Yes, Estela had attached herself to the place. To the Muisca tradition. To its culture. The land where the house was built was sacred. Ricardo had cut into Muisca territory to please her. But Antonia had never thought it was done out of responsibility, not in earnest. Why would it? Was it because feeling responsible for the place gave Antonia's mamá a sense of power? A sense of control? Like she was ruling it while lost in the delusion that she served Bochica herself? That she'd been some sort of servant, with a holy mission?

As Antonia brewed through all these questions, something else began to take shape. Darker, more gruesome, but after what they'd just witnessed, it didn't seem so out of the realm of possibility. Doña Pereira had revealed to Antonia that she'd seen Antonia's mamá the day she died. Antonia's papá had mentioned Doña Pereira had been there. Could it have been Doña Pereira who'd killed Estela? The svetyba was an evil entity that preyed on souls. And Doña Pereira appeared to have been calling on one just mere minutes ago. Plus, she was obviously capable of murder. Had it been Doña Pereira who'd brought a svetyba inside the house?

Antonia tried to form words, but they came out as barely audible whispers, betraying the deep turmoil within her.

"Did . . . you know about this, about Doña Pereira?" she managed at last.

Alejandro pressed to his feet, his leather shoes no longer shiny black but coated in wet grass and mud. "Listen, I know a lot of things about her, but this was not one of them. I've been investigating these cultlike practices for a while now. It's how I got my job at the station, and sometimes we get tips from the police, and other people who witness or think they've seen actual things. . . ."

"Someone was killed," Antonia hurried on, her voice a little hoarse. "We need to call the police; we need to ask for someone's help—"

"Antonia, do you think the police will believe one of the richest women in the city is capable of this?"

Of course not. It had been silly of Antonia to even suggest it, but she was desperate, and they were running out of time.

"Besides, the police have the murder weapon, but of course a bunch of silly carvings on the handle of a pocketknife mean nothing to them. What we need to do is link this"—he pulled the knife out of his pocket—"to what happened that night. What I'm saying is, we need to stick to our plan. It's the only way we'll get your father out and expose all that is happening here."

"Really? And how do you propose we do that? What we need to do is get back to the hotel before they find us here, then we'll figure out the rest." Antonia looked around wildly in fear and took baby steps back to the mansion, moonlight illuminating the path.

An animal-like shriek broke across the field, stopping her abruptly in her tracks. There was a pause, and then a second one erupted. What if Doña Pereira was killing someone else?

Alejandro positioned himself in front of her as they moved swiftly through the beds of grass. There was another scream, but this time, it was more of a thick groan than a high-pitched sound. Neither Antonia nor Alejandro turned around, both of them kept their eyes locked on the hotel in front.

◁▸— — ◅▷

They rushed up the stairs to the main floor, where the party was still in full swing. Antonia had lost track of time. She didn't know how long they'd been away and hoped that no one had noticed their absence. Their attire wasn't immaculate anymore, but under the dim glow of the candelabras, it was hard to notice anyway.

Antonia and Alejandro stood in silence as they peered at the crowd inside. She scanned the busy ballroom, searching for Doña Pereira. "She's not here." Which relieved and bothered her at the same time. What if they were executing more people? She hoped she and Alejandro had been right in not going straight to the police.

Antonia turned to Alejandro, a trace of mud marking his face like a scar. She placed her hand on his cheek, his skin cold to her touch, which took him by surprise. She smiled and swiped the mud off as gently as she could with her bare hand, banishing any trace.

"Is my face clean?"

"Don't worry. You're presentable now."

"If you think so, even better," he replied, a slight smile on his lips.

Antonia then kept her eyes on high alert, searching for familiar faces. If Alejandro and she were right and Doña Pereira was a member, the leader, of a cult, what were the chances some of the guests were part of it too?

"What about León? He must be in it too, right?" Antonia asked Alejandro. "There's a reason why he's trying to keep Papá in jail. You said you knew a lot of things about her, but you didn't know about this. . . ."

"No, I didn't."

"What else do you know?"

Alejandro parted his lips, but he didn't speak. Instead, he stared at something behind her. Something she had to turn around to see.

She spun, only to catch Doña Pereira swiftly gliding onto the dance floor, with the easiness that only someone who knew she could get away with anything could have. It was as though she hadn't just killed someone.

Thrill was written all over her features. If Antonia didn't know any better, she would believe Doña Pereira's contentment was due to enjoying her time *at the party* . . . or the man who now accompanied her. He was much younger, by at least a couple of decades, and upon closer inspection, Antonia could see it was one of the servers. A colorful embroidered tunic crossed over his chest, tightly tied on his right shoulder. He wore no shoes, and his head was adorned with a crown-like bandanna made of the most colorful feathers Antonia had ever seen. Doña Pereira grinned at him and pressed her body against his with a strangled laugh. There she was, using the servers as objects for entertainment, and judging by the onlookers' eyes around them, she was getting exactly what she wanted.

Antonia turned away from Doña Pereira—it was clear that she hadn't seen Antonia or Alejandro, or else she wouldn't be dancing as joyfully—and noticed Padre Juan. The middle-aged man stood beside the band as they played. He was dressed in his uniform this time; otherwise, from that far, Antonia would've missed him. When Antonia swept her eyes over him, the man nodded and gave her half a smile. She averted her gaze, afraid to meet his eyes again. What was he doing here? How many times did a man need to bless a place? This was no party for a priest like him. But more important, had he recognized Antonia?

Antonia clasped her fingers around Alejandro's. "We need to get out of here before any of them recognize us. I have keys to our room—it's on the fourth floor." She pulled him away from the iron railing and back inside through the high archway. His fingers clasped tighter against hers as she shouldered them out of the way of the dancers still gliding across the room.

Upstairs, against the thick cedar door, a gold plate read ROOM 417, shining as though it had been carved the day before. The glossy numbers were accompanied by delicate serpentlike golden figures with feline heads, a recurring theme throughout the house.

She stumbled back. This was *her* bedroom. She reached out and gently rubbed the smooth gilded surface of the coiling figures where their heads merged. A ritual she used to perform to invite good fortune before she walked in and out of her room. She could use some of it now—something that could guarantee her that she'd survive again this time.

But blood seemed to drain from her body as her eyes raked over the familiar but now terrifying figures; she was scared to take another step into her old life. She found no comfort in her past life. Nothing that could soothe her.

Antonia stood still as Alejandro twisted the golden doorknob in front of them. He stepped through the doorway, pushing the thick cedar door to the side, and turned around to face her. "Is everything all right?"

Antonia's limbs trembled, and when she spoke, her voice was shrill. "It's . . . this was my bedroom."

When Antonia booked it, she didn't ask for details. She hadn't considered the possibility of sleeping in her old space. The suspicion that someone had done it on purpose tainted her thoughts, but she immediately scratched her own theory.

No. No one knew they were at the hotel. No one could've known.

Alejandro's lips parted in surprise. "This was your . . . ?" He trailed off as though he didn't want to say anything else. And he didn't need to. Nothing he said could possibly help put her at ease. She couldn't shake off the feeling that the real house, the raw bones beneath the glitz, was welcoming her back to her own hell.

Antonia's eyes scanned every single corner of the room. Instead of the warmth she anticipated, there was a cold, unsettling sensation. On opposite sides, pairs of silver sconces hung on the whitewashed walls, and hard-to-make-out shadows gathered in the corners, dark, unmoving, as if the room itself held its breath, anticipating her every move.

No red eyes . . . not a svetyba. Everything was okay. She was safe.

The flames flickered in that vulnerable way that fire did, pushed by the wind sneaking inside from the open door.

Antonia had never liked the room, its large floor-to-ceiling white cedar windows, and the tiny balcony facing the waterfall beyond. The view wasn't as special as the one from her mamá's balcony, but it came close enough. The wild water from the falls lashed against the crystal windows of the room. She'd gotten used to the *tack-tack* every night, had relinquished the idea she could escape it, regardless of how high up she was. She'd gotten so used to it that she could hear it clearly along with the incessant chiming of the waterfall. The *tack-tack* made El Salto del Tequendama feel even closer than it was. As though its slippery tendrils could reach for Antonia, grab her, and never let go. Now, the sound of it remained, but this was not her room anymore. There was hardly any trace of Antonia left.

Her bookshelves no longer framed her bed. Her hardcovers were no longer victims to the humidity that came from the falls just across. Her stack of unread Gothics wasn't piling up on her nightstand, gathering dust. The dark wood upright piano her parents had gotten her for her quinceañera wouldn't fill the room with Chopin and Bach. Not that it ever did. (Antonia hated the piano—Carmela was a patient teacher, but Antonia never felt like her fingers could go fast enough.) The old rag doll she used to pull apart at night when she couldn't sleep was nowhere to be found.

Now, the white wooden queen-size bed almost reached the side walls, leaving barely any room for bedside tables, let alone shelves. Alejandro's and Antonia's suitcases were placed by a wooden stool by the closet, where Antonia's green velvet reading chair used to be, and her mustard leather messenger bag rested on top of the stool. Everything was new, except for one thing. On the right corner sat her old cedar dresser, adorned with carvings that matched those of the rest of the house. She ran her fingers over its surface, an electrifying tingle immediately rushing all the way up her arms, as though the past were reaching out to her.

Antonia's heart pounded with a mingled sense of melancholy and fear. The vague familiarity of the space was distorted by the ghostly shades of what once was, leaving her with a haunting reminder of how time had irrevocably changed everything.

When the family left, everything had stayed at the house for a while. There was no time to waste on packing, especially after Ricardo had attempted to burn down the house. Trying to hold on to their belongings at that point would've made everything more painful, and additionally more complicated, given the state of her papá's sickness.

She'd seen her life's possessions in disarray, the house itself a monstrous, burning reminder of Ricardo's actions, of what she had lost: Antonia's book collection, the photographs that were a window to their past (to the brief moments of happiness), her mamá's oil paintings that hung all across the five stories, her papá's studio with mock-ups and blueprints, their expensive custom-made furniture.

For months, their things lay under the high roofs. Stillness overcame the place for the first time in years. Some of Estela's paintings, victims to the dampness in the air, began to decay. The lush thicket turned brown, and weedlike vegetation snaked up the walls and over the orange tiles. When Antonia finally mustered the energy to come back, she didn't step foot inside. She hired movers to pack up all of their things and drive them back to the city. They took almost everything from the house, except for most of her mamá's belongings.

But the past was simply that, the past. And there was no point in mulling over what once was. They were in this room for a reason, a really important reason, a fact that came back to her when she noticed Alejandro coldly assessing every detail in the room, contemplating their next move.

The party would go on for at least one or two more hours, until just after midnight, and even though she wanted to set her plan in motion, she knew it was best to wait. Especially with Doña Pereira roaming around the halls still.

"We need some more time in here before we go to Mamá's room," she said. "Doña Pereira won't leave until the party is over. It might be safer for us then. I know how to get down there, but we can't risk being seen. Not by anyone. But her especially."

He nodded. "So, what should we do in the meantime?"

"Get in bed?" The smirk crossing Alejandro's face made her realize it might've sounded like she wanted to get *in* bed with him.

"I-I mean, we should rest, at least for a little bit?"

Alejandro smiled. "Sure."

Antonia perched on the edge of the bed and watched him, his movements deliberate, almost languid. He shed his garments, revealing the contours of his form in the dim light. His strong shoulders and the subtle play of muscles beneath his skin captured her attention even more, and Antonia couldn't help but admire the way the shadows accentuated his physique.

Alejandro's eyes caught hers in the mirror's reflection on the dresser, and a subtle grin tugged at the corner of his lips. Embarrassed, she shifted slightly, clutching the folds of her dress tightly, trying to quell the heat that rose within her.

Antonia realized she was going to be sharing a room with a man. If only briefly. A very handsome man at that. She'd not shared a bed with anyone in years. The nuns would fire her in a heartbeat without any hesitation if they were to find out. It would be unladylike to share a bed with a stranger. Still, her heart yearned in a way that was both exhilarating and tormenting, a secret longing that she could only cherish in the quiet of the night. What if, for once, she wasn't the proper young woman everyone expected her to be?

Antonia didn't have any reservations when it came to intercourse. The physicality of it didn't bother her—she was interested in intimacy and the way she was able to fully give herself to someone else. Whether a stranger or someone she'd gone out with a few times. She liked that it allowed her to open up, without restraint. For a brief moment she felt unleashed, wild, like a force no one could control.

But despite how much she desired to explore their connection further, she forced herself to leave the bed and make for the stool by the dresser.

Antonia removed her leather bag and plopped on the stool. Trying to find a distraction, she turned her eyes to the waterfall across the window, and her mind traveled back to her papá. A pang of guilt hit her like a dozen rocks. She'd thought he'd done it. She couldn't believe how confused she'd been, drowned by the betrayal of her own memories.

She would make amends. That was a promise.

The sound of rustling sheets caused her to steer her eyes over to Alejandro, who was now lying comfortably on his side, eyes closed, succumbing to the call of sleep. Perhaps she should join him, if only her racing mind would allow her to give in to the exhaustion soaring through her body.

Choosing against the temptation, she began to wander around the room again, eventually landing back in front of the dresser.

Her curiosity piqued, she carefully pried it open. Inside the scent of old linens and lingering perfume mixed with a musty smell. As she shifted aside a stack of comforters, her hand brushed against something else, an ornate hand-painted wooden box, partially hidden underneath a thick layer of dust.

Hope sparked in her eyes, and with a deep breath Antonia lifted the lid. Inside, nestled beneath a pile of old scarves and gloves was a small doll-house, one Estela had given her as a gift months prior to their move to El Salto.

Briefly, the room around her blurred out and faded, her mind trans-porting her back to the sunny Sunday afternoon in which her mamá delivered the news to her that they were leaving Bogotá.

Antonia was sitting on the floor of her room surrounded by her porce-lain dolls and a castle-like structure she'd built of books. Her nose pricked with the scent of fresh paint and wood shavings, alongside Carmela's steam-ing hot chocolate con queso.

Estela, in an apron and with a warm smile, was working at a small table, carefully painting the dollhouse's exterior. The tiny structure was a replica of what would soon be their new home. A sumptuous five-story mansion, surrounded by nature, a retreat from the realities of the city life. A new beginning for her family.

"Nona, look," her mamá had said softly. "I hope this house brings you as much joy as you bring me."

Antonia's eyes filled with excitement. "I can't wait to play with it!"

"It's just as special as you are." Estela's lips gaped into a wide grin, her voice full of love. "And now, there're two of them. Both belong to you and are for you to take good care of."

Antonia now focused her attention back on the dollhouse. The paint was chipped, the windows fogged with grime, and cobwebs draped over the tiny structure, giving it an almost haunted look. Antonia's hands quivered as she pulled it carefully out of the box and set it on the floor, its weight heavier than she remembered.

Antonia knelt beside it, her eyes taking in the delicate but disheveled furnishings inside: tiny faded wallpaper; cracked mini porcelain dolls modeled after her family, from when her family remained whole, as one; a parlor with dusty velvety furniture, decorated with Estela's Muisca paintings; a grandiose fireplace; a bedroom with a faded quilt on the tiny bed, a set of shelves framing it; and her mamá's sanctuary with stacks of books and tunjos.

As she opened the dollhouse's tiny front door, a chill ran down her spine. The air around her felt colder, more oppressive, as if the tiny house had been waiting for her return. Her heart ached with a mix of nostalgia and a creeping unease.

This dollhouse had once been a beloved toy for her. But now it seemed like a look into a darker and distant past.

Antonia's eyes were shining with the threat of tears, and a lump formed around her throat. She wished they'd all survived as the tiny house had.

Antonia continued her exploration of the dollhouse and brushed her fingers along the inside, eventually landing against a hidden compartment in the back of the parlor—a tiny space she didn't remember ever existing. Her curiosity spiked, and she opened it. Inside was a small, yellowed piece of paper, her mamá's handwriting scrawled on it.

Excitement slowly consumed her. Could it be that this tiny house held answers for her as well?

The gatherings are getting out of control. A sense of distrust has burrowed its way inside, polluting the unbreakable bonds that link us with each other. We're birds forced in the same narrow cage. Is it on me to make a choice? Was I in the wrong for thinking that purpose would force us to remain together? Whole? No. Instead, we point fingers at each other, like cutthroat daggers ready to slice. We've lost our horizon. We've forgotten where it all begins and where it all ends.

It's not for us that we're here. It's to serve Her.

But I'm no leader when the flock is scattered, when some of them are escaping with the fox.

Perhaps I brought the wrong sheep in. Maybe it is me who is to blame for the cracks in the fortress. I could smooth out the cracks. Heal them.

But perhaps the cost would be too high. Perhaps the chances of fixing anything are too gone now. And all I have left is to embrace the flock, force them together like a shield, and anticipate the strike coming from just across.

⊷— —⊶

Antonia dropped the charred piece of paper. She glanced around the room, the familiar surroundings now tinged with an eerie sense of dread.

The sheep? The flock escaping with the fox?

Fear squeezed the air from her lungs, and her breathing grew shallow as she perspired through her every pore.

The words of Estela written in such earnest fear seemed to linger in the room. Antonia read the note again, searching for something, anything to counter the chilling implications of this one.

But I'm no leader when the flock is scattered, when some of them are escaping with the fox.

Could the fox be a svetyba? And if someone, a sheep, part of Estela's flock, close to her had escaped with the fox . . . ?

Antonia scrambled through every out-of-place occurrence that had happened tonight, eventually stopping at what had transpired right outside . . .

Doña Pereira.

Antonia had been right. Doña Pereira was summoning svetybas. But which had pushed her mother? Or had Doña Pereira saved that act for herself?

The shadows in the corners of the room seemed to shift and elongate, as if responding to the fear that had settled in Antonia's chest.

In the corner of her vision she caught a glimpse of something—perhaps a shadow or a trick of the dim light—that made her freeze. Her heart raced as she turned quickly, but there was nothing there, only the familiar room now imbued with an unsettling sense of malevolence.

The journal entry was a dark harbinger of the evil her mamá had feared. Estela had seen what Doña Pereira truly was, what she'd become. And Antonia had seen it too just mere minutes ago.

Antonia felt restlessness leaving her trapped in a sleepless vigil against the darkness she could no longer ignore.

CATORCE

Antonia pressed her back against the tall white velvety bed frame, her eyelids heavy with sleep. She glanced at the old pendulum clock resting next to the dresser, which indicated that only an hour had passed since they'd entered room 417. Beside her, Alejandro still rested on his side, facing the window, his bare back exposed to the wind sneaking in through the cedar door, but it didn't seem to bother him. His chest inflated and deflated silently.

The flickering light on the wooden nightstand caught Antonia's attention, the yellow flashes in sync with the water slapping against the crystal windows. Antonia's body felt like lead, and her head dropped as her shoulders slouched forward. She stared down at her lap. Her body was enveloped in a long white robe stained with freckles of shiny red blood. Her crumpled handwritten note to the svetyba was lying on top of her lap. The words flashing before her eyes, one after the other. This time, she could read them, understand them, utter them. Her mouth moved, as if against her will, and she heard the sound of her own voice.

Antonia desperately tried to wipe off the stains on the white cloth with her hands and shove the note away.

Outside, the water struck harder and harder each time against the glass, until it managed to creep inside. Runnels of dirty water dripped eagerly down the walls, streaming over the room as if El Salto del Tequendama had been invited in.

As she scurried to get out of bed, something pulled her back, pinned her against the bed frame. Seized by panic, she pressed her hands to the mattress, her fingernails clawing helplessly at the sheets. Antonia strained her neck trying to turn in Alejandro's direction, shaking with desperation. How could he lie so still?

She could feel her muscles constricting as warm blood pooled over her dress. Her pressed spine was sending waves of pain from her tailbone to the base of her skull. As she struggled to detach herself, several sets of bony hands found her, keeping her in place. She twisted and screamed loudly. . . .

Antonia sat up abruptly, her breath coming in ragged gasps as if she had been running and fighting for her life. The remnants of the nightmare clung to her consciousness like a fog, its horrors still playing out in her mind's eye.

She swung her legs over the side of the bed and winced as her feet reached the cold floor. The chill serving as a stark contrast to the heat of her nightmare.

Her eyes scanned the room again: the windows were securely latched, the floors were dry and pristine, no muddy hands pushing and shoving. No white robes. Had there been anything at all? She didn't remember falling asleep. The dream, if that was what that was, had taken her back to that same murky place she'd been revisiting in her nightmares recently.

Antonia felt an urge, a craving, something boiling inside her. More than freedom, what she wanted was revenge. That she understood. Svetyba or not. She'd make Doña Pereira pay for what she'd done.

Alejandro breathed heavily at her side. She considered telling him what had happened moments ago. To tell him about her new revelation. But would it be better to keep it all to herself?

She didn't have more time to ponder about it further, for a telephone she hadn't noticed hanging behind the nightstand rang so loudly, it made Alejandro jolt out of bed.

Antonia tensed at the ringing sound, considering if she should pick up. Had they been caught? But the high-pitched, jarring sound would make her eardrums bleed if she didn't. So she reached for it with shaking hands, then pressed the black plastic hanger against her ear. Music was blasting on the other end of the receiver, making it hard to listen to the muffled voice.

It was someone at the front desk. "Señora Lina, we have a call for you. Would you like me to transfer it?" Antonia didn't answer right away. At first, she'd forgotten that Lina was the fake name she'd used to book their stay.

"Yes, please." She managed to make herself sound as clear and steady as possible. They couldn't afford to give themselves away.

Antonia forced herself to calm down and waited for the voice to come through before she said anything. She glanced briefly at Alejandro, his eyes locked on hers, and she shrugged.

"Aló, Nona—"

Antonia's mind began to spin. If Carmela was calling her, something must have happened. She wouldn't call her at the hotel just to say hello.

The first thought was her papá.

"What happened?"

"León was here," Carmela muttered. "He was looking for you desperately."

Again, she thought of Papá. Why else would León be looking for her? Unless . . .

"W-what happened?" Antonia stuttered. "Is Papá all right?"

"Your father is okay, but León is looking for you. He came by this evening, and he's been calling to see if you're home yet. Nona, he said he needs to talk to you to make sure you aren't screwing things up. He's furious. He said that your father won't see the light of day unless you let him do his job and put your father in an asylum. He thinks you're making a scene and acting like a kid and wants to see you before you do something you'll regret forever. . . ."

Antonia felt her insides knotting, a gathering storm of tension and discomfort settling in her stomach.

"I didn't tell him anything. I told him you'd gone out and hadn't come back, but I'm not sure he bought that. Nona, I think he knows you are onto something. . . ."

Carmela's last words replayed in Antonia's head. If León knew, or thought he knew, they were at the party, Alejandro and Antonia were in great trouble. And there would be no place left to hide.

"I'm calling because I have the feeling that he's going to the hotel to find you. Please come back soon. I'm worried about you both."

Antonia couldn't, not even if she wanted to. They were stuck at El Salto del Tequendama at least until dawn. "We can't, not yet. If he's coming, I'll make sure he and Doña Pereira don't see us. If he goes back home, please just tell him I'm not there yet and you have no idea where I could possibly be. Thank you for calling." With that, Antonia ended the call and turned to Alejandro. She didn't have to explain anything, he already knew that they were in big trouble.

It would take León at least three hours to get to the hotel, but once there, he would tell his mother, if she didn't find out first, and it wouldn't be hard for them to find Antonia. It was time to descend into the basement of the house. It was time to face the reality of what she came for.

QUINCE

Antonia pressed her ear against the door. If they wanted to escape detection, they'd have to move as swiftly as a cat, even if it was close to three in the morning—she didn't expect the other guests to be roaming around.

Alejandro watched her as he stood, awaiting further instructions from her.

Just then, something heavy slammed into a wall with a crashing thud, like shelves toppling to the floor. Antonia had a feeling something big filled the hallway just outside, something coming up from the depths of hell itself, and was heading directly for them.

Relief washed over Antonia when the thudding stopped, but it didn't last long, for it was quickly followed by some whispering. Someone was nearby. She pressed her ear to the door again. The sound of her own breathing felt impossibly loud, louder even than El Salto outside.

When Alejandro finally spoke, an unpleasant grimace cut through his face. "What was that?" He rushed next to her.

The sound, whatever it was, stopped.

"I don't know," she said. "But one thing is for certain—we can't be here anymore, we need to go to Mamá's room."

As if on cue, the noise was back, only louder this time, coming from right next door. She could hear clearly the sound of loud steps going up and down the spiral staircase. Firm and determined.

Antonia and Alejandro were running out of time. They needed to get to Estela's sanctuary, now, and find what they needed to stop Doña Pereira! Antonia knew that's where she'd find the rest of her Mamá's missing pages. The place was saturated with the Muiscas, with Bochica. Every entry Antonia had discovered since arriving at the house had been connected to them.

Thinking of the old woman made Antonia's blood boil with rage. She vowed, again, to make her pay, for bringing the svetyba in the house . . . for tainting the land . . . for killing all of those people . . . for killing Estela. For sealing Antonia's family's demise. She only hoped her inklings about her mamá's missing entries were right . . . that they held the key to killing a svetyba in order to cast it away for good.

She snagged Alejandro by the arm, pulling him toward her. "Listen, there's a window at the end of the hallway. I think we can go out through there. It's the closest to the stairway outside. I used it all the time when I was younger to try to get a glimpse of whatever Mamá did all day in her room—"

Alejandro ducked his head and grabbed a wrought-iron candlestick from the dresser. He gestured at the sconces hanging behind her, and Antonia reached for the flickering flame to light her white candle. He snatched the second one and lit it as well.

Having no more time to waste, she opened the door slowly, the light from their candles the only thing illuminating the corridor.

A wave of nausea overcame her. Beads of sweat covered her forehead and nose, and a warbling voice echoed in the stone archways above.

Something was calling her name.

Nona.

She felt momentarily stunned in place.

"Did you hear that?" she whispered.

"Hear what?" Alejandro said without turning around.

Antonia swallowed dry. "Nothing, just keep walking."

Nona, the voice said once more, and this time the loudness of it engulfed every inch of her body, and her steps came to a halt.

Nona.

NONA!

It was no longer just loud, it now sounded like a strangled animal. Antonia moved a hand to her mouth, holding back a shriek and the bile threatening to surge from inside.

She felt unsteady and disoriented, as though her legs were failing her. But they had to keep moving forward, they had to make it to the floor below. They couldn't afford to get caught roaming around.

She shot her gaze upward, but Alejandro was nowhere to be seen. The hallway seemed to have narrowed after her every step, pressing in on her ominously. From the thick walls, bony arms covered in dried-out mud jutted out and reached for her from both sides.

Antonia struggled to duck away from them, but there was no space left. She tried to run, but underneath her now-bare feet a trail of thick sludge covered the floors, and every step she took felt as heavy and slow as the one before. She tried to hide under her coat, but a sharp pain spread through her like electricity. She screeched, defeated and dejected as the slime glided toward her.

NONA! NONA! NONA!

The voice was harsh and raspy.

Shock turned to dread and dread to horror.

What came next was Estela's voice. Feathery, soft, like a warm embrace.

Nona, welcome home!

"Mamá?" Antonia's voice cracked. Tears streamed down her face before she could stop them.

But no answer echoed back.

Antonia closed her eyes, and like that, gloom fell over her, and everything around her was consumed by it.

Alejandro's voice was slowly creeping through, but she couldn't tell if she was really listening, or if he'd been there all along.

"Antonia," he called. "Antonia, please, what's happening?"

Antonia strained her eyes trying to recover, trying to make out Alejandro's face, just a few inches from hers. Was he really here with her? Was she safe?

"Antonia, for God's sake, say something. I'm here." He shook her by the shoulders. His voice sounded foreign, as though it didn't belong to him anymore.

Her thoughts remained scrambled; she felt as if she were there and somewhere else at the same time.

Nona.

STAY!

Antonia stopped in her tracks once again. The beckoning was getting closer and louder, refusing to let her go. She instinctively put her hands to her ears to try to mute it out. There were several voices now, but they all belonged to a single person: her mamá.

Could she stay? If the house wouldn't let her go, and with the svetyba haunting her, why not give herself to it? She was tired of sacrificing herself. Of getting nothing from it. Of looking for light when nothing but blinding darkness was dancing around her. Darkness she didn't know she was capable of fighting back anymore. Perhaps that was where she belonged after all. And power, she'd do anything for it. A svetyba could grant her that.

No! Fight it, Antonia. This isn't what you want anymore. It's tricking you! Take a hold of your thoughts. Don't let her inside.

Antonia's mind gibbered to itself. The svetyba was tainting her, messing with her emotions and desires. Antonia wouldn't let it. She would banish it . . . even if that's the last thing she did on this earth.

Alejandro must have noticed her glassy eyes, staring off into the distance, for he said, "Hey, don't listen to it. Whatever it is that you're seeing or hearing, it's *not* real. I'm here with you. We need to go."

Antonia let Alejandro's grip tighten around her waist and didn't resist when he pulled her toward him and back to the safety of the empty hallway.

Then, a familiar voice, a very real one, came from below.

"It's time. Find her and bring her to me." Doña Pereira's command was loud and sharp, cutting through the silence.

Antonia exchanged a look with Alejandro, who stood just as still as she did.

There was no way they'd make it through the window and down to Estela's room now that people were after them.

"Antonia, she—"

"We take the elevator." The elevator was off-limits for the hotel guests, mostly because it was unsafe, but Antonia had used it with no issues.

Antonia hurried on, grabbing his arm and pulling him beside her. They'd have to go out through the window and head to the old elevator outside. If it worked, they'd be on the basement floor in no time, inside the only place where they wouldn't be found.

Her mamá's sanctuary.

DIECISÉIS

⬥——— ———⬥

The elevator stood just as it did the last time Antonia had seen it. The iron handles were covered in rust, and vegetation had crept in, threatening to devour the boxlike structure. Moss and dirt dusted the now-darkened white tiles inside.

Wind rattled the branches of the wild encenillos sprawling over the Andean Hills, reaching to the darkened sky.

Antonia leaned closer and wrapped her fingers on the handle, sliding the iron door to the side, making a shriek. They squeezed themselves in, and Antonia pulled the pulley on the floor to the side. Relief washed over her as the elevator descended. Water pelted the rocks, and she was thankful that the sound of the falls masked the high-pitched noises the elevator made moving down.

Once the elevator came to a halt, Antonia recognized the view. They were deep inside the mountain. Estela's sanctuary was a few steps away. Anyone wanting to come find them would have to climb down the rock itself to get to the bottom floor.

She squinted her eyes, surrounded by darkness, illuminated only by the light of their flickering candles. With a quick movement, she pulled the keys from the right pocket of her coat as her left hand scrambled to find the lock.

Finally, she found it and twisted the doorknob, hearing a satisfying click-ing sound. The door was heavy, and with the assistance of Alejandro, they pushed it open together.

The first thing that hit them was the frigid air, slashing through their clothes and seeping into their bones. Before she could change her mind, she stepped inside. Every corner of the room was infused with her mamá's scent, and Antonia felt Estela's lingering presence enveloping the space. The expansive room was adorned with pairs of sconces with intricately carved Muisca and Bachué designs. A long, narrow cedar table, accom-panied by ten chairs, extended to almost both sides of the room, and her mamá's paintings were hung all over the walls. Above the throne-like chair at the room's end, a part of her collection of gold tunjos rested on floating shelves, creating an aura of serene grandeur.

The space, one that had been so lovingly maintained by Estela, was both comforting and painful.

Antonia's eyes welled with tears as she sat in Estela's chair. The blanket on it, so warm and soft, still carried the faint scent of her essential oils. An-tonia clutched it to her chest, letting the tears fall freely.

But after a few moments, her grief and sadness morphed into some-thing more complex. The realization began to take root within her: this room, so meticulously built and cared for, was proof of her mamá's pref-erence for solitude, for this quiet, untouched retreat, while seemingly ne-glecting Antonia's needs.

She stood abruptly, pacing the room with increasing agitation, until she approached the bookshelf by the entrance. Crafted from dark nogal wood, the set of shelves carried on them gold ornaments and delicate engravings of the Muisca serpent and Bochica's staff. Perhaps she could find more of Estela's journals on it, like she'd done the day of the party in one of the rooms above.

Upon closer inspection, Antonia could see scratches, the wood of the nogales a little paler where it had been dinged. She ran her fingers across the roughness, thinking it made the structure more interesting. They were just like people's scars: clues to a bigger story.

A woody, faint vanilla aroma filled her nostrils as her eyes scanned the old leather spines of books on the shelves. From first-edition Jane Austen to books on Muisca lore and culture to occultism and cults, the selection was quite broad.

As Antonia whirled around, reaching for her candlestick, her eyes caught Alejandro examining the tunjos.

"She collected them," she told him. "They were expensive. I never knew where she got them from."

"I don't think she simply collected them—"

Interest sparked inside her. "What do you mean?"

"These tunjos are the kind Muiscas would use for ritualistic purposes." Alejandro pulled one out of the shelf carefully.

"Mamá always told me stories about El Salto and los Muiscas. I always wondered how much of it was real and how much was her fabrication."

"I think that more than telling you stories, she was preparing you for what she thought was your mission—"

Mission?

Could it be the duty she needed to fulfill according to her mamá's journals?

"I didn't say any of this before because I wasn't sure. But from what you've told me, from the things I've witnessed . . . I think your mother intended for you to be an Hija de Bochica." Alejandro lowered his gaze. "*Your mother* was an Hija de Bochica. At first I thought you were lying, hiding it from me because it was supposed to be a secret, so I went along with it. I figured I wouldn't say anything unless you brought it up, but it didn't take long for me to realize you really did not know."

Words eluded her, confusion washed over her. Her mamá the daughter of Bochica, the goddess of the Muiscas?

"Your mother was the leader of a cult, Las Hijas de Bochica. They considered themselves a group of women bound to protect this place, El Salto, from those who want to corrupt the land. . . .

"This room was the place where they met regularly. That's probably one of the reasons why your mother did not allow you here and why your father had this place shut down when she died.

"After your grandma passed, your mother was left in charge. Doña Pereira and your grandma had been running it up until then. The members chose your mother over Doña Pereira because she was young, full of life. And because she had an architect as her husband who could build them an altar of their own. Estela was too young when she was appointed the leader. La Lideresa. That's why your mother wanted to live here, that's why your father built her this place. . . ."

"No, *no*, Mamá just enjoyed the story and the cultural background of El Salto. . . . She was a fanatic. But the leader of some sort of . . . cult? That can't be. You're wrong! It was simply a group for like-minded women! Women who break the rules."

The sheep.

The flock.

The sheep escaping with the fox—

"Your father built this house because he loved her," Alejandro continued, ignoring her outburst. "But also because he knew the truth. She was about your age when she had to assume this position, to protect the place."

"Protect the place from *whom?*"

"Those who corrupted the land over the years. Antonia, this is a sacred Muisca land. It's full of energy, good and bad. The necromancers, the practitioners, they come here to perform all sorts of rituals, like the one we witnessed a few hours ago, to channel the bad energy. You're sitting on top of a graveyard, the perfect place to summon the dead. . . ."

The sound of blood pounding in her ears briefly drowned out Alejandro's words.

"There's an equilibrium that needs to be preserved," he continued. "This place is not inherently evil, not at all. It wasn't always haunted . . . the hauntings began when that equilibrium was broken, when people started to wake the spirits. And it only got worse when the svetybas—"

"Is this part of your job too? You know all of this because of your investigations?"

He shook his head. "My mom . . . she was also one of them."

Alejandro's mother was a member of Estela's organization too?

There was a moment's pause, a frantic silence exchanged between them after Alejandro's reveal.

"So our mothers did this . . . *work* . . . together?" Her mind went back to what Carmela had said about Alejandro and them having met before. His mother was friends with Antonia's, and they stopped seeing each other after Alejandro's mother passed. There were so many questions Antonia wanted to ask, but there were more pressing issues at hand.

"They practiced magic to protect the place and maintain that equilibrium. Your mother . . . she had a mission—"

"A mission?" Antonia interrupted, starting to realize something. "What made them think they were any better than the rest of the people coming in to drain energy from the land? Mamá said it in her journals . . . she knew the land was polluted, but she wanted to take it regardless. To appoint herself as its protector. But what if the place didn't need her protection, or anyone's? What if all it wanted was to be left alone?"

Antonia felt a sickly lurch of disappointment. What else did he know that he wasn't telling her?

"What else do you know about her? Why didn't you tell me this earlier?" Her voice cracked. "I told you more than I've shared with anyone else. And you knew all of this and didn't say shit."

"I told you. I didn't know you didn't know about your mother. And about the svetybas, about the place being haunted by them. I had no idea. . . ."

Antonia opened her mouth, but Alejandro interrupted her before she could let anything out.

"Antonia, I don't know if you understand what I've just said. . . . You're the next in line!"

DIECISIETE

A lejandro's words trailed through her mind. They sounded off-key, distant and slightly dissonant. She wanted to speak, to say something, but she'd lost the ability to say or do anything but process what she'd just heard.

She was next in line? To do what exactly? And whatever that was, could *she* do it? Antonia was surprised to feel an odd flash of excitement washing over her. Could she reinstate the equilibrium and fulfill the destiny Estela was too weak to realize? Finally have a role in this town besides babysitting girls at the escuela?

Antonia began picturing herself running the city council. Telling Madre Asunción what she could do with her prayers. But the images evaporated as quickly as they'd appeared.

But what would I owe the house in exchange for my freedom?

Alejandro's fleshy forearms rested on the long, narrow table. His dark gaze was locked on her, questioning, assessing.

When Antonia finally managed to speak, her voice came out choked. "I don't want any part in it. I don't wish to continue the evil work Mamá and her friends were doing all for power. For a fake sense of superiority. This wasn't her land to take."

Alejandro shook his head. "It's not about that. They were trying to protect Bochica, to *protect* the land. You're next in line to protect it . . . which might be why the place, the house, welcomes you, almost like it knows you're here. . . ."

Antonia quivered with frustration. Alejandro didn't realize that the place she was supposed to call home had tormented her for years. That she never wanted any of it, that within her was only resentment and anger. Antonia didn't want to protect it.

"Welcomes me? You think this place welcomes me? It was a nightmare. I never liked living here. The walls told me things, secrets at night. I could hear them whispering in my ears. Things I didn't want to hear, things I didn't want to know. Uninterrupted sleep? I didn't know what that was until we left and I was able to sleep again, but in here, I never could. . . . I'd try to sleep and this creature, this thing . . ."

She'd never told anyone about the old bearded woman. But before she could stop herself from spilling her secrets, the words escaped out of her mouth. Why would her mamá subject her to that?

"She'd wake me up every night. I felt a weight over my chest when I tried to sleep, and when I did manage to fall asleep, the only thing I saw was an old bearded woman with a scythe staring at me with red eyes from the corner of my room. Perhaps it wasn't even female. I don't know. But I know it was a svetyba. I'm certain now. So, no, Alejandro. This place doesn't welcome me, and my plan doesn't include staying."

Gathering the last remnants of resolve she had in her, she worked her attention back toward the bookshelves. The only benefit of Alejandro's story for Antonia was that she now felt more hope that her mother could've known how to stop the svetyba . . . or at least had a spell or something that could banish it.

She began rummaging through a pile of books placed beside the bookshelves, her hands working faster than her brain.

"You can stand there, contemplating the legend of our mothers, or you can help me grab some of these books."

Alejandro joined her and pulled out a few from the pile and placed them carefully on the floor next to him.

Antonia desperately rifled through the fragile pages, her brows furrowed in distress. Her breath came in quick, uneven gasps, her chest constricted with the weight of the pressing urgency of finding Estela's journals.

Antonia's eyes darted from page to page, her fingers skimming the worn edges of the old tomes.

Alejandro worked beside her, his calm demeanor contrasting with Antonia's frantic energy, as he sorted through the stack, trying to keep pace with her search.

"Look at this," she told Alejandro. Her mamá's name was delicately carved on the spine of a leatherbound journal.

Estela Rubiano.

A tingly sensation stretched across her as her fingers untangled the dusty lace keeping the journal whole. She crouched on the floor and placed the diary in front of her. Alejandro followed, carrying a candlestick with him, beaming the flame carefully at the now-open book.

Antonia eyed the pages, filled with Estela's handwriting. The ink slowly fading, smudged, but she would've recognized Estela's handwriting regardless of its condition.

Pictures were securely glued on some pages, little captions written for each. One of those was a photo of Antonia standing at her mamá's balcony staring at the falls. Next to it, one of Antonia as a baby, the next one Antonia on her quinceañera.

Reading the little notes below each photo was enough to flood her cheeks with tears.

My little girl, you're the smartest girl I know. If you could only see yourself through my eyes . . .

Antonia traced her fingers along every one of the words, which offered her a delicate comfort, one Antonia didn't think she needed until she read the words Estela herself had written for her. Antonia stopped at each and read every word over and over, as though making sure they really existed. As though she could know the feelings were real. She wiped the tears from her cheeks and parted her lips to say something, but then closed her mouth again.

Alejandro placed his hand delicately across her back. "Hey, it's okay. Take your time."

Antonia let the tears fall to avoid choking on her feelings, but she kept on turning the pages, finding pictures of her papá and Carmela, as well as her dead abuela. Antonia wanted to keep the journal for herself, she wanted the scribbles of her mamá to soothe her in the long nights when she'd cried herself to sleep.

As Antonia flipped through Estela's memories, one page in particular caught her attention.

"Look." She pointed at a photo, securely glued in place with the heading *Las Hijas de Bochica.*

Could those be . . . ?

"That's my mother." Alejandro pointed at the woman standing beside Estela. Among the group of women, Alejandro's mother was the tallest. Her black curls fell over her shoulders, with a few strands framing her face, just like the ones dusted over Alejandro's tousled hair. His mother's face, much like the other women's, was adorned with a wide grin. They all wore matching sack-like dresses with a low cut. El Salto del Tequendama in the background.

Antonia scanned each of the women's faces. Those were her mamá's friends, the ones who'd come over regularly.

"So all these women, they're—"

"Dead?" Alejandro stole the word from her as Antonia's eyes went back to the group photo. "Yes. The only one left is Doña Pereira."

Antonia flipped through the remainder of the journal, looking for any shred of information, something—

Suddenly, her eyes locked onto a familiar-colored page hidden between other pages. Her breath hitched. She pulled out the paper, eyes widening with a mix of hope and desperation.

One by one I've lost my hermanas. Eight of them. Gone. First came Teresa. I shouldn't have listened to the complaints. Mere gossip, driven by ill intentions. Esperanza followed. Margarita, whom I wanted to make next in line, to rid Antonia of such responsibility, found dead in her bathtub back in Bogotá.

All except one. Eleonora was the only one left standing. It made sense that I'd hand the power to her, but I feared her intentions no longer aligned with our purpose.

Willingly, Eleonora had lifted the veil, inviting the uttermost evil creature in. Our fortress… its doors were wide open, and I didn't have the strength or the will in me to fight. Antonia is not ready, and I frankly don't think she ever will be.

She's better than me. She deserves better than me.

I don't want to hand this over to her. I don't want her to walk around this cursed land. To devote herself to it. For what? For nothing. I couldn't protect my hermanas. I couldn't protect my family. The svetyba. I'm not strong enough to cast it away. And I refuse to live a life with it standing by my side. I don't wish to put any of them at risk. Antonia. Carmela. Ricardo.

No.

But how can I stop it, before it comes for me?

I don't have much time. Bochica, please, reveal your path.

◆— ◆—

"Mamá was cornered." Antonia's tone was flat, empty. "No one could help her. The svetyba got to her before she could find a way out."

Antonia was a jumble of emotions. With this new revelation, there was also relief. At least Antonia hadn't had a part in summoning the darkness that took Estela. Svetyba or not, Estela loved her.

"Antonia, what are you talking about?"

"Doña Pereira is handing these souls to the svetyba." What was intended to be a thought slipped off her lips. The missing pieces were finally clicking with each other. "I think, no, *I know* she's the one that summoned the svetyba, the thing that haunts this place. I began suspecting this to be true after we stumbled upon her murderous ritual, then even more so while you were sleeping and I found another of my mamá's entries. But this, this one right here, proves I was right. Take a look at this and tell me you don't agree." Antonia handed the entry to Alejandro and waited patiently for him to read it through . . . once, and then again a second time.

"You may be right, Antonia. It makes sense, doesn't it? Doña Pereira betrayed the clan when she brought it in. She got rid of everyone." Alejandro followed.

Antonia's face flushed with a deep, burning anger. Her steps were heavy and erratic as she stomped around the room, each pace driven by a torrent of raw fury.

How could she have been so oblivious all along? How couldn't she have seen what was truly happening?

"Speaking of getting rid of things—what about getting rid of the svetyba? Doña Pereira invited evil in, how do I . . . ? Never mind, what matters now is that Doña Pereira won't get away with anything else. I won't let her if it's the last thing I do. With everything we've found so far, I think we could make a strong case and get Papá out of jail too. I won't let him get punished another day for her crimes. She'll pay for all of it—your mother, mine, those other women, and all the innocent people that followed. . . ."

Antonia's eyes blazed as she wrestled with the intense wave of emotions crashing through her. She couldn't protect her mamá anymore, but she would avenge her death.

Alejandro's mouth was set in a firm line, then he spoke again. "If we don't shut the hotel down, if we don't expose what's been happening here, more deaths will follow. The bloodbath won't stop, for the svetyba is always hungry for souls."

Antonia wiped the tears off her face. But before she could fully devote her attention to Doña Pereira, she had one last lingering problem to address—she still needed to eliminate the svetyba.

There had to be something else. Something they might have overlooked. Estela mentioned she lacked the strength to cast it away, or the knowledge to do it. Antonia might not have possessed the strength, but she was charged with anger. She clung to the hope that it would be enough.

DIECIOCHO

ime was not on their side, and they had already wasted more precious minutes looking for answers on how to stop the svetyba. Just as they were about to head out, among the remaining tomes Antonia's eyes caught sight of a book called *Evil in the Times of Bochica*. She picked it up and scanned the table of contents fast.

Inside, an image spread over two pages, the watercolor had almost completely faded, but the strokes remained. Stitches secured the creature's lips in place. Red eyes. A scythe. Its face almost completely covered in a thin veil. A ragged robe.

Antonia knew what it was.

She fitted the book carefully inside her bag. Yes, she needed to find a way to get rid of what haunted her, but getting her papá out of jail was more pressing, especially since she'd gathered enough evidence to prove his innocence.

She draped her mustard messenger bag across her chest, carefully securing a couple of Estela's journals. Twisting the silver knob ever so slowly, she cautiously poked her head outside. The soft glow of the candle flickered as a gentle breeze wafted in. Suddenly, a burst of loud chatter caught her attention, causing her to raise her head. Neck tense, eyes wide, Antonia scanned the area, trying to determine whether someone or something was approaching. A rustle in the grass below the base of the house prompted her to rush forward, but to her surprise, there was nothing there. The chatter didn't resume, but she could feel her insides constricting like a tightly wound piece of string. If someone was descending upon them, they had to move fast.

"We're basically in the forest. That sound could've come from anywhere," Alejandro said reassuringly.

But she knew what she'd heard. It wasn't just the rattling sound, there were human voices too.

Alejandro followed her as she crossed the threshold and stood in the narrow hallway that led them back to the old elevator. A wave of fear surged in her chest. In response, she adjusted her posture, drawing her shoulders back like her mamá used to.

Before she could regret it, Antonia unlocked the elevator's pulley, and soon they were descending farther down into the rock and to the deepest part of El Salto.

At the bottom, the forest came as another form of night, the vegetation cloaked in white velvet. The nogales and wild encenillos were shrouded in the lightest of mists, their trunks somber brown with sable cracks that gnarled the bark. Antonia drew her gaze up; the house and its roof blurred like an old watercolor painting.

Even though the house overlooked the falls, Antonia had never, willingly, stepped foot in the dense forest that sprawled just below it. Estela had always warned her of the dangers that lurked within.

The forest released the sound of a plethora of nocturnal ghosts, those who moved safely within the hug of the shadowed night, to the rhythm of the thunderous cascade. Alejandro's right eye pressed behind his camera as the shutter went off.

"What are you hoping to find down here?" Alejandro asked.

His face remained behind the lens, the forest briefly illuminated by the flickering flash.

"A pile of rotting bodies," Antonia mumbled. "The bodies of all of those that Doña Pereira and her necromancy cult have disposed of. We not only have to get Papá out, but we also need to get everyone away from here. You're right, the hotel, the place must be shut down for good. Finding those bodies will give us even more proof than what we already have."

"What do you mean—?"

Antonia drew out a breath and remained silent, as though looking for the right thing to say. Finally, she said, "This place harms people. If the svetyba is linked to me. To us. To this place . . . You implied it yourself—if the evil spirits keep crossing to this side, people won't be safe, ever. Whether it's Doña Pereira or someone else bringing them in.

"I meant it when I said I don't plan on taking the role of the new Lideresa. Yes, this land may be sacred, so it should be protected . . . but not by us, the living. We are all too corrupted, too greedy. Los Muiscas can protect the land on their own. It doesn't belong to us. Mamá and her group . . . her cult. They may have started out with good intentions, but they were—are—part of the problem. I won't stand by and let people get killed knowing I could do something. Papá must have known, about the spirits, about the land and how cursed it was." Antonia wasn't sure about that last point. Her mamá had always been so mysterious, so Antonia wouldn't be surprised if Ricardo didn't know the whole story.

"He tried to warn me when I visited him, and I didn't listen. Instead, I had all these doubts, I pointed fingers at him, and for a second, I seriously considered he'd gone mad and killed those people. I will never forgive myself for doubting him."

⊷— ⊷

As Antonia and Alejandro immersed themselves farther into the forest, Antonia's leather shoes sank into the makeshift muddy path more and more as she stomped forward. Alejandro offered her his free hand, and she took it as gracefully as she could. She wondered what was going on back at the hotel, if Doña Pereira and León were chasing after them.

"El Lago de los Muertos," Alejandro said, pointing his candle at the body of water several feet across from them. It wasn't quite a lake, but that was the name that the locals had given to what formed when the waters of El Salto hit the rocks below it. The Lake of the Dead seemed like an appropriate name to Antonia now that she knew she'd lived on top of a graveyard half of her life.

A fit of nausea swept over her; before, El Salto del Tequendama had been nothing more than a pithole from which rancid and rotten smells infused the air she breathed. But now, she understood that all this time she'd been filling her lungs with the stink of death itself.

The wind rattled the wet branches of the withered encenillos sprawling over the decay of forest rot. She angled her hand next to her candlestick to prevent the flickering flame from extinguishing.

Antonia followed Alejandro as he led the way through the trail, his figure a shadowy silhouette against the swirling haze. Grimness clouded his face, but there was something softer in the way he carried himself, a subtle fragility that spoke of his inner turmoil.

Alejandro seemed like the type of man who carried his emotions like a cloak, not easily shed, but today the cloak must have been particularly burdensome for him, heavy. He'd found out Doña Pereira had gotten his mother killed . . . she'd been snagged away from Alejandro just like Estela had been from Antonia.

Their shared silence was laden with an unspoken understanding that passed between them, a shared empathy forged from the same devastating loss.

Antonia brought herself to a halt as questions escaped her. She wasn't sure it was the right time or if she'd get an answer from Alejandro at all, but the words left her mouth before she could think to hold them back.

"Your mother . . . she died at the hands of the cult. Was that also a reason why you agreed to help me? To get some answers to your own questions?"

Alejandro didn't regard her; instead, he walked on past her and remained silent.

She opened her mouth to say something, but words evaded her. She wasn't certain she was capable of making any sound. She should've kept her mouth shut.

"I started working in paranormal investigation because of her. For years I wanted to know what had happened. Her cremated remains showed up at our door. A month after she'd gone missing. I never bought it. When my aunt told me about what she did at the cult, when she told me that story, I couldn't help but think that El Salto del Tequendama had the answers I looked for. My aunt tried to convince me otherwise, and I ultimately pretended like I was leaving the subject behind. But how could I do that? I needed closure. I knew the house had the answers I was seeking. So I dove headfirst into an investigation that led me to working at the station and eventually here."

It was then Antonia realized the story he wanted so desperately was a story of his own. Of his mother.

Antonia quickened her pace behind him and reached for his arm gently. She swallowed dryly. "I'm sorry. I really am. I know how hard it must've been for you...."

"I know I told you that I came here because of my boss and his fascination with this place, and that is still true, but I also came looking for answers. I came for my own personal interests.

"My mom discovered something, I don't know what—my aunt said she never told her. But it was something bad. Something that could put the cult at risk. But then there was a misunderstanding, and the blame was put on my mother."

Alejandro's voice was cold, and a hint of sorrow tainted his features. Antonia reached for his hand and squeezed it.

"She'll get what she deserves." Antonia's voice came out determined. For the first time in a while, she was making a promise she knew she would keep.

DIECINUEVE

—◆»———— ⊷————◆⟩—

Above, as they advanced through the trail, the moon, obscured by wispy clouds, cast faint, shifting shadows across the rocks covered in slick moss. There was a musty scent, mingling with the aroma of decay from fallen leaves and wet ground. Antonia's breath formed plumes in the bitter cold, and her eyes darted through the dense shadows.

The water churned and roared with an unsettling intensity, echoing off the sheer rock walls of the gorge with a hollow foreboding rumble. A tangle of twisted branches and dense underbrush seemed to close in on the small clearing.

Within the embrace of the veil of fog, Antonia strained her eyes to see if there was something behind them, but among the vastness of the night, horrors could lurk around her in plain sight without her ever noticing. But she sensed a faint, almost imperceptible presence behind her—an unseen observer of sorts that made the hairs at the back of her neck stand on end. The sensation came in waves, at times fleeting yet persistent.

Antonia straightened in place, and a gasp escaped from her lips.

Alejandro's march came to a halt. "What is it?"

"Did you hear that?"

A voice came again. Just like the ones she'd heard inside the hotel. Except this time it felt closer.

Alejandro turned in her direction. "Antonia, don't allow the place to mess with your head," he said between gritted teeth.

Nona. Nona. Nona.

"Mamá?" The ground felt like quicksand under her feet, but she broke into a sprint, closer to the base of the falls before Alejandro could stop her.

"Antonia, don't . . ." He struggled to catch up to her. "Antonia, please . . . ," he yelled, but Antonia no longer listened.

Her body was acting as if through its own accord. Almost as if subconsciously, Antonia needed to see if Estela was here. She needed to see that El Salto was not playing games with her this time.

Nona! Welcome home!

Every sound, every shadow, and every ripple in the water seemed to conspire to ensnare Antonia's soul and cast over her pure dread.

Alejandro wrapped his hand around her arm and yanked her backward, pulling her out of her daze. "Do not run away like that. Don't you see where we're at!"

"There's something here. Something's watching. . . ." Antonia's senses heightened. Her ears became more sensitive to every noise. Slowly, she turned her head to her right, looking over her shoulder. Even among the white canvas stretching on the backdrop of their night, her vision felt sharper. She twirled to the left, expecting her eyes to come across something. *What something?* That question she was unable to answer. There was nothing behind her, behind them. Nothing but her lingering and familiar sensation of being followed, of being watched, haunted.

"I-I . . . there was something . . . ," she said again, this time slowly. "I think this was a bad idea. Coming down here . . ."

Then she heard it. Shallow breathing beyond the mist. She lunged toward the sound and brushed Alejandro's shirt with her fingertips, failing to usher him toward her. She reached back for his arm and felt wet fabric caked with sand and dirt. His flesh was cold, his skin was stone, and as Antonia realized that this was not Alejandro at all, he was already pushing his rough fingers inside her mouth, toppling her to the muddy path.

It was almost as if she had stepped into a strange, soundless dream. Antonia tried scrambling away, but terror gripped her with an ironclad hold, as if invisible hands were clutching her tightly, preventing her from making the slightest sound, the slightest move.

Around her swarmed faceless figures like the ones she'd seen the night of the opening party. Limbs and flesh hanging in tatters.

As she shrieked and cowered, Alejandro's silhouette came into view, his back to her as he stood as tall and still as carved wood, but he gave no indication of having heard her, so she pressed her hands at her sides and staggered to her feet, wiping off the mud against the fabric of her woolen coat.

The creatures swarmed around them, dense with filth, blocking her from any sight of the falls beyond, and they gave no sign of relenting.

She inhaled and exhaled a few times in an attempt to force her thoughts to slow down. She knew the svetyba was near . . . playing tricks with her mind.

This is all in your head. Breathe, she thought.

Antonia gathered strength and seized Alejandro, but he didn't move an inch. Instead, his eyes shot open, lost somewhere she couldn't see without turning around. His face was gray, his eyes felt hollow, empty, and even though Antonia shook him hard, he gave no sign of being there.

As desperation began to take hold of Antonia, a familiar face stepped through the crowd of ghosts. Seeing it triggered a quick shift between anger, shock, and fear, then back to anger.

The svetyba.

Antonia stumbled back; Alejandro's body pressed against hers. Across the sodden earth, a figure akin to a woman advanced with deliberate steps, each footfall resonating ominously. Its skeletal fingers, tightly clenched in a macabre grip, oozed crimson. Shadows draped its countenance, shrouding a face etched with solemnity and obscurity.

Antonia glanced around, trying to find a way to escape. If only Alejandro were awake.

"Please. Please. Wake up. Wherever it is that you are, come back," she muttered against his ear. Alejandro gave no sign of listening to her, but at least she could hear his shallow breathing. "Alejandro, damn it. Say something. Please."

Antonia needed Alejandro to wake up. She might be an Hija de Bochica through birthright, whatever that meant, but she didn't know anything about cleansing spells or witchcraft. She wasn't strong enough to face the svetyba alone.

NONA! NONA! NONA!

Antonia shot a fiery stare to the svetyba, and its mouth, a grotesque array of crude sutures, twisted upward in a sinister grin.

Alejandro had said svetybas couldn't speak, but they could infiltrate the minds of those who'd been cursed, eventually taking full control over them.

Antonia knew that no matter what, she had to keep control. She couldn't let the svetyba inside her mind.

The svetyba stood close, so close its arms could've reached Antonia at the minimum movement. And that's exactly what happened next. It snatched Antonia's hand firmly. Its flesh was clammy, and with its proximity came the same putrid stench that had wafted through the halls of El Castillo de Bochica.

Was this how dying felt?

Cold and empty.

Antonia struggled to slip her hand off the creature's grip, but its fingers wrapped tighter against her hand, so tight its nails pierced Antonia's flesh.

Antonia swallowed a scream as pain coursed through her body. Her wrist soaked in blood.

But she couldn't give up. Not now. She gathered all the strength she had left in her muscles and attempted one final pull, but the svetyba gave no sign of relinquishing its hold. Instead, it leaned forward, and its voice reached inside Antonia's head.

NONA!

"What do you want from me?" Antonia cried. "Leave me alone! Please—"

I AM HERE FOR YOU.

The sounds were a nauseating blend of wet slurps and discordant growls, echoing eerily in her head.

I know what you want.

I can give it all to you.

You will be seen. You will be heard. People will listen to you. They will follow you. You will exert your influence upon others—

You can be like Huitaca, the strong-willed goddess who rebelled against Bochica, even at the cost of her glory.

You can become what your mother never could, a real ruler, a real Lideresa....

It was all tempting. *So very tempting!*

"I said no! No, no, no! Take me, kill me if you must. I don't care!"

May the shadows have no mercy on your soul.

Antonia twirled instantly, and her eyes met the same faceless figures from before, except this time they didn't stand still, they tramped in her direction across the makeshift narrow path. Antonia didn't know what was real anymore. She couldn't tell where she was, if they'd crossed to a different realm, or if El Salto simply had a world of its own.

She'd failed. She knew she shouldn't give it the power of corrupting her mind, but it was simply much stronger than her . . . and she wasn't sure how to cleanse herself from it, how to cast it away.

Antonia dropped her eyelids and forced herself to keep them shut.

The chanting stopped, but the sinister screams did not. The figures were coming after her. Antonia tried to mute the sounds, to concentrate on the slashing sound of the water.

Then it all went pitch-black.

VEINTE

A ntonia's eyes strained to see the silhouette emerging before her. With her heels underwater, she marched closer, her legs shaking, at the achingly familiar figure across. A gust of wind slashed through her, carrying droplets with it. In her chest, each beat a heavy thud of anticipation. "Mamá?" she mumbled.

Estela looked exactly how she did the day she died. Her brown hair was pushed back, secured in a high bun. Her knee-length olive velvet dress was fitted around the waistline and opened on an A cut, her shoulders bare. Her expression was smudged, smeared, as though obscured by a shadowy veil.

"Má?" Antonia cried as she ran toward the silhouette standing at the edge of the clearing. "Is it really you?" Antonia almost choked on her words as she reached for Estela, her arms trembling as she stretched out to touch her. To feel her.

Estela's arms closed around her in a tight embrace. Her love seeping into Antonia's entire being.

A delicate, familiar scent—Estela's scent—prickled in the air, mingling with the shroud of mist around them.

"Nona, I'm here. I'm here with you." Her voice as comforting as Antonia remembered, almost like a balm to the ache spreading in her heart.

Was she dreaming still? Was this real?

"Mamá, what happened to you? What is happening to me?"

Estela reached for Antonia's hand. Her touch was a continuous gentle reassurance. Her calloused fingertips settled softly on the back of Antonia's hand, exuding a warmth that cast away the fear she'd experienced what felt like only seconds ago.

"Shhhh," Estela said. "I'll get to that, Nona."

As they pulled back slightly, Antonia's eyes brimmed with tears. "I love you so much, Má. I've missed you every day."

Estela looked at Antonia with a mix of sorrow and love and offered her a gentle smile. "I've missed you more than words can tell. I adore you, Nona. Always. Do you remember the first time you saw the waterfall—from up there?"

Antonia nodded. "We watched cóndores fly across the sky, like they put on a show for us to enjoy."

They had marveled together at the beauty of El Salto; Antonia's young eyes had never witnessed something as majestic before. Her face was illuminated with awe and excitement as, high above, a pair of cóndores glided effortlessly against the clear skies. Their massive black-and-white wings spread wide, casting fleeting shadows over the shimmering waters below.

Estela had squeezed Antonia's hand, sharing in the magical moment. "Look at how they soar, so free and powerful," Estela had said softly, her voice full of reverence.

"It was amazing, wasn't it? It's one of my fondest memories of us together. Seeing how your face lit up in fascination. I felt like you understood what I'd been feeling all these years. What this place meant to me," Estela said, bringing Antonia back to the present.

"It was. I'm so glad we could see it together. I'm so glad you showed me."

Estela readjusted in her spot, and her tone shifted to a flash of urgency. "You have no idea how much this means to me. Being here with you again. Seeing you again. And as much as I wish we could extend our time together,

I can't be selfish. Nona, you need to leave. Your father needs you. You have a life to live that's not in this place."

But Antonia wasn't sure she could let go a second time. Perhaps she could stay with her, if only a little longer. She had so many questions, so many things left unsaid. . . .

"Mamá, I can't leave until I know what happened. What happened to you, to our home, to our family? . . . What is happening to me?"

"Evil plagued the land, and I was a fool to believe I could do anything about it. When Las Hijas de Bochica formed, we made it our mission to protect it. To steer people away from the sacred lands of Bochica. But evil spirits seeped inside our society. And even worse, it seeped into our family, into our home. I should've listened to Teresa when she came to me with her suspicions about Eleonora, about the svetybas. Instead I sentenced her, condemned her body and soul. I should've noticed the signs earlier. The way you behaved, the way you handled yourself. The tunjos, the night-mares. I should've never exposed you to any of it. By the time I tried to do something about it, it had been too late. I couldn't stop it. I couldn't protect you. I'm so sorry. I simply wasn't strong enough.

"The power . . . it was intoxicating. I was so caught up in the influence and control that it granted me that I entirely lost sight of our true mission. As my influence grew, as my power became bigger than anything I would've anticipated, I became obsessed with holding on to that, expanding it. I was so engrossed with the facade of the grandeur. The more I sought control, the more I was pulled away from our real purpose. And in turn, I lost con-trol of myself entirely."

The thought had crossed Antonia's mind before. Estela's deluded ambi-tions for power had driven her to do the same thing that everyone else did. Estela had drained the life out of the place, justifying herself by saying the cult was here to protect it.

"When Eleonora summoned a svetyba into our home, it was all too late. Bochica stripped from us our power. She turned on Las Hijas. . . ."

Estela closed her eyes, her face contorting with anguish. "I should've been vigilant."

Tears welled in Antonia's eyes as she listened. Her chest aching for the pain in her mamá's voice.

That was why Estela couldn't get rid of the svetyba. That must be why she thought her only choice was to die and hope her family would be safe at last. Guilt and fear consumed her, like it was threatening to do with Antonia.

"Then you left. You did well escaping. I never thought you'd be back. But, Nona, Eleonora planned all of this. She orchestrated it. Your father's sudden change of mind, his insistence on coming back to the house was no coincidence. She messed with his mind, with his will, she put him under her spell. She poisoned him, and she got you both to come back."

The weight of Estela's words pressed down on Antonia like a suffocating fog. The idea of witchcraft would've seemed far-fetched mere days ago, but it all became clear now. Ricardo's sudden decision to return to the house, the one he'd vowed to never step foot in again, it was also Doña Pereira's doing. She had used dark means to manipulate him, to lure him back to that cursed place.

Shame washed over Antonia once again; the weight of her doubts toward Ricardo felt like a betrayal. "I thought he was guilty in some way. I thought he'd killed—" She didn't dare say it out loud. "He brought you here, he built the house for you—and then he wanted to come back to the party—I asked him what had happened, I begged him to tell me something, anything."

"I confided in him, Nona, not about everything—he didn't know about Eleonora—but it was too late. I probably should've told him about her, but I was scared of what he would do to her, and what she would do to him and you in return." Estela paused for a moment, as if reliving those days. "So instead of telling him all of it, I lied—I told him I had everything under control, but I didn't. He knew there was something else to it. Something I was hiding, but I never could tell him. He then started to believe I was sick—ill in a way, sickened by my own delusion. And he wasn't too far off from the truth. But I still couldn't tell him."

"I found some of your old journal entries, hidden around the house—the dollhouse, the tunjos, the music box. Did you leave them for me to find?"

"No, at least not in the beginning, but I guess subconsciously I must have hoped you would find them one day if you were still in the house. Perhaps it would force you to leave. I just didn't want Eleonora to get ahold of them. Some I managed to burn away in time, but when I couldn't, I hid them in the nearest place I could find, a place I knew she wouldn't care to touch, for she no longer cared about our goddess Bochica, or los Muiscas. I was scared. You don't understand how powerful she is. She spared Ricardo because she had nothing to gain from him, and other than the house, she had no real interest in messing with him. But you . . . you would be the one to take my place. I needed him to be there for you, to protect you. So, instead, I said a curse had been placed on the land and the women of our family, but I convinced him I could cast it away. That's why he seemed so dismissive of your nightmares. I didn't want him scaring you more than you already were. But my efforts proved fruitless. That's when the idea came to me, that maybe the only way to cast it away was if I died. I thought it was haunting me, so my death should rid you all of it. But it didn't."

"Oh, Mamá, I wish more than anything you hadn't."

Antonia was newly flooded with regret and anguish. The police had been right the whole time. Estela had jumped.

"Please tell me . . . how do I get rid of it? The svetyba . . . it's after me," Antonia pleaded, a tinge of desperation in her voice. There had to be something she could do.

Estela was right. Antonia did have a life to live. She was certain she didn't want anything to do with cults or hauntings. What she wanted was to kill the svetyba, to get back at Doña Pereira, to rebuild her life, or what was left of it.

"Once a svetyba is summoned, there's often no going back, Nona."

"No. No, I can't live with it, there must be a way," Antonia cried. "I'm scared." She allowed herself to be vulnerable in front of the one person who had given everything, even her life, to protect her. With Estela, Antonia could undoubtedly let her walls down.

"You may have to live with it." Estela's tone shifted, flattened a few quarters below its usual key. Why wasn't she telling Antonia to fight back?

"Mamá, no. What about your books, a spell, something—? You said these waters could cleanse. They're sacred."

"They once were, but they aren't for us anymore."

As much as Antonia wanted answers, those were not the ones she expected. She'd spent her entire life running away from whatever there was to see.

Antonia had come this far, she couldn't give up. She would exhaust every resource she could find. She'd do anything. "What about Bochica? She's a goddess, she saved the Muiscas when the savanna flooded, didn't she?"

Couldn't she save Antonia too?

"Nona, I meant everything I said. Bochica doesn't trust us anymore, and Las Hijas don't pull from the places a svetyba comes from. We never did. The only person who would know how to reverse such a curse would be . . ."

Antonia's heart sank as she noted the gravity in Estela's tone. "No. *No. No—*"

"Eleonora summoned it. She should know how to send it away. There's always a way in and a way out of a curse. She must know, Nona."

Antonia's eyes widened, confusion and fear swirling in her mind. The person after her, chasing her down, that cursed her . . . No. There had to be something else, some other way out. Doña Pereira wouldn't help her. And Antonia didn't trust her. Not at all.

"What about the balance? How can we restore it? Bochica's trust?" Antonia pressed.

"It's too late, Nona. There's nothing we can do. You need to leave. Nona, I'm so sorry I left. I'm so sorry for not being there when you needed me the most, but I will always be around to take care of you. I had to sacrifice myself if I wanted to save you two. I'm so proud of the woman you've become, of everything you've done. I love you more than anything in this world. And I always will, but right now I need you to leave. This place is not safe for the living. Especially not for you."

"I don't want to leave you."

"You must. For your own sake. Go back in the house and get people as far away as you can."

Their hands clasped together, Antonia's heart heavy with the weight of another goodbye. For four years, she'd wished she could've prevented Estela's death. She wished she would've had a chance to talk to her, to say goodbye. She was grateful she'd had that chance now.

Antonia struggled to hold back her sobs. "Me too, Má."

"Goodbye, Nona."

Estela's face softened, and she offered Antonia one last loving smile. Antonia closed her eyes, as if trying to capture this memory, to lock it away in her brain like her most precious belonging.

"Goodbye, Mamá."

When Antonia opened her eyes, she realized that a part of her was missing, and she didn't know how to fill the void. She was standing there, her heart wrapped in a bittersweet blanket of memories and love.

◆——◆

It took her a few minutes to remove herself from her grief. Estela was gone, again, for a second time. But Antonia couldn't dwell on her emotions much longer.

She wanted to restore the balance. She wanted to have the power to do it.

She wanted this. She wanted to make things right. But she also didn't want to become the new Lideresa. She didn't want to rely on Bochica's powers, to prey on it. So if she was going to protect the land in some way, she'd do it on her own terms.

Estela was wrong. Antonia wouldn't end up like her. She also wouldn't let Doña Pereira win. Whatever it might cost, even if she had to live with the svetyba following her around, she would.

The hotel. It had to be taken down. But before she could do that, she needed to find Alejandro and get her papá out of prison before the corpses kept on rolling down El Salto. And she wouldn't be able to do it if she got trapped in the same hell her mamá was in.

Antonia was going to miss Estela, but she couldn't look back. She had to let go as much as her papá needed to.

"Alejandro," she screamed, hoping to hear his voice. To see him peeking through the mist. Praying that he'd give her a sign that could tell her where in this hell he could possibly be.

"Please, *please*," she cried. "Please, Alejandro, where are you?"

Deep inside, Antonia knew that it was pointless. He wouldn't hear her unless he was really close. The waterfall drowned out every single sound, and she wasn't sure she had the strength to keep going. But she had to. She didn't want to glance back because she was afraid to the core that the faceless figures would still be there, hunting her down. That the old bearded woman would come back preying on her soul.

Antonia had lost all sense of time as she traveled deeper into the forest's foreboding embrace, her footsteps muffled by the damp, decomposing leaves under her feet. Just when she was about to succumb to despair, Alejandro's voice pierced the oppressive silence somewhere above. She looked up to where the sound had come from to catch Alejandro standing at the edge of the falls.

Pain carved in her stomach, and a gasp stole the breath from her lungs. He was on the verge. El Salto would swallow him whole.

"Alejandrooooooooooooo," she screeched. *"NO! NO! NO!"*

She had to move fast.

Antonia kept her eyes locked on him as she rummaged to find a path across the forest and up to the falls. She held on to wet branches and lunged her legs across rocks, until she eventually pulled herself up onto a narrow ledge. Her arms were on fire, and her legs threatened to fail her, but she commanded them to keep moving until she said it was time to quit.

"Alejandro, I'm coming." She continued screaming as she made her way across the mountain. "Please talk to me. It's me! Look at me!"

She wouldn't let the place feed off him as well. She wouldn't let it take anyone else from her. As long as he listened to her, as long as he at least heard her, he would be fine.

Alejandro slowly craned his neck toward her, but he didn't speak. It was as if he was unable to. He looked frozen, his entire body stiff, just standing there.

"Alejandro, look at me, talk to me, *please*," she tried again, this time a more desperate plea, tears and all.

When she reached the falls, Antonia was hesitant about getting too close—she was afraid that any movement she'd make would make him plummet to his death.

"Alejandro, whatever's happening . . . it is *not* real. Just like you said to me, remember?" Antonia's voice was tender, laced with an undercurrent of profound concern.

She assessed her situation. A wrong step and they'd both trip and inevitably fall. But she'd rather fall with him than stand still and let someone else die.

She didn't allow herself to rethink the situation and lunged forward against him, shoving him to the side of the ledge. She guarded him with her body, and they tumbled against a pile of rocks and mud. She stifled a groan as a sharp pain spread from her knees to her chest.

Alejandro's eyes fluttered open. "Antonia," he managed.

He was back.

She wrapped her hands around his head. "You're here. You're fine."

Antonia pressed her lips against his forehead and didn't let go for a bit. She'd saved him, she'd not failed him like she'd failed her mamá.

Alejandro looked up at her, still dazed and disoriented. "W-what happened?"

Antonia's hands moved carefully over him, checking for scratches or more severe injuries. "You're safe now, it's okay."

He stirred, groaning in pain. His eyes filled with confusion and shock. "I was so close, I thought I was going to jump, but I didn't want to. I was not myself. It was as if I was seeing myself from the outside. . . . Someone, or something, was whispering in my ear. It's like the falls—"

"I'm sorry, Alejandro. It's this place. It's happened to me too. But you're with me now, you're fine. I won't let anything happen to you."

He grasped her hand tightly. "Thank you; you could've gotten yourself killed."

"I won't let anyone else die here."

Alejandro winced in pain as Antonia helped him sit up, her touch tender and reassuring.

"There's so much I have to tell you, but we need to find a way to get everyone out and the hotel shut down. Then I need to go get Papá freed."

It took Alejandro a few minutes to compose himself, for his face to finally recover some of the color that had been snagged from it. And Antonia waited patiently, running her hands down his back, hoping to ease him back to the present.

Eventually, Alejandro nodded. "I have enough evidence to scare people away, to save Ricardo. I have the photos of Doña Pereira's endeavors in the after hours. The dozens of people that have died under her hand. There's no way anyone would want to come back here after we spill the place's dirty secrets."

Antonia hoped that Alejandro was right. A horror story could attract even more people than a luxurious hotel ever would.

"Do you think they'll believe us?" she asked.

"People dying here has never been a secret. People already believe it's haunted. Now we have the proof and a plan to get the story out. I have a friend at *La Gaceta de Santa Fé*. We can get this to them. I could go to my boss as well, but I don't think he'd be of much help. They'll think it's just another aficionado thing. But *La Gaceta* is reputable, and thousands of people read it every day. . . . That's just what we need. News that spreads not only in Bogotá but all over the country. *La Gaceta* won't say no to something like this, to news about the most popular place in Colombia involving a murderous cult."

"It's almost dawn, I don't know how we'll be able to leave. I need to go back to the hotel. I told Emiro that I'd call him to pick us up, but if we go back, I'm afraid we might get caught. We've come this far, I don't want to make any mistakes now that we got what we wanted."

Alejandro took in a deep breath before he spoke again. "We can walk. There's a house not far away from here. . . . I know the family who lives there, and they'd let us use their phone. If we get caught right now, they'll take all the evidence away and we'd be back to square one."

He was right. If they let Doña Pereira or León catch them, they'd be even more screwed than they were before.

But Doña Pereira wasn't her only concern.

The svetyba. She still had to find a way to cast it away.

VEINTIUNO

◆━━━━━▬ ▬━━━━◆

Antonia dragged on her feet, her legs threatening to fail beneath her, as they walked on the empty road, heading toward the house Alejandro had mentioned. She'd lost track of time, but the piercing pain on her heels told her that they'd been walking for an hour at least.

In the distance, the little house lit up its corner of the forest. Antonia didn't know where they were headed, but she was glad it was far away from the hotel. She kept glancing back just to double-check that no one was coming.

"I'm so tired," she told Alejandro. "It's like being down there completely drained my energy...."

Encountering Estela, having to say goodbye to her afterward, grieving her once more, had drained Antonia as well. She didn't think she had it in her to go through the emotions and her absence once again. Yet she had.

She thought about telling Alejandro what she'd experienced, but just as she was about to say something, he broke in first.

"We're almost there. See, look, just a few more minutes."

Alejandro was right. Within a few minutes, they were standing in front of the house. Up close, it looked more like a shed. It was covered in moss, as though the vegetation of the forest had claimed the place as part of itself. All she wanted was to feel safe, and this felt about the only place where she could.

The door was ajar and Alejandro let himself in, Antonia following right after.

A long-haired woman came through one of the doors across the short hallway. Her black eyes—framed by a set of long lashes—contrasted against her dark olive skin. Her lips, painted a burnt-rose color, curved into a smile.

"What happened? Jesus, are you all right?" The woman rushed toward him, opening her arms as she got closer.

Alejandro opened his arms to her as well.

"Antonia, this is Rosalía. . . ."

Rosalía stood tall in front of them, glancing at Antonia, then back to Alejandro.

Antonia stared briefly, but quickly responded, "Hi, sorry to come in the middle of the night, we . . ." She fumbled. "I'm Antonia Rubiano." She leaned forward, offering her hand to the young woman.

"No apologies needed, my God," Rosalía chimed in. "Please, take a seat." She gestured toward the big velvet poltrón chair in the living room. "Do you want to clean yourself up? Do you want something to eat? Are you hurt? I can patch you up."

"Some coffee and some water would be enough. We need to get going soon," Alejandro said, then sat on the coffee table in front of Antonia as she watched Rosalía get lost through the hallway. "Are you okay?"

"I can't not think about everything that happened. What we're about to do . . ."

He chuckled. "We're safe now. I'll ask Rosalía for her car, and we'll be back in the city soon."

"Can we trust her?"

He nodded. "She's my cousin Berta's partner. She's also a reporter, like myself. We're colleagues, although she does the very serious, real news. She's the one that works at *La Gaceta*."

"She's the one who's going to help us?"

Alejandro nodded once again.

Rosalía's voice came from behind them; she carried a wooden platter with two cups of coffee, water, and some cheese bread on it. The smell of queso fresco tinged the air, Antonia's mouth immediately pooling with water, and the scent of freshly baked bread made her feel as if she were almost at home.

Home! She had to call Carmela.

"Do you have a phone I could use?"

"Sure!" Rosaliá said. "It's right in the kitchen."

Antonia left her chair and started toward the kitchen. Rosalía and Alejandro's chatter faded away as Antonia put the hanger against her ear.

"Carmela, it's me," Antonia said hurriedly once Carmela came through on the receiver. "Are you okay?"

"For God's sake, Antonia, where are you?"

"I'm safe. I'll be back home soon, okay? In the meantime, if anyone asks, you still don't know where I am."

"But what happened?" Carmela sounded so distraught that Antonia felt as though she could see her worried expression through the phone. "Where is Alejandro? Antonia, please, don't leave me like that—"

Antonia went over briefly what had happened last night. She didn't have time for details, but she wanted to assure Carmela that she would take care of everything.

"I'll explain everything later, but I'm okay. Listen, I have to go, we're heading back to the city now."

"Please, come home soon, Nona."

"See you soon, okay?"

Antonia put the phone back. Knowing León was at the hotel sent a sense of urgency to Antonia. They had to leave now.

"Alejandro, I think we better head back. . . ."

"I'll drive you both. I need to be at the paper earlier than usual. Alejandro has requested this to go out as early as possible."

"Are you sure about this? You could get in a lot of trouble. . . . There's money, lots of money, involved. Doña Pereira and her son are one of the richest families in the city, and they have a lot riding on the hotel. I fear something could happen to you if they were to find out your involvement. It's too risky," Antonia said.

"I'm not scared. Besides, I owe this one more favors than I can keep count of." Rosalía smiled, pointing at Alejandro. "Don't worry about me, Antonia. I know how to take care of myself."

◆━ ━ ━◆

The sun was peeking through the sky as they drove down the cobbled streets of La Candelaria, a few blocks from Antonia's house. The memories of what had happened replayed in her head all through the drive back. How would she ever get over everything? The goings-on at the hotel, Doña Pereira being the leader of a necromancy cult and the person responsible for dozens of deaths, even the death of Antonia's and Alejandro's mothers. Going back to Estela's sanctuary, seeing her at the bottom of the falls, the faceless figures, the svetyba. The memories alone were going to haunt her a lifetime, but the feeling of helplessness, of not knowing how to rid herself of the evil that haunted her, was what truly perturbed her mind.

Minutes after, Rosalía killed the engine and they stopped across from Antonia's doorway. Rosalía glanced at Antonia over her shoulder. "Antonia, it was nice meeting you."

"Thank you for the ride." Antonia shot her a smile from the rear seat.

Alejandro stepped outside and shut the door behind them.

Antonia watched as Rosalía's orange truck disappeared around the corner and gave him a questioning look. "What are you doing . . . ?"

"I'm staying here."

"But the station, the photos, I thought . . . You must be tired too."

He crossed his arms over his chest and leaned toward her. "I'm not leaving you alone in this," he said curtly. "I'm staying with you and going with you to get your father out of that place."

"I don't want to get you in any more trouble. If León finds out that you, of all people, are here with me, things will get even messier. You already have the story that you wanted to tell, you know what happened to your mother . . . and Rosalía, she has the evidence. You have your answers. You've done enough."

Alejandro shook his head and reached for Antonia's hands. "I'm not leaving you alone, but also, I want to face Doña Pereira as much as you want to face her. She hurt us, she killed our mothers. I need to see that old lady's face when we uncover her grotesque charades."

"Rosalía will take care of everything, at least for now. The evidence is safe with her, far safer than it could be with either of us. But once that's out, you're going to be in danger. Doña Pereira and her son will come after you.

"Though I must admit, that's not the only reason why I'm staying." His voice was low and rusty, his eyes tracing every corner of her face.

Suddenly Alejandro's lips were pressed against Antonia's, and she didn't pull back.

"Please don't kill me for this, I just had to do it. I had to kiss you. . . ."

Antonia placed a finger to his lips, then closed her eyes and kissed him like she'd longed to be kissed, like no one else had ever kissed her, soft and moist and hot and breathy, not trying to win a battle but seeking union and closeness and the sharing of one breath. She found herself lost in the rhythm, savoring the way their lips met and parted, only to come together again. It was sweet, it felt effortless. Antonia could taste their shared breath, feel the thud of their combined heartbeats as their bodies enveloped each other, refusing to let go.

Somehow Antonia eventually managed to pull away and shot her gaze up to him.

"Whatever this was, it's exactly what I needed."

Alejandro curled his full lips into a smile. "Me too."

VEINTIDÓS

Carmela stood below the white arched doorway, motioning them to step inside. Her face was adorned with dark under eyes, her platinum hair secured in her usual braids.

"You both look like hell," she said. "I have some clothes for you to use, Alejandro. You can take a shower and freshen up too if you wish."

Carmela gave directions to Alejandro, who listened intently. When they were inside, he walked into the guest bathroom on one side.

"There are fresh towels and everything you may need. I'll fetch you some clothes from Don Ricardo," Carmela told him, before glancing back at Antonia, who followed closely after them. Her eyes were still locked on Alejandro as he disappeared behind a mahogany door, the scene of them kissing replaying in her head like a mirage.

Carmela cleared her throat. "Hello, Antonia. Are you there?"

Antonia swallowed, and Carmela's broad voice pulled her out of her daze. "Yes, I-I was just thinking . . ." She trailed off, unsure what to even say. How long had she been staring?

"Uh-huh," Carmela said mockingly.

"Did you go to see Papá?" Antonia asked instead.

"Yes. He's not okay. He's full of sadness. He barely said a word. It's like he's given up all hope, like that place is sucking the life out of him. I told him that you were going to get him out, but I think he thinks all is lost."

"It's not. We're going to get him out. I promise."

"I know you are, Nona. Now, tell me what happened. I feared for you both. When León came here, he was acting like a lunatic. I'd never seen him like that, so angry, so desperate. . . ."

León was scared. Perhaps he knew by then what Antonia was up to and he had only come looking for her at the house because he hoped that he was wrong. For his own sake, but especially his mother's.

"Has León been here again? Has Doña Pereira come around?" Antonia asked.

Carmela looked at her intently for a moment before she spoke again. "He hasn't, but he could come back any minute. Did you see him there?"

"I didn't see León at the party, but I suppose he could've gotten there at some point, looking for me. Doña Pereira was there, but I'm not sure she recognized us."

"Padre Juan was there too. He has a thing for parties apparently. . . ." Antonia still wondered whether he'd recognized her at the ballroom. Perhaps he had been the one to set the alarm for Doña Pereira of Antonia's presence at the party.

Antonia watched as shock cut through Carmela. "He was at the opening too—I remember he said something about blessing the place. Cleanse it or something, but I think he said that snidely. To tease you."

"Uh-huh." Antonia nodded. "He's turned into Doña Pereira's shadow, as though he's become her personal bodyguard. Perhaps she thinks that having a priest by her side will spare her from a trip to hell. Speaking of hell . . . We also went to El Lago de los Muertos," Antonia blurted.

Carmela staggered backward against the wall. She placed a hand on her chest, as though preventing her heart from escaping her rib cage.

"You both did what?" she grumbled. "So that's what the filthy clothes and that horrible smell is all about. You were down there?"

Antonia had gotten used to the odor after carrying it around for hours. She'd gotten so used to it that she'd forgotten about it. Now it was as though she'd brought El Salto and the house with her to the city.

"I'm going to need some coffee." Antonia started to the kitchen, Carmela keeping pace just behind. "We're going to get Papá out of that place. Then, I'm tackling the hotel. . . . We're kicking them out. I hate how much of a fool I was. How ignorant I was of the truth. How couldn't I realize that—?"

"Nona," Carmela began to say, with that dismissive warm tone Antonia knew so well. "Stop blaming yourself. For all of it. You couldn't have known what was all going on. We all went through so many things at that house."

"I know. You're right. I'm sorry. It's just . . . Carmela, there's so much we didn't know."

Carmela's eyes narrowed slightly. "Like what?"

Antonia hesitated, but she pushed through. "Doña Pereira is the leader of a necromancy cult. She draws power, energy, whatever, from the dead. They kill people. She summons svetybas . . . she summoned one on me . . . or the house. I'm still not sure which one it is. . . ."

Carmela looked at Antonia with fear in her eyes. Her face paled, and her braids seemed to take on an eerie stillness. "Nona, I didn't know, but go on," Carmela urged, her voice barely above a whisper.

Antonia quickly filled Carmela in on everything else she'd found out about Estela, about the house, and about Doña Pereira. The air around them felt heavy, charged, as though the very walls were holding their breath. As Antonia recalled the events of the past days, her mind was inundated with the thought that even once she got her papá out of prison, she still had something to take care of.

And the worst of it was that she didn't even know where to begin.

Perhaps, once Ricardo was out of jail, she could make some time to go over the journals and the book she'd brought along with her. Maybe they could point her to a potential solution. One that didn't involve her asking, pleading with, Doña Pereira to cast the svetyba away.

⊸—⊸ ⊸⊸

Later that morning, Emiro drove Antonia and Alejandro to *La Gaceta* to meet Rosalía. Alejandro's photos were ready to be featured in her special story in the most important national newspaper. If Doña Pereira wanted to make the headlines across the country, she'd get her wish granted. There was no place in Colombia where her story wouldn't be heard.

Loud chatter and the clack of several typewriters filled *La Gaceta*'s offices. Every worker was either bent over a piece of paper or ran desperately across the room carrying a stack of papers. From the green wooden windows, La Plaza de Bolívar came into view. A sea of people gathered around and inside the city square as Sunday's farmers' market was in full bloom. The cathedral, with its double doors ajar, welcomed believers as they strode inside while the ringing bells announced the midmorning mass. Antonia thought about Madre Asunción and the job at the escuela. She was getting her papá out of prison just like she'd promised the old nun she would, but she wasn't certain whether her job was a concern to her anymore.

Rosalía waved at her and Alejandro, a smile forming as she welcomed them into the office. The walls were lined with framed headlines and press clippings, while the hum of the printers drowned out almost every other sound.

Rosalía extended her hands, each holding a pile of glossy photographs, the edges slightly bent from being handled.

"These are all I got from Alejandro," she said.

Antonia flipped through them with increasing intensity. Images of the ritual that had taken place outside the hotel, but also pictures that Alejandro had managed to take as they explored the forest down from the falls, and snapshots from his previous investigations, including some from the night of the hotel opening. There was a picture of Antonia and her papá and a close-up of the murder weapon.

As Antonia eyed them, one of the images caught her attention briefly. Padre Juan had been in the ritual at the hotel the night before. At first, as they watched the scene unravel from behind those bushes in the middle of the night, Antonia hadn't recognized him, but from the picture in front of her, up close, his uniform gave him away.

"Alejandro." Antonia poked at his back. "It's Padre Juan. He's in this picture."

Alejandro took the photo from her. He stared for a second or two, and then his mouth gaped in shock. "How did we not see it? That's why he was there—"

"If we recognized him, other people will too—"

Alejandro whispered something to Rosalía as he handed her the picture. Rosalía recognized him too. Padre Juan was the priest at the Cathedral of Bogotá, the old church standing on a slope across from them.

"These people sleep with God and wake up with the Devil," Alejandro muttered.

"A special edition of today's paper will go out this afternoon," Rosalía told them as they headed to her booth, which was framed with posters of the stories she'd covered—from the assassination of a presidential candidate to the Hundred Days of war to the roaring twenties in the United States. "As soon as I told my boss about this, he gave me the green light." She grinned. "This is going to be big."

"They won't see this coming. If somehow the Church is involved with all of this, all hell will break loose. In no time, reporters from across the country are going to be piling up at the doors of the hotel, and people will see no rest until the doors are shut down," Alejandro said eagerly.

Antonia understood the implications, not only for those responsible but also for her and her family. Soon, even with the hotel shut down, El Salto and the gates of the house would be filled with hundreds of dozens of curious onlookers, polluters, the murderous cults run by rich people in town. She had to do something to stop that from happening.

Alejandro glanced at Antonia. Under the golden light sneaking in from the open windows, his features appeared softer, almost too delicate, almost childlike. His black hair was combed back, only this time, not a strand was out of place.

"I'm taking this to the police now. You should go and see your father, make sure he's okay. I'll meet you there."

Antonia nodded. "Do you think this will be enough?"

It had to be enough. The plan couldn't fail. She wouldn't let it.

"Antonia, it will. Don't be scared, we are getting your father out of that place. Doña Pereira and her son won't prevent us from doing what's right."

"I'm just worried. . . . What if León went to see Papá and did something to him out of spite? What if we get there and they tell us he's been transferred or he's been sentenced already, and that I missed the trial? What if . . . ?"

She couldn't say another word, not if she didn't want to cry. She could feel herself wavering. She felt as though she'd break at any moment, if she wasn't broken already.

"I'm coming with you to the police," Antonia said, "then we're going to get Papá out of prison."

Alejandro beamed. "Let's go then. . . . We have to rescue your father."

⋯ ⟶ ⟶ ⋯

Antonia turned in the evidence to the new pair of lawyers that she'd hired to take care of his case, which had been more than enough to prevent Ricardo from going to trial. Her new lawyers went over the autopsy report and found out the timeline of when her papá was with Alejandro didn't match with the time the chief of staff was killed.

At the police station, things went smoothly: they handed to the police a copy of the material they'd gathered that incriminated not only Doña

Pereira and León, but also the hotel's other investors, along with the people that accompanied Doña Pereira at her rituals.

At first, the officers in charge were hesitant, but Antonia threatened to gather press outside the station's doors if necessary in order for them to sign Ricardo's release. He'd still have to go to trial, but with all the proof that they had, he'd come out of it clear.

Antonia recognized a few faces upon closer inspection of Alejandro's photos, but the police would take care of the rest. The hotel would be emptied out later that same day, as there was now an ongoing investigation at the place. Antonia hesitated for an instant at the thought of having her house, Estela's sanctuary, rummaged for clues and hints that could clear up what had gone on there. The picture was as clear as ever to her eyes, but the police still needed to find out things for themselves. She was fine with them being there if that was the price she had to pay to keep everyone else away. The detective in charge of the case told Antonia and Alejandro that a letter informing the investors and the owners of the hotel of what was happening was going to be sent immediately, and that the police already had cars heading to the hotel.

⊷— ⊷

Later that afternoon, Antonia was able to sneak Alejandro and herself inside the city prison after Antonia bribed a guard with a few pesos and Alejandro promised to write an article about the penitentiary and the guard.

Inside, a blanket of darkness covered the long stone hallways, illuminated by dim kerosene lamps hanging on the walls. The ward was as massive as Antonia remembered, but she felt it narrowing toward them as they walked. An agonizing pain pierced her heart as she thought of the possibility of not finding her papá alive in his cell, of finding insects swarming around his rotting corpse.

No. No. She snatched a few long breaths to still her racing heart. She was going to save him. She already had.

When they arrived at Ricardo's cell, and Antonia got a glimpse of him, she burst into tears. He sat back, his eyes distant, fractured, lingering somewhere else.

"Papá?" Antonia called.

He looked even more frail than last time. His clothes were dusted with a coat of dirt that went along with the mud caking the corners of his cell. He seemed as though he'd lost a few pounds since the last time she'd been here.

She had promised him that she'd get him out. She was here to deliver on that promise.

His expression lightened as he rushed against the bars and stretched his hand toward Antonia.

"Nona, you really are here?" His voice bounced off the walls.

Antonia wished she could tear the cell and open up space for him to crawl outside. He did not deserve any of this. And it pained her to have thought he ever had.

"I am. We're getting you out," she said.

Antonia glanced briefly at Alejandro, a sly smile appearing at the side of his lips.

"What happened—how?" Ricardo asked, as if not as interested that he wouldn't stay locked up. "Did you go back?"

Antonia nodded. "Papá, I had to. I'm sorry I dismissed everything that you said, but I must confess that I was scared. Scared that you'd done it. That the house made you in some way. I thought you were sick. I thought you were confused, clouded with grief and sadness. I'm sorry I doubted you. I . . . we need to shut the hotel down. Things are worse than we thought. We saw things, we . . . Doña Pereira and León, the reason why they want the hotel for themselves goes way beyond everything we could've imagined."

"No, Antonia, I should've insisted to your mother before it was too late. I should've seen the change in her, her devoid of life. It was only after I lost her that I understood what it all meant, what her plan was."

"I know. Mamá . . . I found it in her journals. It was Doña Pereira all along."

"What are you saying, Nona?"

"Papá, the reason why you're here is not because of the house, it wasn't El Salto's doing. Doña Pereira has turned it into a refuge for murderers. She's been the puppeteer for years, and now she's ready to build her dark community on our land. But reining her in won't be easy. She has León, the whole town."

Ricardo glanced at Alejandro, then back at her, then back at Alejandro, then back at her. "That fucker—" Ricardo's jaw clenched, and his nostrils flared with each rapid breath. The veins in his neck, barely visible under the dim light, strained.

"I know this is a lot to process, Papá. And I'll give you the time to do so, but right now, what we need to do is shut down the hotel and find a way to destroy what she summoned there." Antonia's stomach churned with dread.

Was her mamá right? Was it impossible to exorcise the svetyba?

Antonia reined in her thoughts, focusing on what she could control. "We have enough evidence not only to have them discharge you but also to shut the hotel down. This place isn't meant to be a tourist attraction. It's a sanctuary, a sacred place, and it should've remained that way."

As she spoke, the truth that had been clawing for her attention came to the surface. The mansion, an emblem of opulence, had been built on a land that rightfully belonged to the Muiscas. Ricardo had seized the land to pave the way for his grandiose project. But those last years at the house had been a prison for Antonia, a gilded cage of privilege built on foreign land. And it was up to Antonia to put an end to it all.

VEINTITRES

———◆———■—■———◆———

Antonia stepped inside her bedroom, a palpable sense of unease tugging at her. She closed the door with a soft click and locked it firmly.

A chill swept over her as she moved quickly to her bed. On it were the pile of journals belonging to Estela that she'd brought back from the sanctuary, along with the old yellow leatherbound *Evil in the Times of Bochica*. On its cover, the title was framed with engraved geometric Muisca shapes.

Antonia sat on the edge of the bed, her heart racing as she opened the book. She'd skimmed over the table of contents back at her mamá's room, but she hadn't had the time to actually try to find what she needed. Now she did.

She flipped through the brittle pages, their edges frayed, determined to find something, anything that could answer her questions regarding the haunting of the svetyba and how to get rid of it.

When she landed on the page with the svetyba illustration on it, her eyes then fell upon notes, their hurried scrawl standing out starkly against the smudgy text. They were chaotic, as if scribbled down in a frenzy, with ink blotches and smudges, but the words were legible.

Phrases like *The house must stand*; *Make them leave*; *Poison their minds*; and *The house is the heart* jumped out at Antonia, the unsettling nature of the comments cementing her to the mattress.

But . . . the handwriting. It didn't belong to her mamá.

She flipped back to the beginning, just before the table of contents, and there was the name of the owner, written down in the same handwriting found in the rest of the book.

Eleonora Pereira—Octubre 1930

If Doña Pereira had used this book to place a svetyba upon them, to try to seize the house, take hold of it . . . then how to get rid of a svetyba might be jotted down somewhere within. If there was a way in, there had to be a way out. Isn't that what Estela had told her?

Whatever fear she might've had left in her began to recede, replaced by newfound clarity.

Antonia stood up briefly with resolve, as if she'd tapped into an inner reservoir of knowledge she was never meant to possess.

The house must stand.

The house is the heart.

Doña Pereira never wanted the house solely for its beauty; her money could've gotten her an exact replica, if not a better one, anywhere, anytime.

She wanted this house, Antonia's house, because it was the heart. An artifact through which the power she was drawing from El Salto traveled . . .

An artifact just like the tunjos, which were said to harness divine power, which Estela used in her rituals.

The house had become Doña Pereira's tunjo, an artifact to appease and empower the svetyba.

Antonia took a deep breath, the reality of her situation crashing upon her. She needed to restore Bochica's balance to, in turn, save herself.

She had her answers, and like that, the weight of her burden seemed momentarily lifted. Her papá . . . he'd been right all along. Antonia shouldn't have prevented it.

The house couldn't stand anymore.

VEINTICUATRO

⟨⟩————⟩ ⟨————⟨⟩

When Antonia showed up at Madre Asunción's office, unannounced, the old nun twisted in her throne-like chair. Her eyes, magnified by a pair of glasses, followed Antonia as she crossed the thick doors. A faint scent of incense and burnt cigar lingered inside the old nun's office. Antonia was certain that Madre Asunción didn't think Antonia would ever come back, that the shrew didn't believe Antonia capable of getting Ricardo out of trouble. But she had.

Antonia was relieved to have found Madre Asunción on a Monday. These days she was hidden at the convent part of the school at this time in the evening. But Antonia needed to get this over with. She needed to tie every loose end before they could all move forward.

Antonia shifted her weight, feeling suddenly pinned under Madre Asunción's unwavering look. A thick cigar lit between her fingers.

When Antonia locked eyes with the nun, Antonia didn't cower. Determination moved alongside her steps and toward Madre Asunción.

"Miss Rubiano, it pleases me to see you back." The old lady motioned for her to take a seat.

Antonia flashed a crooked smile and slipped onto the gold ornate stool across from Madre Asunción. "I am guessing, you must have heard the news?"

How could she not? In the city, news like this spread like wildfire. People gave in to their most morbid cravings.

Madre Asunción's eyes slid across the table to her. "We all did," she said flatly. "And we are all very pleased to welcome you back. It brings us joy to see that your father is finally out of that hell pit of a place. Such a fine man like him doesn't deserve such treatment, especially if he's innocent." Madre Asunción's face looked cold as she uttered the last words. A strand of gray hair moved along the smoke being blown out from her mouth. "I knew you would get it done. Too much at stake not to—"

Antonia gestured for her to stop, and it broke her speech to a halt. Now she believed that Ricardo was a decent man after all, after having accused them, even Estela, of living an indecent life?

"I'm not here to listen to how you always knew my father was innocent, or any sudden words of love and kindness that you want to express toward us. I don't believe a word that comes from your mouth."

The tension thickened around them, and the nun's voice appeared to cut through it when she spoke again. "I was not doing such a thing." Madre Asunción tapped her cigar against the crystal ashtray just beside her. "All evidence was against him, yes. But in my heart, I knew he was innocent. I've known him for a while. The poor thing, he's always had such bad luck, especially when he drifted away from church." She placed her hand against her chest, as if showing her devoted concern for Ricardo.

Antonia took in a few breaths, trying to calm herself and keep from lashing out viciously against the bitter old woman. "I'm here to tell you that I quit." With that, Antonia felt as though a huge weight had been lifted off her back. This is what she wanted all along. "I'm doing you a favor, am I not? You said that parents didn't want the daughter of a lunatic as the teacher to their kids, so I'm making it easy for them, for you."

Madre Asunción's eyes flashed a flicker of surprise as she heard Antonia's words. "I know what I said, but your father's innocent. You've proven that—"

"I did, but I didn't do it so I could keep this job. I did it for myself, for him, for our family. I did it because he was not guilty, therefore he had no business inside that place."

Without warning, Madre Asunción's chair scraped loudly against the floor as she pushed it back and stood up, her movements sharp and disjointed. Her habit swished around her as she began to pace. Each step a testament to her agitation. Her usual calm demeanor had been shattered by Antonia's news, replaced by a flurry of panic.

"That's nonsense," Madre Asunción said dismissively. "We were expecting you back. You're one of our best teachers, and your job is here. Do you think La Escuela para Niños will take in a woman as a teacher? Especially one who's unwed still?"

Antonia hadn't thought of seeking a job at the school for boys. She didn't know if it was worse to have a woman such as Madre Asunción as her boss or a priest who thought himself better than anyone else as the head of the institution. She'd rather serve women, even if those women were serving men at the same time.

"I'm sorry for the girls. I've grown quite fond of them, although I'm not quite certain if it is because I genuinely like them or if it's because I pity them and their poor lives and everything they have to endure within these dull walls."

Antonia was right. One of the things that had always kept her from leaving was the girls. She felt for them; she felt like she had to be there to protect them. But protect them from what? And how? If they were not exposed to Madre Asunción during school hours, they were exposed to far worse than her outside these walls: abusive parents, fanatic adults who would suppress their growth and their development. A world that would censor them merely because of their being female. To have been born a female in this world that punished women, that was their haunting. It was Antonia's as well.

Madre Asunción cast her a sideways glance. "You're out of your mind. What are you going to do? Are you going back to that madhouse of yours?"

"I don't think that should be a concern of yours."

"So you're going back? You've convinced your poor father to go back there!"

"What I do with my life from now on is not of your concern—it certainly should've never been."

The nun's expression shifted once more. This time it was vacant, like a void. "Such a tragic past. Jobless. Motherless. Manless. You really want to further ruin your life," she said snidely.

"We clearly have a very different understanding of what ruining one's life is."

Antonia rose from her stool and started to the door. Her steps measured and deliberate. She didn't look back at Madre Asunción, who remained standing at her desk, her face a mix of shock and frustration. The nun's rusty voice, muffled and increasingly frantic, failed to penetrate Antonia's determined silence.

VEINTICINCO

I t had been a few days after her papá was released from jail that the police
called to break the news. Doña Pereira was on the run, and the police
were tracking her down, but no attempts at catching her had yet been successful. Antonia had tried to join the hunt but quickly discarded the idea
after talking to her papá and Alejandro.

Not until early one morning, while Antonia was getting ready to leave
the house, did opportunity come knocking at her door . . . or her phone, if
she was being accurate. She received a call from Lucía, who'd found León
severely injured inside his own house.

"Antonia, please, you need to help me, he's been acting strange, he's not
himself, and he has this—" Her voice broke in a shriek.

Antonia had no reason to help León, but Lucía had always been so kind
to her, she didn't deserve to deal with any of this. Antonia also thought it
was an opportunity to get to Doña Pereira. As evil as she was, she cared
deeply about her son, even if she'd turned him into her puppet. Perhaps
Lucía had information on her whereabouts that Antonia could then take
to the police.

"Alejandro, it's me," Antonia said when Alejandro answered from the
other side of the line. "I need you to do something for me—"

Antonia believed that if Doña Pereira found out about her son, she wouldn't hesitate to make an appearance. So Antonia laid out her plan to the officers in charge, and even though doubtful, they agreed to her conditions.

Antonia's next step was to convince Alejandro to run a story.

Alejandro agreed, and shortly after, the news of León Rivera dying spread like wildfire.

Now all they had to do was wait for Doña Pereira to bite. The police couldn't come with them, or else it would raise alarms. This could be their last chance, and Antonia wouldn't forgive herself if they didn't at least try.

So, resolved, Antonia knocked at the door twice while Alejandro peeked through one of the half-open wooden windows and signaled to Antonia that no one was inside.

Panic flared at the thought of León and Doña Pereira escaping their punishment and not having to face any consequences to their actions, but Antonia forced herself to calm down. If all went according to plan and Doña Pereira took Antonia's bait, the police would finally apprehend her and put her where she belonged. Then, and only then, would Antonia be able to have ownership of the house again . . . and get rid of it for good.

Alejandro knocked the door down after they got no response from Lucía, who was supposedly at home with León.

"Lucía, it's me, Antonia. I'm here."

No response came rippling back, but Antonia did hear something over Alejandro's determined steps as he made his way inside.

"Help!"

Alejandro heard it too; she could tell by the look they exchanged and how he dragged her inside almost immediately.

"Help!"

Alejandro and Antonia ran up the stairs. She knew whose voice it was.

The door to León's studio was ajar. Lucía was kneeling by his body, her face hidden inside her hands. She didn't react to their presence, but Antonia could hear a faint cry.

Antonia's eyes widened in horror, and she recoiled at the sight, her hand flying to her mouth as if to ward off the stench.

A shiver of disgust ran down her spine as she surveyed the scene, but she waved it off and rushed to León's side, knelt beside his body, and placed a hand over the shoulder of Lucía, whose vacant gaze was fixed on her husband. Antonia pressed her lips tightly to suppress bile threatening to come out.

León's once-strong frame was now emaciated and gaunt. From up close, his skin was a grotesque canvas of injuries—patches of his flesh were discolored and eroded, revealing raw, oozing wounds beneath. His skin seemed to be dissolving in places, leaving gaping, ragged injuries that pulsed with an unsettling, rhythmic throb, as if they were alive, eating him from the inside and out.

In Antonia's eyes, León appeared like one of the creatures in her nightmares. Could it be that this had something to do with the svetyba? Had it taken hold of León's body, sickening him from within?

"What is happening, Antonia?" Lucía managed, snatching Antonia away from her theories. This poor lady, she was oblivious to anything her husband and her mother-in-law ever did.

León groaned at the sight of Antonia, preventing her from answering Lucía, although Antonia wasn't even sure León could see her.

Antonia pressed her hand against his cheeks. "León, it's me, Antonia," she managed firmly.

"Ay—" he said in a choking voice. "Help me . . ."

Antonia scanned León's body—his pale skin was covered in ulcers and other cut-like injuries, as though he'd done it himself. His face was as pale as she'd ever seen in a man before. She grabbed one of his wrists and almost jumped at the sight of a hole that went all the way through his hand.

Stigmata. In her dreams, in her nightmares. Was this what the svetyba did to its followers once they stopped worshipping it?

A mockery; an imitation of the Church's divine miracles.

Antonia looked at Alejandro and gestured for him to come closer.

As soon as he was next to her, seeing what was in front of him, Alejandro ripped part of his shirt and placed it around the wounds on León's hands, applying pressure to them. Antonia wasn't sure if preventing him from bleeding out was worth the try, given the state of his wounds, but she wouldn't let him die. That would be the easy way out, regardless of his current physical state. He needed something much greater than a priest, or a doctor, could provide, anyway. If anything, Antonia's inner voice seethed, he needed to stay alive to face the families of those he and Doña Pereira murdered.

"What do you think this means?" Alejandro asked.

"I think these people were playing with far darker things than we can imagine," Antonia said. "I think Doña Pereira must have pulled from far darker places . . . and things bit her back."

"But—why him? Why not her—?"

"She's greedy. She'd put herself first over everything else. Even her own son. He didn't know what he was getting himself into. She dragged him along with her. She, or her evil hag, must've cast a spell to protect herself from the wraths that awaited her, and she chose her son to take the brunt of it all."

Antonia glanced back at León, his mangled features changing him by the minute. That Doña Pereira had dragged him in, Antonia was sure of. But she didn't think he'd been a victim, that he was less guilty because he was her puppet, and she was the puppeteer. Antonia was tired of finding reasons to justify the actions of men. Some people were bad, and there needn't be any more reason than that.

"Mother . . ." León's voice emerged in short, labored whispers as if the weight of his words matched the burden of his condition. "It's Mother."

Antonia and Alejandro shared a look, then she said, "Where is Doña Pereira, León? Where is she?"

Antonia glanced at Lucía, her expression vacant. "Where is she, Lucía?"

"I don't know, I swear—she just left a phone number, I found it in León's office. She didn't answer when I called, that's why I turned to you. I don't know anything else."

Antonia didn't have a reason not to trust her.

"She did this," León managed hoarsely, clots of thick blood spilling from his mouth. "You all did."

Even at the sight of him, Antonia wouldn't pity him. He knew exactly what his mother was doing all along and he just stood there. Allowing her to do it all.

"Maybe she's onto us and thinks the newspaper article was a trap. Perhaps we could try summoning her again, tell her the svetyba came for her son," Alejandro said.

Antonia nodded. "Lucía, the call should come from you."

Lucía pressed to her feet and reached for the phone hanging on the wall.

Antonia was willing to try anything, would play her every card to get to Doña Pereira.

Now all they had to do was wait.

⊰•—•—•⊱

Minutes seemed like hours as they waited for Doña Pereira. They were growing restless, and things weren't looking so well for her son.

Antonia glanced at León. If there had been at least a flicker of hope in his eyes, it had vanished.

She pressed to her feet and left the room to find Alejandro. Lucía chose to stay with León, a holy rosary on her lap as she dutifully prayed for her husband's forgiveness. But perhaps her Christian god wouldn't be able to do much. As the svetyba had no business with him.

Alejandro was waiting outside the door. As soon as he saw Antonia, he wrapped his arm around her shoulder and escorted her downstairs. She stared at her hands, covered with León's dry blood. She thought about crying, as a way of releasing her emotions, not out of pity for León, but because the past days had been too much on her. But she couldn't bring herself to do it. She'd cried so hard for the past years that no tears were left in her, especially not to be wasted on people who'd become the real demons in her haunting story.

When they stepped through the hallway, Antonia's gaze met Doña Pereira's. The old woman's face was shadowed with wrinkles, as though she'd aged ten years since Antonia last saw her several days ago.

Relief washed over Antonia briefly, and then it was replaced with anger.

"What are you two doing here?" Doña Pereira spat out. "Isn't it enough with everything you did at the hotel?"

"You took the bait," Antonia said simply.

"You think they have reasons to put me in a dungeon, but unfortunately for you, they don't." Doña Pereira's voice was sharp. She held a cane in her right hand and hit it hard against the waxy wooden floor, then pointed the stick at them. "Don't you dare think I will let you get away with this. Your career, kid, is ruined. No newspaper or radio station will want to work with you. And you, Antonia, you're an entitled brat, just like Estela was."

"You killed all those people. Las Hijas, you made them turn on each other, those people you sacrificed at El Salto. Alejandro's mother's death is on you too. If you think that a piece of shit like you is going to make me feel any worse than I already do, you're wrong."

"You have no clue what you're saying. You're nothing but a dumb child after all. As to his mother, I did it for the benefit of Estela. I thought that would make her a stronger leader, and instead, it made her a weakling. Much like you. Teresa's death was a waste, but it had to be done." Doña Pereira paused, gazing briefly at Alejandro.

Antonia could tell he was fighting hard to keep himself calm.

"As to León, I didn't do anything to him. The svetyba is taking hold of him. He's a weakling, all men are. When he didn't want to join me, when he turned his back on us, darkness was cast upon him. Entirely his fault."

Antonia was disgusted by the thought that Doña Pereira would sacrifice her own son for the sake of her quest for power.

"If you hadn't ruined our plans, if you hadn't meddled with things that shouldn't be a concern to you, this wouldn't have happened. You want to make me feel guilty for my son? Well, you should feel guilty as well." Doña Pereira dropped her cane and melted to her knees. "This is your fault. This is his fault too. I had to complete the ritual, and he wouldn't let me—you ruined everything."

She rushed toward Antonia, and Alejandro angled himself in front of her, shielding her from Doña Pereira's wrath.

"*Step away* from her." He emphasized each word slowly, his face twisted with fury.

"Hah." Doña Pereira laughed in a loud shriek. "I see what's happening here. You are too deluded by her beauty—"

Antonia swallowed.

"You're wasting your time with her, boy. Look at her. There is no way she'd ever make you or anyone happy. She's miserable and petulant. She doesn't think anyone is good enough for her, let alone a poor aficionado like you," Doña Pereira said snidely.

Anger surged through Antonia, thick and suffocating, as her fingers curled into fists. Doña Pereira's brown eyes glinted with a twisted satisfaction, a smugness that made Antonia's blood boil. She thought about Estela, Alejandro's mother, and all the other people Doña Pereira had killed.

In a sudden rush of adrenaline, Antonia jolted forward, her hands reaching out instinctively. Her fingers found Doña Pereira's neck, and tightened around it viciously, her whole strength shoving the old woman's body against the cold cement wall.

Doña Pereira's eyes widened, pupils dilating in shock. The corners of her mouth quivered, but no words escaped her lips. Instead, Doña Pereira's breath came in hitches, each inhale a struggle against Antonia's firm grip.

An urge took over Antonia—a desperate need to make Doña Pereira pay, to silence the echoes of her own pain, her anger.

This is all her fault. She shattered my family. And now she stands here, unrepentant . . .

Doña Pereira's face transformed. Her skin, already weathered and pale, flushed with a sudden rush of color. Her wrinkles deepened, carving new lines into her expression as panic spread across her features.

Antonia's pulse throbbed in her temples. She had to make the old lady suffer like she'd suffered. How could she live with herself if she didn't?

Antonia felt her resolve hardening.

If I don't do this, who will?

But as the world narrowed down to that singular moment, Alejandro's arms wrapped around her waist, pulling Antonia back with a strength that startled her. In that moment, the clarity of the consequences washed over her.

But if I do, I'd be just like her.

"Antonia, stop," he urged. "Please. She's not worth it."

Antonia hesitated, torn between her thirst for vengeance and the dawning realization of what she was about to do.

Doña Pereira's face, now marked with horror, seemed to mock Antonia.

I am not like her.

"You won't be seeing anyone again," Antonia muttered, her hands trembling as she released Doña Pereira from her grip. The old woman slouched slightly, her hands flying to her throat. Her chest heaved, each breath a struggle, and then she looked up at Antonia.

Antonia opened her mouth to say something, but a group of stern-faced police officers, along with paramedics, entered through the open door, right on time, interrupting her. The lead officer, a tall man, stepped forward, his gaze fixed on Doña Pereira. He cleared his throat, then firmly announced, "Eleonora Pereira, you need to come with us. You're under arrest—"

Doña Pereira's brown eyes widened in a flicker of fear once again, but she quickly masked it with a veneer of defiance. The officers advanced steadily, their movements synchronized as they approached her. "What—" She turned her attention to the officers, then back to Antonia and Alejandro. "What did you do—?"

Antonia followed Doña Pereira's line of sight as the paramedics and a pair of officers took León outside on a stretcher. The sight of the two being apprehended did little to quell the storm of anguish within Antonia.

"You're going to rot in hell like you always wanted. It is time that you and your son start to pay," Antonia said. But in that moment, the justice she had sought seemed elusive, hollow, failing to fill the void left by her mamá's loss.

Instead, Doña Pereira's acts seemed to echo a more disturbing truth: malevolence was a shadow that could fall on anyone.

Real horror lay not just in the actions of one person, but in the pervasive, insidious presence of evil that lurked in every corner of human nature, even masked under a disguise of good intentions.

Doña Pereira's heinous crimes were a grim reminder that darkness could reside within the hearts of many, Antonia's even. . . .

She jerked herself out of her darkened thoughts and brought her attention back to Doña Pereira as she was being taken away. Her once-imposing figure seemed diminished and frail in the stark light of the doorway. The old lady didn't struggle, as though energy had completely drained from her. On her face a mask of resigned bitterness. Antonia had expected more resistance, and she found it a bit unsettling to see Doña Pereira give herself in to the police like that. Perhaps this was all part of whatever plan was gestating inside her evil mind.

Alejandro turned to face Antonia. "Are *you* okay?"

"Yes."

He offered his shoulder to her, and she cried. She thought she didn't have it in her anymore, that throughout the years she'd spilled enough tears that her eyes had dried up. That so many years of hiding her emotions would make her strong enough to face anything. And she was, but the tears escaped her before she could stop them.

ANTONIA'S JOURNALS

29 Noviembre 1936

I carried a gasoline canister, the heavy metal container weighing me down. But its weight was lighter than the burden of being haunted, and I was fueled by anger, loss, love.

A sharp scent of petroleum filled the air inside as I unscrewed the lid. I poured the liquid generously at the base of the house and watched it as it spread quickly, soaking into the dry wood, and seeping into the cracks of the old stone.

Each of my strides was calculated, each of them a step toward liberation. A mask of grim determination, eyes steely and focused, gave no hint to the turmoil within me.

With a final glance, I struck a match and tossed it onto the drenched foundation. The flames ignited with an immediate ferocity, leaping up as if hungry for the house's old bones. The fire spread rapidly, the noise of the five-story structure beginning to drown out the distant sounds of nature. My heart pounded. I had orchestrated this moment, with precision, to set it ablaze, to purge myself of the haunting, of the svetyba that had clung to me, to my family, like a shadow. I was fulfilling Mamá's mission.

I watched from the waterfall. The water that cascaded down a stark contrast to the violent consuming fire taking away my past. Liberating me from the svetyba. Cleansing the land.

My eyes were drawn to something unsettling happening before me. Amid the shifting waves of orange and yellow, a shape began to emerge. Flares seemed to morph into a face, a familiar one, with malevolent red eyes. A svetyba. I watched as its features twisted in a cruel mockery, framed by the violent dance of flames. Its eyes staring back at me. As if they were the very essence of the burning house.

The vessel.

The heart.

The svetyba burned away along with the structure, as the fire continued to consume the last traces of my past.

The windows exploded in showers of glass and sparks, the sound of the flames testament to my resolve. The walls buckled and groaned under the pressure of the conflagration, the roof collapsing in a thunderous crash that sent a plume of embers into the air.

With the house a seething mass of fire and fumes, I turned away from it. I moved slowly, almost reverently, acknowledging in my thoughts the finality of what I'd done.

Sliding into the driver's seat of the Packard Eight, I glanced once more at the burning ruins in the rear window. A radiant figure, unlike the one before, shimmering through the blaze with an ethereal light, appeared before my eyes. The silhouette moved with a commanding grace, briefly cutting through the smoke and chaos like a beacon of divine authority. Regal and resolute. My heart swelled, brimmed with satisfaction.

The land finally lay in the right hands.

As I started the engine and drove away from El Salto, the car's headlights cut through the encroaching night. The steady hum of the motor was a soothing contrast to the mayhem I'd left behind. And as the road unfurled in front of me, the weight of my burdens lifted. The future now stretching out before me gave me a newfound sense of freedom.

ACKNOWLEDGMENTS

I first got the idea for *Bochica* in 2019, but I didn't start drafting it until 2021. In a time when we were all grappling with our own fears, I decided it was time to write a horror story of my own. During that time, writing became my anchor. Amid isolation, I found light in the form of this book. Not a day goes by when I don't think about the people who stood beside me as I followed my lifelong dream—especially those who made this book possible.

To Janine Kamouh, my biggest champion. Thank you for saying yes when I told you it was time to pivot into something darker, scarier. You saw something in *Bochica* that I couldn't always see myself, and your expertise turned it into something bigger than I could've ever imagined.

To Caitlin Mahony, Gaby Caballero, Oma Naraine, Suzannah Ball, Carolina Beltrán, and Olivia Burgher, thank you for being part of the incredible team behind the making of this book.

To my editor extraordinaire Michelle Herrera Mulligan: you helped me turn this story into something I could believe in. Thank you from the bottom of my heart. *Bochica* wouldn't be what it is today without you.

To Yezanira Venecia, thank you for pushing me to make every line, every paragraph, and every page as best as it could be. I'm a much better writer because of you and I'm beyond grateful.

To the entire team at Atria Books / Primero Sueño Press, not limited to but including Norma Pérez-Hernandez, Chelsea McGuckin, and Annette Pagliaro Sweeney, thank you for gracing this story with your gifts. An extra big thank you to Maria Mann, for helping me take *Bochica* places, and for loving it as much as I do.

To Jessica Parra, my best friend, who is also the most brilliant writer I know, you believed in this story before I did. This book exists because of you. More stories of mine will likely exist thanks to you. Your friendship means the world to me, and I couldn't have gotten here without you.

To María J. Morillo, thank you for always showing up when I need you the most. Thank you for the countless hours of shared writing frustrations as well as victories. I'm so grateful to have you beside me, both in life and in writing.

To Carlyn Greenwald and Robin Wasley, thank you for going on this wild ride with me. Your support and understanding mean the world to me. Thank you for giving me a safe space to share the ups and downs.

To Paula Gleeson, for being one of my biggest cheerleaders, and dearest writer friends.

To Elora Cook, Liann Zhang, Gloria Muñoz, Taylor Grothe, Roselyn Clarke, Xan Kaur, Alyssa Villaire, and to all the other fellow 2025 debuts. I'm so happy to share this journey with all of you.

To Sonora Reyes, Hailey Alcaraz, Vanessa Montalban, Isabel Cañas, Cynthia Pelayo, Isabela Livino, Sofía Robleda, Christina Li, Sadie Hartmann, Luke Dumas, Kiersten White, Fernanda Trías, Erika T. Wurth, Ana Reyes, Jennifer Thorne, Hannah Whitten, for your enthusiasm and support.

To booksellers, librarians, book bloggers, reviewers, and readers thank you for your excitement for *Bochica* even before it came out. I'm so honored to share this story with all of you.

To my parents, always. I owe so much of this to you, and I will forever be thankful for the way you've shaped me into the person and writer I am today. This book is as much yours as it is mine.

To my brother, thank you for sharing your love of horror with me. This book is a direct result of the stories we've shared, the movies we've watched, and the conversations that never fail to keep me awake at night.

And finally, to my husband. You've been the strength behind every word I've written. You are, and always will be, the heart of my story. Thank you for being my biggest fan.

ABOUT THE AUTHOR

Carolina Flórez-Cerchiaro is a Colombian author of genre-bending speculative fiction based in Medellín, Colombia. She's always been passionate about stories, whether her own, fictional or not, or those that belong to others. Her work is fueled by curiosity, her love of history and the supernatural, and the desire to give voice to traditionally marginalized perspectives. When she's not writing, she can be found sipping black coffee, puzzling, and listening to audiobooks. Find out more at CarolinaFlorezAuthor.com.